A WINTER'S KEEP

A Winter's Keep

A Novel

David Cope

SUNSTONE
PRESS

SANTA FE

Sunstone books may be purchased for educational, business, or sales promotional use.
For information please write: Special Markets Department, Sunstone Press,
P.O. Box 2321, Santa Fe, New Mexico 87504-2321.

Book and cover design › Vicki Ahl
Body typeface › ITC Benguiat Std
Printed on acid-free paper
∞
eBook 978-1-61139-438-2

Library of Congress Cataloging-in-Publication Data

Names: Cope, David, 1941-
Title: A winter's keep : a novel / by David Cope.
Description: Santa Fe : Sunstone Press, 2016. | "2015
Identifiers: LCCN 2015035697 | ISBN 9781632930965 (softcover : acid-free
    paper)
Subjects: LCSH: Psychiatrists–Fiction. | Forensic psychiatry–Fiction. |
    Mental status examination–Fiction. | GSAFD: Suspense fiction | Legal
    stories.
Classification: LCC PS3603.O63 W56 2015 | DDC 813/.6–dc23
LC record available at http://lccn.loc.gov/2015035697

Sunstone Press is committed to minimizing our environmental impact on the planet. The paper used in this book
is from responsibly managed forests. Our printer has received Chain of Custody (CoC) certification from: The
Forest Stewardship Council™ (FSC®), Programme for the Endorsement of Forest Certification™ (PEFC™), and The
Sustainable Forestry Initiative® (SFI®).

The FSC® Council is a non-profit organization, promoting the environmentally appropriate, socially beneficial
and economically viable management of the world's forests. FSC® certification is recognized internationally as a
rigorous environmental and social standard for responsible forest management.

WWW.SUNSTONEPRESS.COM
SUNSTONE PRESS / POST OFFICE BOX 2321 / SANTA FE, NM 87504-2321 /USA
(505) 988-4418 / ORDERS ONLY (800) 243-5644 / FAX (505) 988-1025

Acknowledgments

My sincere thanks go to my wife Mary Jane, without whose encouragement and patience this book could never have been completed, Keith Muscutt, whose expertise in writing has helped me immensely, Larry Prescott, whose editing is always spot on, and to the many others whose advice on this manuscript was extraordinarily helpful. I'd also like to thank all the authors whose books helped me find my way in unknown territory. Any mistakes of omission or commission in this book are entirely mine.

1

The buildings house the men and women of the Forensic Psychiatric Facility in eastern Washington State. This is where criminals judged incompetent to stand trial for crimes they're accused of committing are kept under lock and key until such time as judged capable to stand trial by the psychiatrists to whom they report. Mostly that means they remain here for life.

Strangely, no windows let those inside look out. As if the mere observation of the meadows and forests beyond would provoke the prisoners to attempt escape.

Inside, where puce-colored walls exclusively pervade, the doctors, janitors, and guards suffer the unbearable ravings of the inmates, made worse by the strange acoustics that reverberate those ravings twenty-four seven.

Mister Barnum?

Yes.

Do you remember me?

No.

I visited you last week. We talked about why you're here. Do you remember now?

No.

I'm Doctor Amador. A-M-A-D-O-R. Ring a bell?

No.

Well, can you spell it?

I-T.

Hmm. At least you've not lost your sense of humor. I meant, can you spell *my* name?

A-M-A-D-O-R. Amador.

Right. I've returned to speak with you a bit more. Is that all right?

Yes.

I see you've been taking your meds regularly.

Yes.

Any problems?

No.

Stomach aches or skin rashes?

No.

And how do you feel otherwise?

Fine.

Good. Anything else you want to tell me before we begin?

No.

Then let's start. Do you know where you are?

Prison?

A kind of prison, yes. But this prison, as you call it, is for people with mental challenges.

Challenges?

Yes. People who've done things in their lives that are not acceptable, though for one reason or another are considered unfit to stand trial for doing those things. Incapable of understanding the criminality of what they've done. Do you understand?

Yes.

Very good. Many people in here have no idea what that means.

Why?

They're incapable of doing so.

Why?

Either they don't remember what they did, or they can't understand that what they did was wrong. Thus, they're here, but can't figure out why. You, on the other hand, have told me you do understand, so that's a step forward. See?

Yes.

So you remember what you did?

No.

You don't remember?

No.

But you said you understood why you're here.

I *do* understand that.

Okay. That means you understand you did something wrong, but don't remember what it is. Right?

Yes.

What do you remember?

About what?

Anything, I suppose. Who you were before you came here. Who your friends are. That kind of thing.

I remember those.

Then let's begin there. What do you remember about who you were before you arrived here?

I worked on a farm.

Your own farm, or someone else's?

Not sure.

Why do you say that?

I lived on the farm, but had to pay someone else for it. Once a month.

Good. Renting the farm?

No. Or maybe, yes. I was paying off the loan on the farm.

To a bank?

Yes.

So you owned the farm, still had a mortgage, and thus had to pay off the bank?

Yes.

Was that the only job you had?

Yes.

This is going well, Mister Barnum. And that reminds me, would you object if I call you by your first name?

No.

'No' you wouldn't mind, or 'no' I shouldn't do it?

No, I wouldn't mind.

You remember your first name?

Yes.

Could you tell me what it is?

Yes.

What is it?

Joe.

Good, Joe. Now, what exactly did you do on your farm?

Ran the tractor in the fields. Milked cows. Stuff like that.

How big was your farm?

Don't remember.

An acre? Twenty acres? A hundred acres? Just a rough estimate will do.

A hundred acres. Maybe more.

So you're a real farmer?

What do you mean?

Sell crops, raise cattle, that sort of thing.

Yes.

For profit?

Enough at least to keep things going. Pay the bills.

Good. Do you have a family?

You mean parents?

No. I know you must have parents. I mean a wife and kids.

A wife.

Where is she?

I don't know.

Do you miss her?

Yes.

But you don't know where she is?

No.

Where was she the last time you saw her?

At the farm.

So, maybe she's still there?

Maybe.

Do you have kids?

One.

Girl or boy?

Girl. About six, I think.

You think? You don't know?

No. When I last saw her she was six. Would be older now.

I see. What's your wife's name?

Missy.

Missy Barnum?

Yes.

Your daughter?

What about her?

Her name?

Carla.

With a 'C' or a 'K?'

A 'C.'

Carla Barnum?

Yes.

Good. Do you miss Carla?

Very much.

She's about six?

Don't know. Last time I saw her she was about six. Not sure any more.

Right. I remember that. Because you don't know how long you've been here.

Yes.

Do you have friends in this place, Joe?

I don't know.

You mean you might have some but don't remember?

Something like that. Actually I do know that I don't know.

Why don't you know?

There are people I think who like me, though I can't be sure they do.

Why is that?

Because they're not exactly honest with me.

You mean they lie?

Yes. Or at least they don't tell me the truth.

Isn't that lying?

Not really, because I don't think they're doing it on purpose. They can't help it.

Why is that do you think?

Because they're in here, that's why. Because they're mentally challenged as you said.

Good point. So you might have friends, but you can't depend on them.

Yes.

All right. Which of these 'maybe' friends can you depend on most?

None of them.

Not one?

No.

Why?

Because they can't be trusted. None of them.

Does that disturb you?

No. It's just the way it is.

How about people on the outside?

What about them?

Anybody you can trust there?

Sure.

Who?

My wife and little girl.

Missy and Carla?

Yes.

Do they come visit you here, Joe?

Missy and Carla?

Yes.

No.

Never?

Never.

Why do you suppose that is?

I don't know.

Do you still love them?

Of course, I do.

Even though they don't come visit you?

They probably have their reasons.

Does anybody come to visit you here, Joe?

You.

Besides me?

Other doctors.

Like me?

Yes.

That's it? Just other doctors?

So far.

Does *that* bother you?

No.

Why not?

They must have their reasons.

What kinds of reasons might they have?

Don't know. Maybe they're too busy.

Too busy for one visit?

Yes.

That doesn't make you angry?

No.

You seem like a generous man, Joe.

Generous?

I mean, not getting mad when no one besides other doctors come to visit you.

They must have their reasons.

They're entitled to them?

Absolutely.

Good. Are my questions bothering you?

No.

Why not?

They're only questions. Why should they bother me?

No reason. Just making sure. Some people might think I'm prying into things I shouldn't be prying into.

Doesn't bother me.

Everything's pretty much open for me to ask you?

Pretty much.

Did you ever harm anyone, Joe?

What do you mean?

Only what I said.

Harm anyone?

Yes.

No. Not that I remember. Why would I?

Well, we're both human, Joe. Sometimes people do things that make us angry. Human nature. You seem like an easygoing person. I myself can't imagine anyone making you angry.

Well, you're right. I don't remember anyone making me angry.

That's all I meant, Joe.

Okay.

Is the food good in here?

Fair, I guess.

For institutional food, that is?

Yes. Not bad, though not good either. Pretty much the same every day.

No special occasions?

Not that I remember.

No special desserts?

Don't get desserts. Not allowed.

Why?

Never told us. Never serve them.

That make you angry, Joe?

No. Why should it?

Don't you like desserts?

Sure.

Doesn't it make you angry they don't serve them?

No.

Because?

Must have their reasons.

I see. That's an interesting reaction. You've said it before.

Said what?

That they must have their reasons.

Makes sense, though, doesn't it?

Yes, it does. And it's a very mature reaction.

I try to be mature whenever I can.

Does that mean you have times when you're not mature?

Don't know. I suppose I must have times like that.

Can you cite an instance when you've not been mature?

No.

Thank you for your time, Joe.

That it?

For now, yes. Though I'll be coming back.

When?

Soon.

How soon?

Probably in the next couple of days. Is that okay?

Sure.

I enjoyed speaking with you.

I did, too.

Goodbye, Joe.

Goodbye.

2

The fluorescent lights throughout the building make a continuous buzzing sound. Day and night. Ever present. Never off.

This has the effect of causing some inmates to lose their bearings, wandering around as if in a coma, or following invisible beings. For others, this sound has a numbing effect, causing them not to hear anything at all.

The lights are also embedded in the walls so that they seem to glow rather than shine.

Joe.

Yes.

Do you remember me?

Yes.

Who am I?

You're Doctor Amador.

Good. So you remember I've been here before?

Of course.

When?

A couple of days ago.

What did we talk about?

Lots of things. Missy and Carla, for example. Mostly about whether I was angry with someone.

Are you?

No.

So things haven't changed since I was last here?

No.

Not one thing?

I guess I've gotten older by two days.

Very good. I again see that you've not lost your sense of humor.

No.

When I was here last, we'd begun talking about your not having any friends. At least ones you could trust. Has that changed?

No.

Would you like to have friends?

I guess.

Does that mean yes or no?

Yes, I guess I'd like to have friends.

But it would have to be someone you trust?

Yes.

Can you imagine trusting anybody?

Anybody at all?

Yes.

I think so. I mean, if they earned my trust. I'd like that.

How can someone earn your trust, Joe?

Not sure. I guess that would depend.

On what?

On whether they lied to me or not.

How would you determine that?

If they lied?

Yes.

Well, if they told me something and it proved untrue, they would have lied. If it proved true, they wouldn't have lied.

Maybe they'd merely made a mistake.

That's different.

So they could still be your friends?

Until they lied.

Until? You make it sound inevitable.

What do you mean?

You make it sound like they would eventually lie to you. Do you believe that?

No.

But you'd keep putting them to the test.

I'd have to. Otherwise I'd never know if they lied or not.

However, if you considered everything they said as a test, they could never be your friends. Isn't that right?

I'm not sure I understand what you're getting at.

Isn't it like cheating? One may not be cheating at the moment, but having to check on them all the time means you think they might cheat at the next opportunity. Therefore, these people can never earn your trust. They're always on trial, so to speak. Do you see now?

It's confusing. But I think I understand what you mean.

Most people test others for a time, and then assume they can trust them from there on if they pass the tests. That's how friends are made.

Yes. I can see that.

So the way you've got it set up, no one can be your friend. Ever.

Missy and Carla are my friends.

Even if they lied to you?

No, not if they lied.

But they've never lied to you before. Is that what you're saying?

I'm getting confused here.

Sorry. I don't mean to do that. We doctors sometimes get ourselves confused. Let's change the subject.

Fine.

Your last name. Let's talk about that.

What about it?

Have you ever heard of Barnum and Bailey?

No.

Well, P. T. Barnum, the first half of the duo, was a nineteenth-century showman responsible in part for founding the Barnum and Bailey Circus.

Circus, huh?

Yes. Really big stuff when I was a kid. They traveled around the world putting on shows.

What's the P. T. for?

Phenias Taylor. His first and middle names. I think he was a magician, too. Some called him a scam artist. Quite a man. I thought you might be related to him in some way.

Don't know.

Your parents never talked about him?

No. Not heard of him before now.

Just a thought. It would be something to talk about for sure. I'm pretty confident your parents would have said something about him if you were related.

I guess.

Do you have any enemies, Joe?

What do you mean?

Does anyone you know dislike you in any way?

Why?

We're only talking here, Joe. I've asked you about your friends. Now it's time for me to ask you about your enemies. If you have any, that is.

I suppose I do.

You suppose?

Yes. Though I don't know anyone who I'd consider an enemy.

Not what I asked. Do you know anyone who'd consider *you* an enemy?

There must be someone.

Why do you say that?

Well, it only stands to reason there'd be someone that considered me an enemy.

So you don't actually know of anyone?

No.

How about friends?

I thought we already covered that the last time you were here.

No. Then we talked about people you considered *your* friends. This question is about people who consider you *their* friend.

I see. Well, I'd have to give you the same answer.

You don't know of anyone?

No I don't.

All right. Let's talk about Missy. She your friend?

She's my wife.

Doesn't that mean she's your friend, too?

Sure, though I wasn't counting her or Carla.

How about your parents?

My parents?

Yes. Are they your friends, too?

Don't know.

You don't know?

No. That was a long time ago. I don't know them anymore.

You don't know them?

No.

Why's that? They dead?

My father is.

When did you last see him?

A long time ago.

How long?

A very long time ago. I can't remember exactly when.

How about your mother?

She's alive.

When you last saw her was she your friend?

Probably.

Why haven't you seen her for so long?

She lives a long way from here.

Where?

New York.

New York City?

No. New York State.

Where? Exactly.

Somewhere upstate. Not a town.

They farmers too?

Yes.

Did you work with them on their farm when you were a boy?

Yes.

That where you learned how to work on a farm?

Most likely.

Why'd you leave home?

Who says I left home?

Well, you haven't seen your parents in a long time. I presumed you left home. Didn't you?

I guess I did.

You guess?

Yes.

Could you be more specific?

What's this got to do with Missy? You said we were going to talk about Missy.

We'll get to Missy. Trust me. For now, I'm interested in your parents.

I don't like to talk about them.

Why not?

I guess I don't remember much about them. Too far back in my life.

Well, what do you remember about them? Even something small would help me.

Help you what?

Help you.

Help you help me?

That's right. Remember, I'm a psychiatrist. And you're in a place where people are sent who need help. If I can help you, you'll be able to leave this place. You'd like that, wouldn't you? Stand trial and eventually go back home to your farm and see Missy and Carla again?

I guess so.

Well, what about your parents?

I remember my parents as being farmers.

Yes?

That's all.

That's all?

Yes.

These answers are what we psychiatrists call somewhat ambivalent.

Meaning?

Meaning that they're neither one way or another. Even though you say 'yes,' I can't tell whether you mean exactly that.

You think I'm lying?

No, it's not that at all. I think you may be skirting the issue. You know, not telling me the whole truth. That's quite different than lying. So, I guess I'll ask my question again. Maybe in a different way. Did you like your parents?

They're my parents. That's all.

That's what I mean by ambivalence. I don't understand what you mean. Can you be more precise?

Like?

Well, did you and your father do things together? Go fishing or hunting? These are only suggestions, mind you, not specifics.

I understand now.

Well, did you?

Did I what?

Did you and your father do things together?

Yes.

Like what? Fishing or hunting?

No. But we farmed together.

All right. Did he teach you things about farming?

I'm sure he did.

For example?

How to operate a tractor.

Good. Now we're getting somewhere. How did you two get along when he was teaching you?

Well, he didn't actually teach me directly.

You mean he taught you more by example?

Yes.

So you watched him do something, and when you got the opportunity, you did it yourself?

Exactly.

Did you two talk much?

Not a lot, no.

Why was that do you think?

He didn't talk much. A lot of work to be done. Too tired afterward to talk about it.

I see. That makes sense. How about your mother?

Same thing.

She was too busy to talk to you as well, and too tired afterward?

Yes.

So. You and your parents didn't converse a lot when you were young. Is that it?

Yes.

But they were your friends?

They were my parents.

Fine. I get that. Were you an only child?

I think so.

What does that mean?

Means I don't know of any brothers or sisters.

Don't you think it's obvious then? Rather than saying 'I don't think so,' wouldn't you more likely say 'No?'

Then no. No brothers or sisters.

I'm still slightly confused over your initial response.

Why?

Indefinite. Did you ever in your life imagine that you might have had brothers or sisters that, for some reason or other, you'd never met?

Why would I imagine that?

Possibly your parents gave you the idea that one had died in childbirth. Or that they'd run away from home. Or maybe he or she had been sent away to a hospital somewhere before you were born. Things like that.

What makes you think those things?

Again. Your indefinite response to my initial question.

Then no, I never thought about any of those things.

Then you're an only child?

Yes. As far as I know.

There you go again.

What?

Indefinite response. Can you give me a definite yes or no to the question?

Yes.

Yes you can give me a definite yes or no to the question, or yes you have a brother or sister?

I don't have a brother or sister.

You're sure of that?

I am now.

Good. Let's go back to Missy.

What about her?

Did you talk to her much?

Some.

What does that mean, exactly?

Well, I spent a lot of time working the farm. She kept to herself mostly, cooking in the kitchen. We'd talk sometimes at dinner, though mostly we kept quiet. Especially around Carla.

Why was that?

We didn't want her to hear about things adults do.

Interesting. Like what?

Like politics. Things like that.

So you talked about politics and things like that later on in the evenings?

Sometimes.

What did you say about those things?

What do you mean?

Give me a sample. Doesn't have to be exact words or anything, just a sample short conversation.

That's hard to do. We'd talk about upcoming elections. Stuff like that.

Did you agree about most of these things?

Like politics?

Yes.

Nothing to agree or disagree about. We reminded ourselves about them, and went to sleep.

Interesting.

How so?

It just is. Most couples talk about a lot of different things. You and Missy seem to have not talked about much.

We didn't. Like I said, we were tired after working all day. Went to bed early.

You must have not gone to sleep early every night, or you wouldn't have had Carla, right?

That's none of your business.

Are you sensitive about issues regarding sex, Joe?

I am when it involves me and my wife.

I see. But not in general.

Don't talk about it much, if that's what you mean. Don't think it's proper to speak about such things to just anybody.

I'm not anybody, Joe. I'm the psychiatrist who's working to get you released from this place. I need to know a lot about you in order to do so. Let's forget that for the moment. We can come back to it later. That all right with you?

Maybe.

Maybe?

As I say, it likely isn't proper.

Okay. Let's get back to Missy in general then. Did you two fight a lot?

Fight?

Yes. I mean disagree, not fist fighting.

Did we disagree about things?

Yes. That's what I mean.

No. We never disagreed.

Never?

No. Never.

That's unusual for a married couple. To never argue. Did you know that?

No.

Yes. Most couples fight and then make up. It's only reasonable for two people of the opposite gender to have their spats once in a while.

Oh.

You never did?

No. Not that I can remember we didn't.

How about over issues of trust?

What do you mean?

I mean did you trust her? Did she trust you?

Sure. I guess.

Didn't the issue ever come up?

Not that I remember.

Maybe because you saw one another every day and were both there on the farm together all the time.

Yes.

Didn't that ever get on your nerves?

My nerves?

Yes. You know, day in and day out, always the same old thing. You and her. Her and you.

And Carla.

And Carla. With no break of any kind. Didn't that get annoying some of the time?

No.

Absolutely never?

You don't believe me?

I do believe you. But that's the point. It's unusual.

From my end, I was too busy to care.

That's an interesting word to use, Joe.

What word?

Care.

How so?

Well, I assume you cared about your wife and daughter.

I did. Still do.

But you were too tired to show it?

Guess so.

I see.

What's that mean?

It means 'I see,' Joe. Simply that. My evaluation is that you and your family had a very special arrangement. Rarely talked and were generally too tired to get involved in things together. Did you take drives in the country?

No need to.

Why not?

We lived in the country. Why drive to see more of it?

You've got a point there.

Yes, I do.

I enjoyed speaking with you today, Joe.

Me, too.

Goodbye, Joe. See you in a couple of days.

Bye.

3

The guards don't carry guns since the Forensic Psychiatric Facility worries about inmates stealing them. This means these guards have to make up for their lack of weapons with brawn and skill. The guards wear red and the patients prison orange so they can be distinguished from one another.

Each building of the facility has only two doors, one at the front and one at the rear. Both doors are controlled by assistant guards to carefully check the credentials of those wishing to enter or exit. Even the ventilation ducts have several layers of crisscrossing metal screens to discourage attempts to escape. Those, and the small size of the ducts themselves, make that route impossible to traverse.

Good morning, Joe.

Morning.

Did you sleep well?

Guess so.

Meaning?

Had a dream.

About what? Do you remember?

Yes.

What?

Is it important?

Might be.

How?

Dreams sometimes tell us something about the dreamer. In this case, you.

No kidding?

No kidding.

So you want me to tell you about the dream?

If you wouldn't mind.

Seems foolish.

Foolish?

A dream's a dream.

Not to us psychiatrists, they aren't. Humor me, Joe. Tell me about the dream.

I was in a jungle someplace. Probably South America.

Why South America?

I'm more familiar with jungles in South America than other places.

Been there?

No, but I once saw a movie filmed there.

Go on.

It was night and quite dark.

So you couldn't see well?

Right. But there was a sliver of moon. I think they call it a crescent moon. Straight above my head. I know that's impossible since you only see those kinds of moons near the horizon at night, so I figured it was a dream.

You figured it was a dream when you were actually in the dream?

Maybe I thought that after I woke up. Can't remember.

All right. Doesn't matter. Go on.

I'm all alone, except for some animals I can't see but for their wide eyes. And these eyes are staring directly at me.

How did you feel?

Scared, I guess. Didn't know what kinds of animals these were, only that their eyes were closer to the ground than mine. That's why I assumed they were animals.

Then what?

I stood there for a time, not sure what to do. Stand still, or run.

So, the animals were on one side of you?

Yes. Right in front of me. I suppose some other ones could have been behind me, though I didn't think to look there. Anyway, everything changed when I heard the larger animal, the one whose eyes were further off the ground and must have been a cat of some kind, growl at me.

Cats growl?

This one did. I figured it was a cat because the sound was different than the sound a dog or bear might make.

The growl make you more afraid?

Absolutely. You had to have heard it. Its eyes grew bigger and had more light reflecting off them. Like in a horror film.

Sounds frightening.

Was.

So what did you do?

I decided the cat would outrun me if I ran, so I screamed and charged directly at it.

That took some courage.

It did. But I had nothing to lose at that point, so I screamed and attacked it. Straight on.

What did the lion, or whatever it was, do?

It's eyes blinked, and it ran.

It ran? How did that make you feel?

Powerful. It made me feel I was strong and fearless.

Go on.

Then the animal with its eyes lowest to the ground hissed at me.

Hissed? What do you mean?

Like a snake. It hissed.

Okay.

I looked down toward it and could see it slithering toward me with a forked tongue slipping in and out of its mouth.

Thought you said it was dark.

I know, but I could still see the snake. It curled back and forth like snakes will.

What did you do?

I jumped in the air and let it slither underneath me.

It must have been going fast.

Not so fast.

Wouldn't you've come down on top of it?

No. It was a dream, see, and I could stay up in the air as long as I wanted.

So you escaped the snake, too.

I did. Except the dog-like thing snarled. Didn't bark, it snarled.

Like the cat?

No, that was a growl. This was the kind of snarl Doberman Pinchers make when they get ready to attack.

Scary?

Very.

So what did you do this time?

I snarled back at it.

From up in the air?

No. By this time I was back on the ground again.

What did the dog-like thing do?

It whined. Like I'd hurt it in some way.

Did it run away, too?

No. Just whined. I felt sorry for it.

So, did you comfort it?

I don't know.

You don't know?

No. That's when I woke up.

Now that was a powerful dream, Joe.

Yeah? Why?

Because it could have many meanings.

Like?

I'm not sure I could tell you without asking you more questions.

Like?

Like, how did you feel about your dream when you woke up?

Not sure. Still scared, I suppose.

Scared? Still? You were now awake and knew it was a dream, right?

Yes, but sometimes the feelings don't go away immediately. You know what I mean?

Yes, I do. So you were still scared. Did something then come to you about what the dream might mean?

Aside from being a dream?

Yes.

Not really. I mean dreams to me are only dreams, not things that have special meanings.

Like a horror movie? Not real? The people and the situations made up?

Yes.

But dreams are not horror movies, do you see that?

Yes. They're only dreams.

And you create your dreams. This means they might have some meaning for you if you take them seriously. Do you follow?

Yes.

So what do you think your dream might mean?

Probably that I'm afraid of animals.

Are you? I mean, are you afraid of large cats, snakes, and wild dogs?

Probably.

Do you think what you did in your dream you could do in real life?

I could do most of what I did, but I couldn't predict what the animals might do in response.

Good answer. However, let's imagine you could. That your dream was a signal of what you should do if you encounter such animals in real life.

Seems right.

Then imagine now that these animals represent something else.

Like what?

Like people you know.

People?

Yes. People. Do you know anyone that the cat you encountered might represent?

Cat people?

No. People who might act in some way like the cat did?

Like growl?

Again, no. Remember, I'm trying to get you to think in terms of symbols here, Joe. Think of the cat as a representation of someone or something you've encountered in real life. So the way the cat looks, the way it sounds, and the eyes it has, all symbolize someone you might know. Do you know anyone who has large eyes, a menacing voice, and who scares you in some way?

No.

You're sure?

Yes. People I know are generally nice.

But imagine your dream is trying to tell you something. That the dream, which is actually your subconscious, is warning you about people, or revealing their true identities. That no matter how nice they may be to you, they could really be threatening.

So, you want me to tell you if anybody I know might act like the cat did, though not exactly like the cat?

Precisely.

I guess.

You guess? That must mean that someone comes to mind, but you'd rather not say.

I suppose.

Who?

I'd rather not say.

Joe, everything you tell me in here is held in strictest confidence. I don't have a recorder and I'm not taking notes. It's just you and me. And my profession as a psychiatrist prevents me from ever telling anybody anything about our conversations. Do you understand?

Yes.

Who does the cat remind you of?

My mother.

Fine. Now we're getting someplace. Did your mother ever act toward you like the cat did in your dream? Did you ever respond to her acting that way by charging toward her?

No.

Never?

No. I mean, yes.

Which is it?

No, she never did anything like that.

I got it.

Good.

Did the snake remind you of anyone you know?

No.

No one?

Yes, no one.

And the dog-like being? He remind you of anyone you know?

Yes.

Who?

My wife.

Missy?

Yes.

In what way did the dog remind you of her?

When I snarled back at the dog, it began whining.

Does Missy snarl at you?

Not exactly.

What about the dog specifically reminded you of Missy?

Missy complains to me in a whining manner.

What does she complain about?

Lots of things.

Anything in particular?

Mostly about my not holding my head over my plate when I eat.

What?

She doesn't like to have to use bleach to clean my shirts when I spill food on them.

I see. Do you?

Do I what?

Hold your head over your plate when you eat?

I try to. Whenever I remember. Mostly I'm so hungry I eat as fast as I can.

Like a dog.

I suppose.

So the dog-like creature in your dream reminds you of Missy?

Not so much.

Then why did you say that?

Mostly so you wouldn't be disappointed.

Disappointed?

Yes. You seem to want the animals in my dreams to be people. Didn't want to disappoint you.

Like you disappointed Missy?

I suppose.

So, the only thing about the dog in your dream that reminded you of Missy was her nagging you in a whining sort of way?

I suppose so.

You suppose so?

Yes.

You're not sure?

No, I'm sure. That aspect of my dream reminded me of her. But only that part.

So you never snarled at Missy.

Never.

All right. That was certainly quite a dream.

Yes.

Anything else about it that you haven't mentioned to me?

No. That was pretty much it.

Do you often dream that you're up in the air and not falling to the ground?

Is that important?

I don't know.

Don't most people dream such things? I think I read somewhere they did.

Most people *do* dream such things.

Then why would my dream be special?

Because, Joe, you're special.

I am?

Yes, you are.

Okay.

You dream often?

I do. Almost every night.

And you remember these dreams?

Yes.

Are they pretty much the same?

Different.

Very interesting. I've got to go now. I'll be back tomorrow. Is that all right with you?

It is.

Goodbye, then.

Bye.

4

ost of the inmates in the Forensic Psychiatric Facility are drugged to keep their violent tendencies at bay. Several sit on their beds staring at walls. Others pace in circles looking at the floor. Still others act more strangely, like crawling around on all fours and whispering unintelligible things. Many sleep, as there is no way for them to tell whether it's day or night. Thus, roughly half the population of the facility is awake at all times. This keeps the guards busy by working in shifts to make sure each building is fully guarded twenty-four hours a day.

Good morning, Joe.

Hello, Doctor Amador.

Good. You remembered my name. How did you sleep last night?

Fine.

Did you dream again?

Yes.

Mind telling me about it?

No.

Good. I'm looking forward to hearing about it.

Good.

You can begin anytime.

Well, my dream last night involved a fight between two people.

Interesting. Do you know the two people?

No.

Could they be symbols like we talked about the last time we met?

Maybe.

But you're not sure *who* these people might represent?

No.

Maybe this dream is a release of emotions of some kind. I'm listening.

The two people were both women.

Now that's interesting in itself.

It is?

Yes. Most men don't have dreams that involve two women fighting. In fact, in all my years of doing what I do, no one has ever mentioned anything like this to me.

That's interesting.

It is. Are you talking about a fistfight here, or two women screaming at one another?

They're actually fighting. On the floor. Screaming as well.

Go on.

One of the women, the one on top and getting the best of it, yelled that the other woman, the one on the bottom, should stop messing around with her husband.

That's interesting.

Yes, and then the woman on the bottom somehow got lose and began beating the other on her face with her fists. That's when it got bloody.

Bloody?

Yes. And this woman on top screamed at the other one that she should start treating her husband with respect.

That mean anything to you?

No.

What happened then?

Nothing. The dream was over and I woke up.

A short one, huh?

Yes.

Are those typical?

You mean short dreams?

Yes.

Not so much. Mostly I have longer ones.

What do you think of this particular dream?

Not sure. What should I think?

I'm not going to tell you what to think of it, Joe, I'm listening to you tell it, and attempting to get you to tell me what *you* think it represents.

I'm not sure what to say.

All right, think of it this way, do you know anyone like either of the two women involved in the fight?

Already told you, I can't figure out *who* they might represent.

Then maybe we should come at this from a different angle. As a situation. Does the situation—two people fighting with one another—mean anything to you, or remind you of anything that's happened in your life?

Two people fighting?

Yes.

Sure. Everyone fights once in a while.

Not what you said about you and Missy and Carla the other day.

Okay, everyone except me and Missy and Carla. But I know people who fight with one another.

Does that include fighting physically as well as using words?

To some degree.

Some degree?

Well, I mean it's mostly words, but sometimes it's physical.

With women?

No.

But you do remember that happening? With men?

Yes. Occasionally.

All right. Can you remember a particular instance when that happened?

Yes.

Who was fighting?

Two guys in a market where I was buying groceries.

What did you do?

About what?

Them fighting.

What *should* I have done?

I don't know. What *did* you do?

Nothing. Just watched them go at it, I guess.

Did one of them win?

Yes.

Did it at one time look like the other one might win?

Yes.

So that particular fight, with the exception that they were men and not women, parallels your dream rather closely.

I guess it does.

What happened when it was over?

The manager called the cops and they arrived.

With their guns drawn?

Yes.

That stop things?

It did.

Did they take the men away?

No.

What happened?

They gave them both tickets like they'd been driving too fast or something.

How did this whole thing make you feel?

Feel? I don't know that I felt much of anything.

Didn't you root for one or the other?

No. Never did know what they were fighting about. I couldn't take sides.

As they were fighting, did you feel an urge to get involved?

No.

Not one bit?

No.

So you stood there and watched.

Yes.

Did the police ask you any questions?

Yes. I told them much the same story I just told you.

What did they say?

Thank you.

And?

They went on to talk with other people there.

That was it?

Yes.

Now, do you think your dream last night had anything to do with the real fight you witnessed?

Don't know. Probably not.

Why so?

Makes no sense. The real fight was nothing much. The dream was pretty dramatic.

When you see violence, like what you saw in that store, how do you feel about it?

Don't feel anything about it. Didn't involve me.

If it had involved you?

Then it would make me think. Real hard.

What would you think about it?

I would think about killing the guy.

Killing? Pretty harsh word to use, don't you think?

I suppose. But it would be difficult to get me into a fight in the first place. So if someone were to manage that, it would probably be over something significant. So I would most likely be fighting for my life. Therefore, taking his life might be the only way to defend myself.

So, it's difficult to get you into a fight?

Yes.

Once there, though, it would be for keeps.

Most likely.

Getting back to the dream you had for a second, the two women weren't fighting for their lives.

I don't know.

Why not?

Because the dream finished before I had a chance to see what happened next.

I see. That makes sense. Can you think of any other time in your life when you've witnessed a fight between two people that might remind you of your dream?

Not off hand.

Do you want to take some time to think about it some more?

Not particularly.

Then let's go back to something we were talking about before.

About?

About Missy. Your wife.

All right.

Do she and your daughter get along well?

Yes.

You seem pretty confident about that.

Shouldn't I?

Sure. If that's the way you feel. But at one point in our conversation you mentioned that you spent a lot of your time out in the fields doing what farmers do. Isn't that right?

Yes.

So you were not always able to see how Missy and Carla got along.

Suppose not. If they had problems, though, wouldn't I have seen them when I was around?

Good point. Did you?

Not at all.

How about your parents?

What about them?

Did they fight?

Sometimes.

Can you give me an example?

Well, they would disagree over how to raise me.

For instance?

They'd argue whether it was best to beat me or reason with me.

How did that make you feel?

I'm not sure.

Well, for example, which side thought which way?

My father was in favor of giving me the belt.

And your mother wanted to reason with you?

Yes.

Who won?

Mostly my father.

Why so?

He was bigger than my mother. If he really wanted something, he'd get it.

How did *that* make you feel?

Feel?

When your father beat you.

It hurt, what do you think?

Did you hate him for it?

I suppose I did at the time he was beating me.

Not afterward?

Got over it.

Your mother?

What about her?

Did he beat her as well?

No.

You sure?

Never in my presence. I don't think he ever would.

What makes you say that?

He didn't appear to be the type.

But he beat you. And you were much smaller than your mother.

Yes, except I wasn't his wife.

That makes sense. Now, does your father beating you relate to anything in your dream?

No.

You sound confident of that.

I am. These were two women fighting.

But they might be symbols, remember?

All right, but I never beat my father. He only beat me.

In your dream, though, only one of the two women actually used her fists as I remember.

I don't remember.

Maybe I'm taking this too far.

Why do you say that?

Because you seem to be tiring of this dream stuff. Besides, we're not getting very far with it.

Sorry.

Don't apologize. It's only one of many ways that psychiatrists attempt to discover how you think about things. Sometimes it works. Sometimes it doesn't.

Makes sense.

Good. Now tell me about your memory of why you're in here.

Come again?

Why do you think you're in this place?

I'm accused of committing a crime. That's why.

But that's not all of it. Is it?

No. The court tested me and decided I was not prepared to stand trial so they put me in here.

For possibly the rest of your life.

Yes.

Why did they do that?

Why?

Yes.

Because they must have thought I was guilty.

That you committed the crime, or that you were not capable of standing trial for it?

Probably both.

Both?

Yes.

Fine. Let's assume you're correct about that. How do you feel about your being here under those circumstances?

I'm happy enough. Given the alternatives.

Alternatives. What alternatives?

I might have been put in a regular prison.

Have you ever been in a regular prison?

No.

How do you know this place is preferable?

I've read about prisons in books. They're dreadful.

Read those kinds of books too and they *are* dreadful. But books also depict places like these. Aren't they dreadful as well?

Not so much.

You didn't decide to come here rather than prison, did you?

No.

Who did?

A psychiatrist like you.

And he said?

That I shouldn't stand trial because I was incapable of under-standing what was going on.

On what basis did he make this determination?

He talked to me like you are.

Did you play straight with him?

Straight?

Yeah, did you tell him the truth?

Yes.

Do you remember what crime you're accused of committing that got you into this mess?

No.

Nothing about it at all?

No.

Didn't anyone ever tell you what it was? Like the lawyer defending you?

Maybe he did, I've forgotten. Even if I remembered, though, it wouldn't matter.

Why not?

Because it isn't true. I couldn't have done what he said I did.

Why not?

Because I'm not that type of person.

What type of person?

The type that would do whatever he said I did.

I see. Would you like *me* to tell you what you're accused of doing?

No. I don't want to hear about it.

Why not?

Because I didn't do it.

How can you believe you didn't do something when you don't know what that something is?

Because I wouldn't do something that was against the law. That would put me in court to stand trial.

So you'd rather me not tell you about it.

I'd rather not.

What if I did anyway? Would that make you angry?

No.

No?

No. It would make me sad for the victim and for whoever actually did it.

What if I told you that the evidence indicating you did it is overwhelming? So overwhelming even you'd believe you did it?

I didn't do it. I know I didn't do it.

All right. We've run out of time. I'll be back in a couple of days. Is that okay?

Yes.

You sure?

Why wouldn't I be?

I was pretty hard on you just now. Maybe you're angry with me.

I'm not.

I'm glad. So I'll see you soon.

Goodbye.

5

Visitors at the Forensic Psychiatric Facility are subjected to much the same types of checks that airport security uses. Shoes, belts, loose change, keys, bags, cell phones, and so on, must be placed in special containers, and visitors have to raise their arms while being x-rayed for possible hidden weapons or explosive devices. Then these visitors must leave their belongings with security personnel until they return from their visits. No one passes into the facility through security with anything but the clothes they wear.

Morning, Joe.
Morning.
How are you today?
Okay.
Good. How'd you sleep?
Fine.
Dream?
Yes.
About?
My daughter, Carla.
Was it a good dream?
Yes.
Nothing much to tell me about?
No, not that I can think of.

No hanky-panky?

Hanky-panky?

Forget it. I'm a little tired today. Bad joke.

Didn't you sleep well?

No, actually, I didn't. But we're here to find out about you, though, right?

Right.

Today I'd like you to tell me something about your childhood. Is that okay?

Yes.

What's the first thing you remember about your childhood?

The first thing?

The *very* first thing.

I guess that would be my boat.

Your boat?

I had a toy boat I played with when I took baths.

What kind of boat was it?

Don't know. A boat. I was too young to know if it was a battleship, cruiser, or rowboat.

Tell me about this boat.

Not much to tell. It made me happy.

Why?

It floated.

So you pushed it around the bathtub?

Yes.

That's it?

Yes. No. I mean it floated and I loved to watch it move with the water as I made waves.

I can understand that.

Also liked to watch the bubbles.

Bubbles?

The ones that came out through tiny holes when I held it under water.

That pleased you?

Yes. They tickled my other hand when I placed it over them underwater.

I see. That it?

No. I liked to watch the boat sink further down when the bubbles stopped.

So the boat sank to the bottom of the tub and just lay there?

Yes.

What did you do?

I watched it for a time, and then pulled it out of the water, emptied the water from the same holes the bubbles came through, and floated it again.

Interesting. Is that the only thing you remember?

No.

What else?

I remember my mother getting mad at me for fooling around with the boat for so long when she'd wanted me to wash myself with soap.

How did your mother get mad at you?

She'd yell at me. Loud.

You didn't like that?

No.

What did she yell?

'Stop playing with the boat, Joe, and wash yourself.'

That's all she said?

Mostly.

Did she swear?

Huh?

When she yelled at you, did she swear?

No. My mother never swore. She said it was the curse of the devil. She'd say 'The devil hath power to assume a pleasing shape.'

Your mother like Shakespeare?

Shakespeare?

Never mind. So, your mother was religious?

I guess.

What did that mean for you?

Mean?

Yes. Did she make you do things you didn't want to do, like praying before meals? Stuff like that?

Sometimes. That didn't bother me much.

Why?

It didn't take long, and it seemed the courteous thing to do.

You mean to thank God for the meal you were about to eat?

Yes.

Did your mother ever make you angry?

Yes.

Can you give me an instance?

Just did.

Besides the boat.

Well, she'd make me come inside when it was dark.

Why did that make you mad?

I liked the dark. No reason for me to come inside.

You *liked* the dark? Tell me about that.

She thought it was scary out there at night. I didn't.

Why not?

Seemed to me that the things you couldn't see couldn't see you either. Sort of put us to equal disadvantage. Besides, it made me excited to think that something out there might attack me.

Did that ever happen?

No.

Why did you suppose that was?

Because the night is like the day without light.

Hadn't you heard that some animals are nocturnal? Like the ones you dreamt about recently? Only come out at night?

Not then, I hadn't. Besides, I liked to watch the fireflies.

So you got mad at your mother for making you come in at night when it got dark.

Yes.

Anything else about her get you angry?

Many other things. Mostly for making me stop something I was doing that I liked doing.

Did that make you want to hurt her?

No. She was my mother. She was supposed to look out for me. I knew that was what she was doing. Her job, after all.

But, you got angry with her.

Yes. But only for a few seconds. Then I was on to other things.

How about your Dad?

He'd only get involved when whatever she was demanding I do I didn't do. Or vice versa.

48

He punish you?

He'd threaten to take a strap to me. His belt.

Did he ever actually do that?

A few times. In the beginning.

What made him stop?

I'm not sure. Maybe I got tired of being whipped and stopped making him angry. It hurt.

How did you feel when your father whipped you?

You mean about him?

Yes.

Mad.

Did you want to hurt him?

Yes.

Did you?

Hell no. He was a lot bigger than me. Would have been stupid.

Did you forgive him like you did your mother?

Not in the same way.

In what way?

I figured he could have done something worse than whip me with his belt.

I meant something like, did you plan to retaliate someday?

Retaliate?

Did you think about when you got big enough you might take a belt to him to pay him back for what he'd done to you?

I suppose. Though not for long. Sooner or later I forgot about it.

But you remembered it long enough that eventually he didn't have to use his belt on you.

Yes.

Do you hold any resentment towards your father now?

After all these years? No. He did what he thought he had to do. That's all. I see that now. I didn't see it then so much.

So all in all, you feel that you had a fairly normal upbringing?

I guess so. I was not particularly unhappy. After all, parents don't have much training to be parents. Guess they do the best they can under the circumstances.

That's a very adult attitude, Joe.

Thank you.

How about your daughter? Do you raise her in much the same way your father raised you?

No. I don't yell at her or even raise my voice. I'd never think of whipping her like my father whipped me.

Is that because she's a girl, not a boy?

No. My father hurt me, and I don't think a father should hurt his children.

Good. But children can be hurt in other ways besides being whipped, don't you think?

You're talking about feelings?

Yes, I am. Hurting someone's feelings can sometimes be as damaging as hurting their bodies.

I try not to do that either. I talk to Carla and try to make her understand what she did wrong and that it hurts other people when she does.

Does she always understand that?

Not always.

What do you do?

I talk to her until she gets tired and goes to sleep.

The thing is resolved when she wakes up?

Yes.

So you let it be?

I do. Maybe that's wrong, I don't know. Seems to me parents can't do much right when it comes to raising a kid.

Very observant. I suppose you're correct.

Do you have children, Doctor Amador?

One. Why do you ask?

Do you have the same problems raising a child?

Sure. But let's get back to *you*, shall we?

It's good to know you understand.

Understand?

About parenting, I mean. It's a tough business when you have no experience. Right?

Right. Now, let's get back to your childhood.

Sure. What do you want to know?

Besides your boat, did you have any other toy you liked to play with?

50

Yes. A teddy bear.

How old were you?

Have no idea. Too young to know those things.

So, about three?

Maybe.

But not too much older than three?

Not sure. I wasn't older than five, though.

All right. Why did you like your teddy bear?

Because I could talk to it.

So you talked to your teddy bear when you couldn't talk to anyone else?

Yes.

About your father whipping you, for example?

Sure. About almost anything. It didn't care what we talked about.

We? Did your teddy bear talk back to you?

No. A figure of speech. Only I talked.

Okay. What emotions did you have toward the toy?

It wasn't really a toy. It was a teddy bear.

Interesting distinction. What's the difference?

Size, I guess. It was small. And it always had its front paws out to its sides. Didn't much look like a real bear. Or a toy.

How did you feel toward the teddy bear?

For example?

Did you give it a name?

Yes. Teddy.

Simple enough. How did you feel toward it? Did you like Teddy? Love Teddy? What?

Teddy was a friend when I needed one. That's all. The rest of the time I stored him away in the closet.

So you knew that Teddy wasn't alive?

That was pretty obvious. It was a stuffed animal that my parents bought for me.

So you didn't love Teddy?

Not in the way you mean, no.

What way do you think I mean?

Like I would love my mother or father.

Did you love your mother and father?

Sure.

Why?

Because they were my mother and father. Loving them was part of the package.

The package?

You're supposed to love your mother and father. They feed you and keep you alive. Sometimes they give you presents, allowances, things like that. You're supposed to love them.

So you did?

Yes.

Not your Teddy?

No. At least not in the same way.

So you might have loved Teddy in some other way?

Suppose so. What does it matter?

I'm attempting to discover what the word 'love' means to you.

Why didn't you ask me that rather than beating around the bush?

Because sometimes people reveal things about the meanings of certain words when they tell stories rather than answer straightforward questions.

I see. So if I asked you the same kind of questions about your childhood, I'd discover things about you that I wouldn't have if I asked you straight out?

Maybe. But I'm trained at this, you're not. Do you see the difference?

Yes. Of course I do.

Good. Now, we've talked about Teddy and about your boat. Are there any other things you remember about your childhood?

You mean like toys I had?

I mean like anything. Any recollections from, say, before you were ten?

Sure.

Can you tell me about them?

Yes. I had a crush on the little girl that lived on a farm near ours.

That sounds interesting. What was her name?

I don't remember. Though she sure was cute.

Did you see her often?

Not very. Her father's farm was about a mile away. A mile to a kid is like forever.

So, when did you see her?

Mostly when her father brought her along when he wanted to speak to my father.

She was cute, you say?

Very.

And you had a crush on her?

Mostly I wanted to be around her, and for her to like me.

Did she?

No idea.

Why?

Well, as I say, I only saw her when her father brought her by. He'd only stay a few moments and they'd leave. We never got to speak to one another.

Never once?

No. But she looked at me a lot.

Did that excite you?

Sure did.

How?

It made me feel like she liked me.

Any other way?

Not sure what you mean?

Did she arouse you?

You mean sexually?

Yes.

God no. I was *way* too young for that. I only wanted to look at her. Watch her. It was very pleasurable.

More like you might watch a sunset or something, not because of anything physical?

Exactly right.

So how long did this go on?

Maybe six months, maybe more.

How often did her father bring her by?

I'm not sure. Once a month. Something like that.

So you saw her maybe half a dozen times, give or take a few on either side?

About right.

You never said a word?

No. Never had a chance.

Would you have said a word if you'd had the chance?

Probably not.

Why?

Kind of scary.

What was?

The thought of actually speaking to her. I wouldn't have known what to say.

What if she spoke to you?

That would be different.

What would you have said?

Don't know. It would probably depend on what she said to me.

Makes sense. Do you remember her name?

Don't think I ever knew her name.

Her father never introduced her to you and your father?

No. She came along for the ride, I guess.

What did your father and him talk about when they visited?

Don't actually know. Lots of words I didn't understand. Besides, I was too busy looking at her.

Reasonable. Did your father and her father seem agitated when they spoke to one another?

No.

Were they friends?

Don't know for sure. They spoke normally. As if they had business to tend to. They took care of it and he left.

So, other than the little girl you thought was cute, didn't speak to, and didn't know her name, nothing much else happened?

No. But I remember the visits.

Because of the little girl?

Yes.

She made quite an impression on you.

She did.

Did you ever see her again? After that, I mean.

Not that I can be sure of.

Children that age do change appearance as they get older, don't they?

I suppose.

So you could have met her later and not realized it?

That's possible.

All right, I think that will have to do it for today. I'll see you again soon. Okay?

Yes.

Goodbye for now, Joe.

Goodbye.

6

The outer boundary of the Forensic Psychiatric Facility consists of a ten-foot high chain-link fence topped by coiled razor wire. Only one gate allows entry. To ensure no one can escape by tunneling under the fence, the chain-links extend some five feet underground. Thus, even if inmates could reach the broad lawn directly outside the facility, their chances of actually escaping over or under the fence are slim to none.

Several manned towers are also strategically located outside the fenced-in grounds to ensure no one can bridge the fence in some way and not be caught. These guards are armed with several long-range rifles. All told, no one thinks the Forensic Psychiatric Facility can be entered or exited—the primary worry—without official permission.

Good morning, Joe.
Morning.
How'd you sleep last night?
Well.
Perchance to dream?
Huh?
Did you dream?
Yes.
Anything I should know?
Doubt it.

Try me.

Dreamt about my farm.

What about it?

Nothing much. Except it was on fire.

On fire? That sounds important to me.

The fields were ablaze, but the farmhouse and the barn were safe.

How so?

They'd been cordoned off from the rest of the farm by the fire trucks spraying water into the fields.

A big fire?

Not so much, but everyone was worried about it spreading to the other farms in the area.

I can imagine. Anyone know how it started?

No, but an electrical storm was in the area. Probably lightning.

And how did it end?

Same way it started.

So it began with a fire, nothing much happened, and then it ended with the fire still going?

Yes. Not much of a dream.

Anything actually happen like that on your farm?

No.

Is it a worry among farmers where you live?

Not particularly. I don't remember ever having seen one during the years I spent there.

No idea why you might have dreamt such a thing?

No.

All right. Let's get started.

Fine.

Today, I want to ask you about the meds you're on.

Okay.

Do they feel right for you?

They don't make me sick, if that's what you mean.

No, that's not what I mean. Are you happy with the way you feel?

Sure. I feel relaxed and generally happy about things. Who could complain about that?

Good point. I guess I'm asking something else, too.

What's that?

Are you happy because the meds give you a feeling of well being, or because you actually do feel happy?

How would I know the difference?

By comparing how you feel now with how you felt before you began taking them.

I see. Well, I'm happier now.

What if I told you I could reduce or stop the meds? How would that make you feel?

I'd rather you not do that.

Because you really do like the way you feel now?

Yes.

All right. Let's take this a bit further. Would you like me to increase the dosage of the meds?

Would that make me feel happier?

It likely would. Yes.

I accept the offer.

It wasn't an offer, Joe. I was simply asking how you'd react, not offering you more of them.

I see.

After all, there's a point at which you can't feel happier. At that point, the meds will no longer have an effect on you.

Have I reached that point yet?

I don't know.

Could we try it and see?

You'd actually like to have a higher dose of medication?

Yes.

I'll review your case and see what I can do. I can't promise anything, but I'll see if it's possible.

Good.

Changing the subject, when you walk around inside this facility, how do the other people look to you?

What do you mean?

Do they look happy?

I spend most of my time in my room, not outside it. When I do go outside they look pretty much the same as I feel.

Do you like the way they look?

What do you mean?

I mean, have you imagined when you see them that you probably look the same way to them? And, if so, how does that make you feel?

I guess it doesn't make me feel good or bad. I see them. They see me. That's all there is to it.

How do you imagine people look on the outside of this facility?

Back on their farms and in the cities? That what you mean?

Yes.

Not as happy, I think.

Does that bother you?

You mean do I worry about them not being so happy?

Yes.

No.

So, you'd rather be in here.

I guess so.

Because in here you're not stuck with paying bills, raising your daughter, farming your land, and so on?

Yes.

Does that bother you?

No. Why should it? I've got it easy.

Yes, but with the hard stuff—the less happy feelings out there—there sometimes come some especially happy ones.

Like?

Like having finished a hard day's work. Making love to your wife. Watching Carla grow up. Those kinds of things.

I see. Not necessarily happier things, but more satisfying?

You got it. Does that bother you?

Not sure. I don't give it much thought.

I guess I'm asking you if you'd give up the meds for a chance to see your daughter again. Your wife again. Your farm again. Your parents again. Out in the fresh air. Out where bad things can happen, yes, though good things can happen too. What would you say to that?

I'm not sure. How could that happen, though? Wouldn't I go to trial first?

Yes, I'm afraid you would.

I see.

Could you give it some thought?

Yes.

And tell me whenever you're ready to answer the question?

Yes.

Good. Now, what would you like to talk about today?

Me?

Yes. I thought it might be a good idea for you to set the agenda for this session.

Wow. I never thought *that* would happen.

Well it has. Can you think of something you'd like to discuss? It could be some problem you have. With me or anyone else. Or maybe it could be something wrong with your room, or somebody you've met in here. A particular guard or inmate. Anything at all.

Must it be something I'm *unhappy* about?

No. It could be something you're happy about. I only mention the unhappy things because most people want to talk about those. They see this as an opportunity to change something about their lives here for the better. Telling me something you're particularly happy about probably won't change anything.

I see.

Something spring to mind?

Well, there is one thing.

What?

The lights. I wish they wouldn't be on all the time.

That bothers you?

Yes it does. I like the dark.

You mentioned that before. I remember.

Yes. Here, it's never dark. Even for a few seconds.

Does that make you unhappy?

Not unhappy. No. It does make me wish for darkness once in a while though.

I'm not sure I can do anything about that, but I'll mention it to those who could make that change and we'll see what happens. Do you want me to do that?

Yes. If it won't make them unhappy.

I don't think it will. Remember, though, don't get your hopes up. There are rules here I'm not aware of. There are other people in here that must be considered.

I understand.

Good. Is there anything else you'd like to talk about? Anything at all?

Well, there is one other thing.

What is it?

The food.

You don't like the food?

No, that's not it. I *do* like the food.

What, then?

There's not much variety. It's like we have three different meals. I can predict what each one's going to be because of that. It gets boring, you know? I'd like more variety.

I can see that. Again, I'll talk to someone about it. It's one of those things that could be changed, I imagine. If nothing else, they could make the order of the meals less predictable to keep you guessing.

That would help. It would help more if there was more variety.

Of course. I'll talk to them.

Good.

Now I'm curious. You told me earlier that you were happy in here. Mainly, I suppose, because of the meds I've prescribed for you. I'm guessing that you're pretty much happy all the time. Is that right?

Yes.

Why wouldn't you prefer more variety in your moods, like you want more variety in your meals?

That's a good question.

Thank you. How do you feel about that?

I guess it means I think one of my answers was about food, and the other about feelings. They're different things. I feel differently about them. Does that make sense?

Yes. In fact, it's a well-considered answer. I appreciate that.

Good.

Anything else?

That I'd like to talk about?

Yes.

You.

Me? What do you mean?

Just that. I'd like to talk to you about you.

Why?

Well, I see you often and you know a lot about me, but I know nothing about you. It seems unfair, don't you think?

Yes, but I'm your psychiatrist. I need to discover things about you as a matter of my profession.

In a way, though, I'm your patient, and it appears to me that I have a right to know something about you as well.

Reasonable, I suppose. Go ahead and ask me anything you want. I promise to answer as truthfully as I can. If, that is, I can answer at all.

Why do you say it that way?

Because I'm bound by certain professional guidelines. I couldn't, for example, tell you about another patient. That would be unethical. I've given my word I won't do that. That's what I mean.

I understand.

So, what would you like to know?

I'd like to hear why you decided to become a psychiatrist.

That's a fair question. It's actually a simple one to answer. When I was in college as an undergraduate student, I took a course in the subject. The teacher was amazingly charismatic, and certainly that helped. But the subject itself, one of learning about how the mind works and what kinds of things can disable some of its functions, mesmerized me. I spent most of my non-class time in the school library reading about it, and at night, when I should have been sleeping, thinking about it. The idea of being able to help people with disabilities seduced me into the profession. Once hooked, there was no way out of it.

Wow.

That's exactly how I felt. Does that answer your question?

Yes.

Good. It was a great question and I'm happy to have answered it for you.

Thanks.

Now let's get back to you. What prompted you to ask that question?

Actually, I've been thinking that someday I'd like to become a psychiatrist, too.

That might be difficult.

Why?

Well, first off, you're a lot older than I was when I began. And

62

second, you're probably going to have to wait a long time before you'll be able to go to school.

I see.

Do you?

Yes. If you decide I'm not crazy, I'll have to stand trial. I may then be judged guilty and sent to prison or to the hangman.

Interestingly, Joe, prisoners sentenced to death in this state can still choose between hanging and lethal injection.

I'd prefer injection.

Do you see how difficult it might be for you to become a psychiatrist?

Sort of. I can still hope, though, can't I?

I can't stop you from hoping. But I should warn you that false hopes can eventually make you unhappy. No matter what meds you're on.

Oh.

I'm sorry to put it so bluntly. Better to be truthful than to lie to you now isn't it?

Yes.

On the other hand, there are lots of things you can hope to do and not be disappointed.

Like what?

Writing, for example. Are you interested in writing?

Books?

Books, short stories, a diary, poetry, any of those things.

I guess.

You don't sound nearly as excited about writing as you did about being a psychiatrist.

I'm not.

Do you read a lot, Joe?

Not so much since I've been in here.

Did you before that?

Whenever I had the chance.

What kind of books did you read?

All kinds, I guess.

Fiction or non-fiction.

Fiction.

Do you remember the titles of any of them?

I remember Stranger in a Strange Land.

That's interesting.

Why?

Do you remember what it was about?

Not really. It was a long time ago.

Do you remember the author?

Yeah. Robert Heinlein.

So what kind of books did Heinlein write?

Science fiction.

Good. The book, by the way, was about an alien and his exploits on planet earth.

Right.

You remember now?

Yes. At least that much. I remember *grok*.

What does *grok* mean?

To truly understand something. With your body as well as your mind. With your whole being.

Good. Were the rest of the books you read of similar type to that one?

Suppose so.

You actually don't remember much about what you read?

I do. Maybe not so much now, though, given the meds I'm taking.

How many books did you read before, say, in a month?

Not that many. Maybe two or three.

That's pretty good. At what age were you when you read the most books?

My late teens.

Before you went to college?

Never went to college.

Oh, sorry, it says here you attended junior college for a time.

I signed up, but I was really busy on my father's farm so I didn't attend many classes. Ended up failing at the end of the first term. Pretty stupid, huh?

No. Not if you couldn't attend classes, it isn't. At least you gave it a try.

I did.

Did your father encourage you to go junior college?

No. It was *my* idea.

What did you want to be when you started out?

Didn't know. Mostly a farmer, I guess.

You already *were* a farmer.

No, actually, I was a farmer's son. That's different.

That makes sense. So you went to college to become better at working on his farm.

Yes.

Did he tell you that you weren't good enough at your job?

No, but I knew I wasn't.

Why was that?

Because I didn't want to do what he wanted me to do. I spent most of the time I supposedly worked thinking about things.

Like what?

Oh, girls I guess.

Anything else?

Well, I thought about the stars. You know, astronomy.

Interesting.

Why interesting?

Just that. Interesting. The undiscovered country. Well, I'll leave you with that thought, and we'll continue next time I'm here.

Sure.

7

The pharmacies of the Forensic Psychiatric Facility have locations in each of its buildings. Each pharmacy is situated in a corner of the main room where inmates gather to hear occasional concerts or other presentations. Located in corners with walls diagonal to the room's walls, each has a sliding glass window in front that can be pulled aside and shut only by the registered pharmacists inside. The single entrance and access to these pharmacies opens to the outside where only authorized personnel can enter or exit.

The meds in these pharmacies are kept in large safes that require unique combinations to open, with only staff members knowing these combinations. The pharmacies are open twenty-four seven, and only doctors can write prescriptions, even for what usually would be considered over-the-counter medications like aspirin.

The staffs in the pharmacies work in four-hour shifts, so there are no chances of them tiring or making mistakes in filling a prescription. From the room side of the pharmacy, it looks very much like a prison within a prison.

Good morning, Joe.
You changed my meds.
I what?
You changed my meds. Why'd you do that?
I *didn't* do that.

The pharmacist said you did. She gave me a cup with different colored pills in it this morning. Why'd you *do* that?

Didn't do that. Sit down and I'll get to the bottom of this.

I won't sit until you tell me why you did it.

All right, don't sit. Wait here until I get back.

What happened?

Mistakes were made by many people.

What?

Yes. First mistake was mine.

How?

Over the years I've come to use initials for my patient's names rather than their full names to save time.

Okay.

Yesterday someone was admitted with the same initials as yours.

They got mixed up?

Yes. And there was a second mistake. Two different doctors whose signatures are both a mess. The signatures don't look much alike, but a mess is a mess and the pharmacist couldn't tell the difference. You got the other patient's meds and he got yours. From now on, both us doctors will have to resort to using your full names rather than initials. And we'll attempt to clean up our signatures. That way it will never happen again.

A mistake?

Yes. Did you take the pills given you yet?

No. I didn't know what they were.

Good. I've brought you the right meds. Here. And a bottle of water to wash them down. And a cinnamon roll besides.

So my meds are now back to what they were?

Yes. Take the cup and water.

That could have been a disaster.

Not really. Both groups of meds do pretty much the same things. You would have felt differently if you'd taken the pills you were given, though not that much different.

Good to know, I guess. But it sure had me worried for a while.

I'll bet it did.

Could have been much worse. What if one patient was taking heart medication and the other taking something for ulcers. Could have killed one or the other of us. Maybe even both of us.

Not possible.

Why not?

Because all the patients in this place are suffering from the same kinds of things. No one's here for either heart problems or ulcers.

I see. I'm feeling better already.

That's good. It was a mistake, mind you, and one that will not be repeated. Proves that doctors are fallible, I suppose.

Does.

Now. Let's begin again. How are you doing? Besides the meds mix up, I mean.

Fine, I guess.

Good. How about your sleeping?

Fine.

You probably know my next question already.

I do. Did I dream?

Yes. Did you? Do you remember it?

No, and no again.

You didn't dream?

No.

Is that something that occurs often?

No.

How often do you *not* dream?

Maybe once a month or so.

Can you associate something that happened yesterday that might have upset your routine?

My routine of dreaming?

Yes. And your routine of remembering those dreams.

Not particularly.

Is it possible that you dreamt and forgot the dream?

I suppose.

What do you think *that* might mean?

Maybe the dream was so stupid it wasn't worth remembering.

Good thought. Does it mean, by inference, that all dreams you remember are not stupid? That they *are* worth remembering?

I don't know.

Something to think about?

Yes. Count myself a king of infinite space—were I not to have bad dreams.

What?

Shakespeare. You seem to like Shakespeare.

I do. Do you?

Yes.

Good to know. Now, beyond those dreams, is there anything new in your life since we last met?

Yes.

What?

You got my meds screwed up.

Apart from that.

Well that was a pretty big thing, don't you think?

I do. But I'd like to look beyond that now so we can get on with our conversation.

Is that what you call them? Conversations?

Isn't that what they are?

Not to me, they aren't.

What are they? To you, I mean?

They are times in which you ask me questions and I answer.

So you consider them more of an interview than a conversation?

I consider them interviews sometimes.

What do you consider them other times?

Grillings.

Grillings? Like what police do to suspects?

Yes.

I'm sorry you feel that way, Joe. I'm a psychiatrist as you know, and it's my job to find out things about you. Important things. Questioning you is the best way to do that, don't you think?

I guess.

But I apologize if my process makes you feel compromised in any way.

Compromised?

That you have a problem with my tactics.

I don't. I think I'm still bummed out by the meds thing. I'm sorry for being belligerent.

You're not. In some ways it's good to hear you talk like this. It gives me some indication of your real feelings about our relationship. I'll work on my approach to discovering these things about you.

All right.

Good. That aside, let's get back to your childhood. Do you feel like talking about that some more?

Sure.

Good. Now let's concentrate on your relationship with your mother.

Are you a Freudian?

If by that you mean do I think that your relationship with your mother is responsible for what you've become in life, then no, I'm not. I still respect Freud, though. Mothers are very important in the development of their children. Many aspects of that relationship set a foundation for later behavior.

Interesting.

How so?

Well, I love my mother very much.

That seems like a healthy attitude. Does she show affection for you?

Some, I guess, but that isn't why I love her.

Why?

She sets a good example for me.

How's that?

Whenever my father got mad at me, her, or the both of us, she stood her ground. Didn't back down. Stood up for me. I liked that about her.

Very good. Mature, too, for such a young man to observe.

Well, I didn't actually see it that way when I was a kid. Then I took it all in. Later on I realized she was the one who held the family together.

Now, that's interesting. Did you have the feeling that your family would fall apart if your mother wasn't there to hold it together?

I don't know if we would have fallen apart without her, but she clearly made my father stand up and take notice. She's quite strong.

A real farmer's wife.

Yes. And a good person.

How would you characterize your father by comparison?

Well, he was strong too in his own way, though not as strong as she was.

So your mother was the alpha in your house?

The alpha?

The dominant figure.

No, actually not. Most of the time, on the small issues, my father won the battles. But when push came to shove, especially when talking about me, she won the wars.

This is excellent information, Joe.

Good.

So, you didn't have as strong a relationship with your father as with your mother?

You could put it that way. Though I think they were both alphas.

Good observation. Now, during those times when your mother had to be an alpha, what were the arguments about?

Me.

Always?

Yes.

What do you make of that?

Not much. I was small and she didn't want my father to whip me with his belt.

Could it also be that she carried you in her womb, gave birth to you, and therefore you had a special place in her heart?

Sure. That too.

How difficult were these arguments between your father and mother?

What do you mean?

Did they ever come to blows?

No. Not that I saw.

Did they *almost* come to blows?

A couple of times.

So your father threatened her?

A couple of times.

How did that make you feel?

Angry.

What did you want to do about it? I mean did you want to fight back against your father?

Yes.

Did you?

No.

Why not?

I suppose because he was much bigger than me. He'd win. I wasn't stupid.

Makes sense. So you did nothing?

Mostly.

Mostly? Could you be more specific about that?

Sure. I wanted to fight him, knew I couldn't, and so I made plans how someday I'd get even with him.

What kinds of plans?

Like when he was old and frail, pop him one on the snoot.

So, physical violence?

No. I only wanted to get even. Maybe bloody his nose a bit and tell him why I'd done it. Not hurt him much.

I see. So none of your plans had anything to do with real violence. Like?

Like breaking his legs or busting his arms. Things like that.

Well, they may have occasionally gone that far, but I knew when I thought those thoughts I was never going to carry them out. Just imagining stuff.

How long did these thoughts persist?

Maybe a few minutes.

Then what?

Then I'd go back to whatever I was doing before the fight.

Fine.

Are my reactions unusual? Does this help you diagnose me?

Yes. But they're not unusual. In fact, I'd say they're typical rather than unusual. Most people would feel the way you did.

That's good, isn't it?

Yes. It is. Did the neighborhood kids visit you often?

Not often. There weren't many neighborhood kids. In fact, besides the little neighbor girl, I can't think of anyone else.

Now, that *is* unusual. Of course you met kids in school, didn't you?

No. I was home schooled.

I didn't know that. Didn't you ever attend regular school?

No, other than the semester I sort of attended junior college.

How did you get into junior college if you hadn't attended regular school?

Took a test.

You passed?

Must have. They let me go to junior college.

Do you remember that test?

Some of it.

What kind of questions did it ask?

Simple ones. I took it and was out of there before anyone else left.

Do you remember the score you got?

No. I'm not sure I was ever given it.

Never saw a piece of paper with a grade?

Not that I remember.

No one said anything to you about it having been good, medium, or bad?

No.

So, you have no idea how well you did?

I had no problems. Does that help?

You mean you think you answered every question correctly?

Wasn't difficult. The questions were simple.

What kind of questions were they?

Many kinds. Some involved numbers, some words. Things like that.

I wonder if there would be a record of it somewhere.

Don't know.

Take a guess?

What difference would it make?

I'm not sure. It could help me help you if I knew the results.

How?

Hard to describe. If you did well, maybe it could help me understand your mind better. Help me get a grip on why you can't remember what the police and district attorney said you did and will try you for if you're released from here. I don't know for sure, but that's a possibility.

Sorry I can't help.

Well, maybe you can. Would you be willing to take a similar test if I could find someone to give it to you?

I guess so. Don't see why not.

Good. I'll see what I can do. As an example, though, could you tell me what twenty times forty is?

Eight hundred.

How did you do that so quickly?

Not sure. The answer just came to me.

Why do you suppose that is?

Don't know.

How about the square root of forty?

Six point three two five. Rounded off, of course.

That answer come to you as well?

Sort of.

Why sort of?

Well I know it's between six and seven because the square of six is thirty-six and that of seven is forty-nine. Once I have the six, the rest appears in my brain.

Like a calculator?

Guess so.

It appears that you have a certain gift with numbers.

Is that unusual?

Hard to tell. I don't know enough math to know for sure. That's why a standardized test would be a better reflection of your abilities. How do you do with words?

Like reading them?

Yes. But more like knowing their definitions.

I read a dictionary once.

You what?

I read a dictionary once.

Are you telling me you started at the beginning and read it through from front to back?

Yes.

Didn't it get boring?

No. Only took a couple of hours.

Do you remember what you read?

I guess. Things come to me when I see or hear words again.

So what did you do in your home schooling?

Nothing much. Helped my father with the chores.

So you didn't actually study anything?

No. I read sometimes, though.

Science fiction?

Mostly, I guess. That and the dictionary. We didn't have many books around the house, and I was too busy working to get to a library.

Too broke to buy any books?

We weren't broke, though I guess we were poor.

How long does it take for you to read a book?

Depends on the book.

An average length book.

A little while.

What would that mean in terms of hours, minutes, and seconds?

Probably an hour or so.

How can you read so fast?

I look at the page and what's there comes alive.

Naturally?

What's that mean?

Means that you don't use any kind of technique to make it happen.

No technique. I've always been that way.

This is quite a discovery, Joe. I can certainly use this in my analysis of your sanity.

My sanity?

Sorry. Your ability to remember what happened.

Why?

Well, you remember everything else, except nothing about this one particular thing. That's quite an interesting phenomenon, don't you think?

Yes. I guess I do. Though how does it help?

Well, Joe, we already know that our minds are capable of remembering everything we experience, at least for a short time. But you've got the ability to remember these things for a long time and access them at will. That's a gift. It means that you *do* remember what happened, though something is blocking you from accessing that information.

How could that happen?

Most likely because it was so horrific that your brain is protecting itself and you from facing it. Do you see?

I suppose.

Are there others things you can't remember?

Don't know. I can't remember.

Good, Joe. You've still got your sense of humor. You've recovered from the anger you felt earlier in our conversation when you thought I'd changed your meds without telling you.

I was angry?

Don't you remember? You were standing up when I came in.

I was?

You've forgotten?

Suppose so.

See? You suppress things you don't want to remember. We all do that to some extent. You'll probably remember that later today. Whether or not you do, though, it will take something stronger to make you re- member the incident.

Like?

I don't know that, Joe. If I did, I'd make it happen right now.

So where do we go from here?

We keep at it. I ask you questions. You answer them. Somewhere along the line we hope that something surfaces.

As I told you when we began doing this, I don't want to know what happened. It will probably make me unhappy.

It might. But it also might make you innocent of the crime as well. And that would make you happy, right?

Yes.

Today has been very productive for us, Joe. I'm looking forward to more of the same next time we meet.

I am, too.

Goodbye.

Bye.

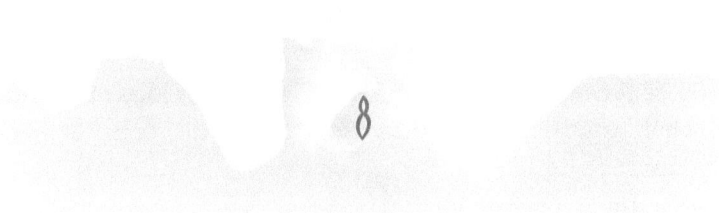

8

The janitors of the Forensic Psychiatric Facility work every other night. Their duties include emptying wastebaskets, cleaning floors, and all the usual tasks required of others in the same profession.

Unlike other janitors, however, the ones in the Forensic Psychiatric Facility have to wear unique uniforms to ensure that any tools or accessories they need cannot be taken by inmates and used to either escape or commit crimes on their follow inmates or themselves. Thus, the janitors' pockets require heavy-duty zippers for small tools, locked containers for cleaning supplies, and secure metal boxes for collection bags, the latter to ensure they aren't used for suffocation.

Janitors are also watched by guards during their presence on site to avoid accidents and injury to others. All told, the process of cleaning the facility is closely monitored and the rules strictly enforced.

Hello, Joe.
Doctor Amador.
Did you dream last night?
No.
Interesting.
How so?
Just one more bit of information about you I now know. Sometimes you don't dream more than once a week.

Yes, I guess so. You know, you're not the kind of psychiatrist I expected either.

What kind did you expect?

Someone like the others. Use a lot of specialized terms, remain quiet most of the time while I talk, things like that.

Those are stereotypes, Joe. Most of us do our jobs differently. Apparently here you've come across a few that use the same techniques.

I guess.

So, nothing new?

Actually, I did remember something I forgot to mention to you regarding one of the dreams I told you about.

What?

I had a dog once.

What kind of a dog?

A mutt. He followed my father home one night after he'd finished plowing the fields. Just a puppy, though a big one. All black with short hair. Had a sheen to it that seemed to glow when the light hit it just right.

How big.

As a cocker spaniel maybe. But he was only a couple of months old. Had big paws. Was going to be a bruiser when he grew up.

Your father take to him?

God no. My father didn't want him around. Tried to kick him so he wouldn't follow him. Mutt thought he was playing around.

So what happened?

My father wouldn't let him inside, so he just whined outside the back door during dinners. My mother often waited until my father went to the bathroom and then gave Mutt the leftovers.

You named him Mutt?

What he was. Seemed to fit.

Pretty dog?

I thought so. But he was dumb.

Why do you say that?

I built him a doghouse the first week we had him, but couldn't get him to go into it. Not even at night when it was cold. Must have been November by then, and Mutt just sat outside the door and whined.

So your mother fed him?

78

Yes. She was a sap when it came to things like that. I think she liked Mutt more than I did.

You play with him?

When I had time. Tug of war with old towels. Those kinds of things. And he loved to lick my face and slobber all over me.

Did he ever get the idea about the house you built for him?

He did when it snowed. Curled right up inside.

And your father?

I think he put up with him. Never liked him though, and Mutt knew it. Stayed the hell away from him when he figured that out.

Sounds like a very interesting dynamic.

Was. Even my mother eventually tired of him whining for food. But she fed him still. Mutt could only depend on me. I'd talk to him sometimes, especially when he first saw me. He'd come running while wagging that long tail of his. Quite a sight.

How long did you have him?

A few months.

Give him away?

Not on your life.

What happened?

I found him in the trees out back one afternoon.

And?

You sure you want to hear this?

We've come this far.

Okay. He wasn't around when I left to go into the field that morning. He always waited for me before then. He'd follow me and then run around while I worked. He seemed to think I was always playing with him.

But you weren't.

No. I was working the fields. But it was fun to see him tire himself out and then nap until I took a lunch break.

And?

He just wasn't there when I left that morning. I waited, but he didn't come. I'd never had to call him before, so didn't even have a special whistle for him.

So what happened?

Nothing at first. I ran the tractor for a while, and then noticed something that smelled bad. So I climbed down and found him in the trees. He was a mess. Everything but his head had been torn to pieces. Blood everywhere. And pieces of fur.

What did you do?

I screamed, cried, vomited. It was terrible. I'd never seen anything like it before. I couldn't believe it. Mutt, my Mutt, had been mutilated by someone.

What did you do?

I ran out into the neighboring field where my father was plowing and told him about Mutt.

And?

At first he wouldn't come. Said Mutt was just a dog. Why the hell should I care?

How did that make you feel?

Terrible. But I cried and pleaded, so he finally got down from the tractor and followed me to the spot. I pointed to where Mutt was, but couldn't go see him like that. Not again. No way.

So your father did what?

Well, he was in there a while. Long enough that I began to pretend it wasn't Mutt. Maybe some other dog. Maybe Mutt would come running after me from across the field like he always did. Barking and wagging that tail of his. I so convinced myself by wishing it weren't true, I thought he might still be alive. So I looked around for him.

But he wasn't there?

No. He wasn't there.

And when your father came out from the trees?

He told me an owl had eaten most of Mutt during the night. Probably while Mutt was still alive.

Good God. He told you that?

Yes.

Why the hell did he do that?

The way he was. That's all.

Did you believe him?

I didn't want to. I couldn't believe him. I wouldn't believe him. Not about Mutt. The day before we'd been playing, and now he was dead. And not just dead, but having been butchered by an owl. Or some bird.

I couldn't imagine anything worse happening. Least of all to a puppy like Mutt.

So?

I asked my father to bury him.

And?

He wouldn't. Just a dog, he said, and walked back to where he'd been plowing. I screamed after him. All he said was, 'If you want him buried, do it yourself.'

So I tried. I went back to the place where he was. But when I got there, a crow was pecking out Mutt's eyes.

Good God. What did you do?

I screamed and ran him off. But when I looked back at Mutt, I just couldn't do it. I didn't have the stomach.

So what did you do?

I ran back to my tractor and began plowing again.

As if nothing had happened?

Right. All I could think of was my little puppy Mutt and what the world had done to him. I kept remembering those times we played together. His long wagging tail. That look in his eyes when we played tug of war with that tail wagging. And now I'd left him to the crows and the owls. I felt sick.

Guilty?

Absolutely.

Why? It wasn't your fault.

I didn't bury him. I left him for the vultures. He deserved for me to at least have buried him. But I hadn't done it. I was a coward, and I didn't love him enough. No one had. Not even me. He deserved a lot better life than I'd given him. And a lot better death as well.

What a story.

It is.

You have a tear rolling down your cheek, Joe.

I know. I suppose I still miss Mutt.

Ever think of getting another dog?

Only one Mutt. It's not like dogs are interchangeable.

True.

By the way, did you investigate the lighting and meals in here?

As a matter of fact, I did. The lights remain on all the time for reasons not explained to me. The cooks, however, have agreed to vary the days on which certain meals are served.

Thank you. No rationale for the lights, huh? Interesting.

Why interesting?

That they clearly have a reason but won't explain what that reason is.

I see.

Yes.

Now, Joe, I have a surprise for you.

What? I hope you're not changing my medications. Again.

No. That won't happen. Or at least it won't happen without my telling you about it beforehand. Which I will never do unless you report some difficulties with the current ones. You have my assurances on that.

Good.

The surprise is that I've brought someone along with me today. She's going to administer a test for you. Something we discussed the last time we spoke.

All right.

This test is likely similar to the one you took to get into junior college.

Not the same?

No. As time changes, so do things like tests. So, I'm sure you'll find it similar, but not exactly the same.

I suppose if it were the same, it would be too easy.

Yes. So, instead of us meeting for our regular amount of time, she'll be giving this test to you in here. I'll be waiting outside the door when you've finished. That is, if you finish before I leave.

Okay.

So, I'll step outside now and wait for you two to work out the details and for you to complete it. And then we'll talk. If there's enough time, maybe, we'll also get to hear the results.

Good.

I'll see you soon.

All right.

Joe?

Yes?

You've finished already?

Yes.

How'd you do?

It was easy.

You knew all the right answers?

Yes.

Amazing.

Why? Did you see the test before I took it?

No. Though I understood from the woman giving the test that the average time for taking it was about an hour. The very best students finish in a little over half an hour. You finished it in less than half that time. Twelve minutes, approximately.

It took time to check the boxes.

Yes, I imagine it did. Well, the woman administering the test told me it wouldn't take long for her to grade it, so we may get an answer before I leave.

Good.

So, not to repeat myself, you found the questions easy to answer?

I did. They also required multiple-choice responses, so it was especially easy. I would have preferred writing the answers myself.

I see. That would have made it harder?

Harder for some people. Not me.

Why would you have preferred it?

Because I'd have felt I'd accomplished something when I finished, rather than simply checking the correct empty boxes.

I can understand that. But you did feel you did a good job?

Yes, I got all the answers right.

That's great. Just a minute, I've got to take this call. It might be the woman who gave you the test.

Right.

Who is it? Yes. I understand. So? What? How can that be? What? It's impossible? Yes. Thank you very much. Goodbye.

What did she say?

I can't believe it.

Perfect score? Like I told you?

No. You didn't get *any* answers right.

What? *None* of them? Something must be wrong with the test.

Nothing's wrong with the test. Hundreds of thousands of people have taken it before and had no problem.

Then what's going on?

She told me that a chimpanzee would have gotten a better score than you did. In fact, probabilities being what they are, you should have gotten some right if for no other reason than by accident or chance.

I don't understand.

She told me that, in her opinion, you deliberately chose all the wrong answers.

Why would I do that? I checked all the right ones. I swear I did.

Then how did the score turn out this way?

I don't know.

She thinks you sabotaged the test to prove some kind of point.

What point would that be?

I don't know. At least I don't know *yet*.

What do you mean?

Maybe you don't want to get out of here.

Why wouldn't I want to get out of here? I *do* want to get out of here. To go to trial and prove myself innocent. To be free.

Maybe you think you do at your conscious level, but you're happy here. You admitted that yourself. After all, you've got a free ride. The meds keep you balanced and happy. Three squares a day without working.

You think I like watching these people stare into nothingness and wondering if I'm doing the same thing? One of the walking dead?

Do you?

No, I don't. It's terrible. I didn't deliberately do what you say I did, or she said I did, and I do want to get out of here. I don't think I could have done it deliberately without my knowing it.

Don't you see? That's the only explanation.

No. I won't believe it. I can't believe it.

Let's slow down a minute. What other explanations are possible? Besides, that is, that the test is screwed up.

Maybe she got the wrong answer sheet. Maybe it's for a different test. An accident.

I suppose that's possible.

Could you check for me?

Sure.

What do you know about the lady giving the exam, anyway? Maybe she sabotaged me.

Why would she do that?

I don't know. But isn't it possible?

Yes. Very unlikely, though possible.

As possible as me getting all the answers wrong?

Good point. I'll check that as well.

Thank you.

Unfortunately, I'm late for my next appointment. I've got to go. I'll see you next time and check those things like we agreed.

All right. Thank you.

Goodbye.

9

The business office of the Forensic Psychiatric Facility stands as a separate building from the psychiatric wards. The staff of this office is responsible for carrying on the daily business of the facility, ensuring that the allotted funding is spent correctly, and dealing with matters involving the individuals, agencies, and organizations that serve the inmates. These include activities such as education, testing, and other matters that may require daily or occasional visitations by independent psychiatrists and experts these psychiatrists may need for specialized focus. The latter individuals, no matter the number of visits they make including just one, must comply with the same requirements made of all visitors. This includes submitting to searches at entrances and all other security measures.

Morning, Joe.

Well?

Thought you might be eager to find out what I discovered. It turns out both of you are correct.

What does that mean?

Well, first of all, the woman who gave the test graded it completely accurately. There's no doubt about that. I've looked it over and can verify that.

I don't see how we could both be right then.

It's the test sheet that's wrong.

The questions are messed up?

No. I meant to say the answer sheet is wrong. Sorry about that.

How do you mean?

Do you remember how each answer had an open square next to it?

Yes. I filled them in correctly.

Actually, you did and you didn't.

How could it be both ways?

That's the rub. There are four answers to choose from, but five empty squares. For each question. Apparently, it was at one time a test that allowed for five possible answers and has been altered to four recently. Thus, each answer has an open square to its left and one to its right.

Strange.

Now most people, in fact all people except you, choose to fill in the square to the right of each potential answer, not the one to the left. They figure, I guess, that we read left to right, and so the empty square to the right must be the one you fill and the first one exists for decoration or something. You must read from left to right as well, don't you?

I don't read in any direction. I look at a page and that's it. It's in my memory.

Like a photograph?

Not so much. More like it's meaning simply comes to me.

How do you write?

Like everyone else does. Left to right. And I answered the questions from left to right, just like the others.

So it was just as easy for you to pick the square to the left of the correct answer as to the right.

I suppose so.

That's it then. When we checked your test by moving the correction sheet one square to the left, every answer was perfect. *Every one of them*, Joe. It means you finished in less than half the time of the best previous test taker who also got one hundred percent. You're a genius.

Interesting.

How so?

It wasn't difficult.

So?

I'd like to take an actually difficult exam to see how I'd do.

That would be interesting, Joe, but the point is made. You have a gift. That may explain some things.

Like?

People who have such gifts are often called savants.

I know that.

Some call them *idiot* savants.

Know that, too.

Well what does it mean?

Means they pay a price for being good in one area by doing less good in others.

Right. So maybe we should look at what areas you aren't so good at.

Like what?

That we'll have to determine by returning to my asking you questions and you answering to the best of your ability.

Okay.

Let's begin with my asking you what you think are your worst areas. I don't mean what you don't like to do, rather what you think you're terrible at doing. Of course, those may be the same thing as we often don't like to do the very things we're no good at. Do you understand?

Of course.

Well, where do you want to begin?

Probably with life.

Life?

Yes. I'm terrible at life.

What, exactly, do you mean by that?

I don't communicate well with people. I don't care what people say most of the time.

Don't you care what I say?

I suppose. I care to the extent that you can get me out of here. That's a big incentive.

So you need an incentive to get along with people.

No. It's not that. I don't get along with people because I ignore them and actually hope they'll ignore me. Maybe a better way to say it would be that I like to stay inside myself. I like to be alone. I don't dislike people, I just find them problematic.

How so?

They think illogically. Answers that come to me are logical. Correct.

Most people I've met think with their emotions rather than their brains.

You don't like that?

I don't mind as long as I don't have to listen to them. If they leave me alone, everything's fine.

I see. And you think this is a deficit?

Don't you?

From a social point of view, it probably is. On the other hand, if you're happy being left alone with your thoughts, it seems to me you have that right. Don't you?

Yes, though others think I'm strange for it.

Ah, now that's very interesting. Does that bother you?

Actually, no. Because thinking that about me keeps them away. Works out better that way for both of us.

I see your point. But doesn't some kind of relationship between you and others make sense?

Of course. Here I am talking to you.

All right, let me ask you this. Do you remember any time, any event in your life that might be responsible for your feeling this way?

I can't think of one.

Maybe a time when you were punished for something by someone forcing you to be by yourself. For example, banished to a closet, a room, something like that?

Well, I suppose so.

For example.

When I was in my teens sometime, my father asked me to put away the horses for the night.

Did he ask you to do that regularly?

No. Occasionally. When he was particularly tired or had something else to tend to, he did. During the time I'm remembering, it was winter.

Did you do it?

What?

Put away the horses?

Yes.

What happened?

I put them away. Only it was winter and very cold outside. I was cold too, and forgot to put out hay for them to eat and put their blankets on them.

Important?

Very. They need the food and the blankets for extra protection from the cold.

What happened as a result?

One of the horses came down with pneumonia and died.

Your father was mad?

Oh, God was he mad.

What did he do to you?

He dragged me outside and into the same barn, put me into the empty stall, chained me to a metal pipe, and left me there for the night.

Make you feel like the horse must have felt?

Yes.

Was it cold?

Probably colder than the previous night when I'd forgotten to feed and cover the horses.

What happened?

I got pneumonia just like the horse did.

You didn't die, obviously.

Obviously.

But you got really sick?

Never been sicker.

Did your father apologize for leaving you out there alone all night?

Never said a word about it.

Did you ever again not put the horses to bed without feeding and covering them?

He never asked me to do it again.

I see. Now you brought this up because you were reminded of it when we were talking about enjoying being alone.

That's because I was out there by myself all night. Didn't sleep at all. I decided the only way to not think about being cold was to think about other things. So I did.

What kinds of things

Mostly about stuff I'd read.

That got you through the night?

Yes, though I still got sick.

Thinking about things you read made things easier on you during that night?

Absolutely. In fact, it so protected my feeling the pain from the cold that I actually enjoyed being out there most of the time.

Interesting.

How?

Because it probably explains the reason you feel so secure when you're alone. In your head. You feel you're protected that way.

I suppose.

Did you end up going to the hospital?

No.

Why not?

Too far away, I guess.

How about seeing a doctor?

No.

Why not? Didn't your father believe in doctors?

Not that. I think he thought I deserved to continue to feel bad. Horses made plowing the fields possible. Having one less made it harder. Even impossible in some cases.

Didn't you have tractors?

This was before we had one.

So he had to buy another horse?

No. We couldn't afford one. He kept us working in the fields twice as long.

How did you feel about that? Were you mad at him?

No. I understood how he felt.

But that's a severe punishment for a kid, don't you think?

Probably. Though I found something I didn't know I had.

What's that?

Myself.

And that made it okay in your mind?

Yes.

I've got to go now. I'll be coming back soon and we can continue this discussion. What you've told me is extremely important. Thank you for sharing it with me.

You bet.

Goodbye, Joe.

Bye. And thank you for figuring out the problem with the test.

My pleasure.

10

Outside the Forensic Psychiatric Facility, the temperature at this time of year averaged in the mid-thirties. On this particular day, the sky had clouded over and the weathermen were predicting a major storm on the way with several inches of snow—maybe approaching a foot—in store for the area. For those coming to visit the facility, this meant making a decision. Chance being stranded until the plows cleaned up the roads, or wait a day or two until the storm subsided. Most visitors came anyway, being psychiatrists and feeling the professional need to see their patients. Some of the business staff and guards phoned in sick. Thus, the wards were understaffed, at least to some degree.

Of course, the pharmacy had to remain open, even if staffed by paramedics acting as pharmacists. Some of the guards were not replaced, others had substitutes—mostly those from the towers outside deemed somewhat unnecessary due to the extreme cold and expected whiteout conditions soon to fall upon the land. This type of thing occurred occasionally during winter months. After all, this was north country, and storms like this were not that uncommon.

Good morning, Joe.

You look as cold as I felt the night I was kept in the barn.

It's going down to zero by evening they tell me. No enemy worse than winter and rough weather.

Can't feel it in here.

One of the advantages of being an inmate.

Then again, there are many disadvantages.

True. Let's begin by continuing our last discussion.

About that night in the barn?

Yes. What exactly did you think about when you were in there?

Mostly about books I'd read by then, especially about mathematics.

You like mathematics?

Yes.

Why?

Puzzles need solving. There's an answer to each puzzle. Simple.

Not like social life?

Not at all like that.

So, you detected that social life's problems are not black and white.

Yes. So I spent my time trying to figure out how things worked. Mathematically worked, that is.

Did you?

Did I what?

Figure out how things worked? Mathematically, that is.

Some things.

Can you give me an example?

Sure. I thought about how many words were possible in the English language. Not just real words, but all possible combinations of letters. After a minute or two, it turned out to be one-hundred and forty six trillion, eight-hundred and thirteen billion, seven-hundred and seventy-nine million, four-hundred and seventy-nine thousand, and five-hundred and ten. Quite a lot of words, though a lot less than I thought there would be.

How long did this take you?

Well the formula's easy. So is the answer. What took time was actually reciting the numbers out loud. That took longer than calculating the result.

And this was interesting to you because?

Because we may run out of possibilities someday.

How many words that we actually use exist now?

That isn't mathematical particularly. It's a counting problem, which *is* mathematical but the results will vary depending on a number of factors.

Such as?

Do we count a word that means many different things as one word or many? Do we count plurals and different versions of one word as one word or many? Things like that.

If we count one word as one word, no matter its number of meanings, and count the plurals and so on as separate words?

Still hard to figure. Even using a dictionary. See, it's like people speaking to one another. What one thinks is true, the other may not. It's messy. Colloquialisms. Dialects. When I'm alone, I know what I mean and everything remains consistent. Otherwise, it's a mess. See what I mean?

I do. But I'm still curious how many words we actually use as compared to those that are actually possible.

It's probably in the hundreds of thousands. Plenty of room for more words to be created if that's what you're worried about. See how much fun this is? It'll keep your mind occupied for hours.

And keep the cold away.

Right.

You told me in one of our earlier discussions that you were only mildly interested in writing things like short stories, poems, and so on.

That's right.

But you just told me about a mathematical exercise to do with words. Writing obviously has to do with words as well.

It does. But, as I say, words are vague. Different people mean different things when using them. Often you have to figure out their meanings by context, or by guessing, or by understanding slang. That doesn't work for me.

I see that. Math doesn't have that kind of vagueness?

Absolutely not. Math is perfect. Every question has an answer.

Is that literally true?

Yes.

How about the Incompleteness Theorem?

You know about that?

Well, I at least know *of* it. 'This statement is false' can never be solved.

Because if it's true, it's false, and vice versa?

Yes.

Well, first of all, words are not mathematical. Gödel's version is and I've looked it over.

Do you approve of the mathematics?

Absolutely. What's your question?

That there are things that mathematics cannot explain.

I see. And why should that matter to me?

Because it means that mathematics cannot ever provide a complete explanation of things.

Doesn't bother me in the slightest. Never expected it to. What I like about mathematics is that for those things that can be explained by math, it gives precise and complete answers.

So you ignore Gödel's theorem?

I do.

So it doesn't bother you?

I suppose it bothers me in the overall picture of the universe. But I'm happy working with less theoretical matters. More content to figure out the day-to-day ones. If you understand what I mean.

I do. So let's get back to your experience in the barn.

Okay.

What else did you think about that night?

Besides mathematics?

Yes.

Nothing much.

Nothing?

Well, I stayed angry with my father for a few minutes, though I realized he was right. I'd killed one of our horses and deserved the punishment. Besides that, I kept doing math.

Did you want to get even with your father?

No. He needed to get even with me. And was.

You didn't continue your anger toward him?

No. At least not once I understood the situation.

Even when you got sick?

Yes. It wasn't about my father. It was about me. Don't you see?

I do. Now, how did your mother take this?

She was angry.

At you or your father?

Mostly him. She yelled and told him he could have killed me.

How did he respond?

He quieted down and let her yell herself out. In fact, he stayed so calm I thought he might fall asleep.

This was when you were sick and in the house? You having no idea how she took it during the night you spent in the barn?

Right.

Can you imagine if she was still as angry as she was when you came into the house as sick as you were, how bad it might have been while you were out there nearly freezing to death?

No reason to imagine something I couldn't know. Doing so would only confuse me.

I understand. Now, let me ask you this. Did it bother you to know you might have died as a result of what your father did to you that night in the form of punishment?

Never gave it much thought.

Why not?

He did what he thought was right. That's it. Whether I thought it was right or not was and is immaterial.

So it doesn't make you angry even at this point?

No.

Never has?

No.

Would you do the same thing to a son of yours?

I don't have a son.

But let's say you did.

Exactly the same thing?

Yes.

No.

You wouldn't?

No.

What would you do?

I don't know, but not that.

Why?

It might kill him.

And you wouldn't like that?

No way.

But your father *did* feel that way.

Yes.

Does that bother you?

No. I'm not my father. He had his rules. I have mine.

You used the past tense.

Yes.

Why?

He's dead.

How do you know this?

My mother called and told me so.

When?

After he died.

When was that?

I'm not sure exactly. A few years back.

How did you feel when you heard that?

I don't know. Sad, I suppose.

You don't sound convinced of that. Did you go to the funeral?

No.

Why?

There *was* no funeral.

Why not?

We weren't a particularly religious family, I guess.

You guess? I thought your mother was religious.

She had her moments. But no, we weren't a particularly religious family.

So he wouldn't have wanted a funeral?

No idea. He never said so either way. At least to me.

He might have told your mother.

He might have.

Did you ask her about that?

No.

Why not?

She would have done what he wanted. So he either didn't tell her, or he told her that he didn't want one. I don't know which, and I don't particularly care.

Do you find this strange?

Strange?

I mean most households have funerals for members of their immediate family. Yours didn't. That's unusual.

Not unusual for our family.

How so?

Well, we heard of other members of my father or mother's families dying and we never went to their funerals. Cousins, and so on.

They have funerals?

I doubt it, though I don't actually know. But I do know that if they did have them, we didn't go.

All right. Let's get back to the time you spent in the barn that night. You said you had no ill feelings or thoughts toward your father.

After my initial reaction, that's right.

Have you ever felt angry toward *anyone* in your life?

Yes. Many times.

Can you give me an example or two?

Sure. I was angry with you when I discovered you'd changed my meds and hadn't told me about it.

What form did your anger take?

Form?

I mean did you want to hurt me?

Like beat you?

Yes.

Absolutely not.

Well, what did you feel like doing?

I felt like changing your meds without telling you.

An eye for an eye in other words.

Yes.

Do you believe that saying?

To a degree.

What degree is that?

Well, if you were to kill me, I wouldn't want to kill you back. I couldn't. I'd be dead.

That's a pretty drastic example. What about less drastic things?

Like would I try to kill you if you tried to kill me and failed?

That's still more drastic than I meant, but it will do for the moment.

Probably not.

Why?

Killing someone doesn't actually teach them a lesson, does it?

No. What *would* you do then?

I'd likely turn you in to the cops.

Hope that I'd be found guilty and put in jail?

Yes.

What if I wasn't? What if I was set free?

I'd probably think you'd try to kill me again.

What would you do about that?

I'd have to stop you.

Up to and including killing me?

Yes. Though that would be a last resort. There are many other things I'd try first.

Like?

Talk to you. Ask you what I'd done to deserve your attempts to kill me. Find out if you were going to try it again.

What if I said I wasn't, but tried it again anyway?

I'd have to do something more severe.

Which would be?

I don't know.

An example?

Probably call the cops again. If that didn't work, I'd hire someone to watch you. Give me some advance notice.

That doesn't seem fair since I'm doing these things to you and not having to pay for protection or fearing retribution from you.

That's true.

Does that change your mind?

Like does it mean I'd try to kill you in return?

Yes.

No.

Why?

Killing is stupid. No point to it. I might beat you. Try to convince you to stop.

So violence is possible?

Certainly. But not lethal violence.

Is there anything that would make you angry enough to kill someone?

I don't know.

What if your daughter Carla was kidnapped, raped, and brutally murdered? What would you do?

I'd let the police do their job. If that didn't work, I'd find the perpetrator myself.

And do what to him?

Turn him over to the police.

What if the person went free again?

You mean he did it, and got away?

Yes.

I'd have to do something.

What?

Not exactly sure.

Would you kill him?

Probably not.

What if he promised to rape and brutally murder your wife, or some other defenseless person?

Where are you taking this?

To the point of last resort. I'm trying to figure out if you would *ever* resort to killing someone. If only to prevent them from killing others.

I see. Like if I were put in a room with Hitler and knew he was about to kill millions of people in concentration camps, would I kill him?

Something like that.

You should have asked that question first. I would certainly kill him. Without a second's hesitation.

You would?

Yes.

That's what it would take for you to kill someone?

Something along those lines. If it were to protect someone from getting murdered, yes, I would do whatever necessary to prevent that.

Murdering the potential murderer being one of those things?

Not murder. I would kill them. There's a difference.

I understand. There is. I meant to say kill rather than murder.

Are you sure?

Of what?

That you made a mistake? Or were you trying to catch me on a fine point?

I made a mistake. That's all.

Good. I'd hate to think we were playing word games here.

You have my word that we're not.

Funny.

How so?

'Word games' and your use of the word 'word.'

I see.

And I understand.

I'm glad you do. I'm going to have to leave now. I've got other patients to tend to. I'll leave you with one thought to consider until we meet again.

What's that?

Are you sure you don't want to know what crime you're charged with committing? The one that's keeping you here? I don't want you to answer me this minute, but that's the first question I'll ask next time I see you. I want you to think about it. All right?

Fine.

Goodbye for now.

Bye.

11

The weather outside the Forensic Psychiatric Facility had not changed much in two days. Snowplows had done their best to clear the roads, and no sooner had they finished than they had to begin again. It was a losing game. Many visitors to the facility had been caught in the storm's wrath and stayed the night. Or two nights. Some slept in chairs in the Administration Building where business was conducted, as far from the inmates as possible. Some stayed in conference rooms designed for teaching and meetings. No one stayed with the inmates. For many it was a matter of fear. For others a matter of necessity, since overcrowding in the facility made finding beds a near impossibility.

Good morning, Joe.

Morning.

How did you sleep?

Dreamt about a man trying to kill me.

Interesting, particularly given our last discussion. What did you do?

Nothing. He didn't succeed.

Why not?

I woke up.

Convenient.

I thought so.

Are you okay?

Yes. Why? It was a dream.

Not what I meant. You seem a little on edge, today.

I'm fine. We can't experience it in here, though the word's out that there's a mighty storm going on out there. Is that true?

It is. But don't worry, you're safe in here.

I know. But it's still worrisome.

Why?

Well, if there are high winds, the electricity or the heat could go out. Make this a dangerous place. The winter of our discontent.

That's not going to happen. There are backups here. One goes out, the other kicks in. You wouldn't even notice the change.

I see.

It still bother you?

Yes.

Reminiscent of the barn you spent a night in so long ago?

I suppose.

Concerns you still, huh?

Yes.

I can understand that.

Can you?

At least as much as anyone can who hasn't experienced it themselves.

Good.

Now, could we get back to the question I left you with the last time we met?

Of whether or not I'd like to hear about the crime I didn't commit?

Yes. That's it.

No.

Why?

I don't want to suffer through something you say is awful. Then hear there are people who think I committed it when I didn't.

That makes you angry?

No. That makes me not want to hear about it.

You're going to have to hear about it sometime. Why not now?

Timing is everything, Doctor Amador, timing is everything. Why should I want to hear something that will make me sad and angry now, when I can wait until later? If I hear it later, I'll have a lot more time being happy between now and then. Don't you see that?

I do. But aren't you curious?

About something I didn't do? No, I'm not curious. Would you be?

Yes, I think I would.

Well, time does not have the same appeal for everyone. I'd rather wait. Who knows, maybe I won't ever have to hear it.

Wishful thinking, Joe.

I'm a wishful thinker.

Well, I won't do anything against your wishes.

Thank you.

Maybe you'll let me ask you what you did in the courtroom to get you sent here in the first place.

I attacked whoever it was that made the accusation.

You remember that?

No. I know that's what I would have done.

I thought you preferred logic to violence?

Not when someone claims I did something when I didn't.

Well, I guess we can skip that part. Can we talk about your wife?

Sure.

Where did you two meet?

At Niagara Falls, believe it or not.

Now that's interesting. That's where many people go on their honeymoons. Why were you there?

Visiting. With another woman I was seeing at the time. And my wife-to-be was there with another man she was seeing at the time.

Interesting. How did that work out?

We eventually dumped our respective friends and got together ourselves.

I figured that, but can you give me some specifics?

Sure. I thought Missy was attractive. My girlfriend gave me some grief about it, and we eventually broke up.

The same day? Journeys end in lovers meeting?

No. Pretty much the next day. At least that's when it began. When she found me and my wife-to-be talking outside our apartment.

She left you there?

Oh, no. We had some very long discussions about it afterward. Then she left me. After we returned to my farm.

How would you characterize the discussions?

With her? Hostile.

Only on her part?

Yes.

You didn't get angry?

No.

Why not?

What would it have accomplished? It was bad enough the way it was.

Did it bother you that she was angry?

No. Well, maybe initially, then I turned her off.

Turned her off? How did you do that?

Just like in the barn. I turned my thoughts to other things.

Like mathematics?

Yes. That and other things.

Like?

Like my wife to be.

So it was pretty serious?

Yes. For me at least.

Love at first sight?

Sort of.

What attracted you to her besides her looks?

When we talked she was reasonable.

Did she like mathematics?

I don't know, or at least I didn't know so at the time.

Later on?

Yes. I mean no, she wasn't interested in mathematics. She was interested in rational discussions about things. No emotional flares. We made a good team.

How did things go with her and her boyfriend?

Pretty much the same way mine did with my girlfriend. Her boyfriend also found us together and began screaming.

Did you witness that?

Sure.

What did you do?

Tried to calm him down, but he wouldn't.

Did he get violent?

No. He called her a few names, and left.

What did you do?

Nothing.

Didn't you defend her?

She didn't need defending.

What did she do?

Tried to reason with him.

He didn't listen?

No.

So you two got together then?

Yes. It was perfect.

Could you describe your relationship with her? Without the intimate parts, that is.

Yes. We never fought. We discussed things, and when we disagreed we agreed to disagree and either did things separately or one of us would give in to the other without any strings attached. It was perfect. A rational relationship.

I see. Love is not love which alters when it alteration finds?

You like to read Shakespeare?

Yes. Was Carla eventually a part of that rational relationship?

She was. We agreed to have a child, and to apply scientific means to discover the best times for Missy to conceive.

That doesn't sound very exciting.

But it was. It was a mathematical experiment of sorts, based on probabilities.

I see. Did that work out?

Do you mean were we happy after Carla was born?

Yes.

Immensely happy. Everything was perfect.

Now, I have to ask you a question that will probably not be pleasant for you to answer.

All right.

Why do you suppose your wife has not attempted to contact you since you arrived here, and neither she nor Carla has come to visit you?

Outside the walls of the Forensic Psychiatric Facility, seven horns suddenly blared so loud that the windows of the Administration Building rattled and threatened to shatter. Sounding these horns meant that one of the entrances to the facility had been compromised. That is, someone without authority to do so had exited or entered a door to a building.

Inside the facility, these horns could easily be heard and, since they had never sounded at any time in the past, everyone, including the staff and guards, were completely confused as to what to do. The inmates covered their ears and mostly sat on the floor hoping it would go away. The guards immediately ran to the two exits and entrances of each building to see what the problem was. The wail of the horns lasted for five minutes before stopping.

What was that?

If you're talking to me, I can't hear you. But, guessing what you're saying by reading your lips, I don't know. I just don't know.

Is someone escaping?

I still can't understand you, though I'm assuming you're asking me if there's an escape. That must be the case.

Who?

What?

Who?

I have no idea. You stay here. I have to report to someone. Do you understand?

Yes.

I'll be right back and let you know what's happening.

When the horns stopped blaring, all went deadly silent. The snow kept falling as it had since daybreak, but no one could be seen in the yard or climbing the fence surrounding the complex.

What's happening?

They think there was an error caused by a brief brownout from the storm. No one's escaped. Everything's fine.

Good.

Now, where were we?

I don't remember.

Ah, yes. I asked you why, if your marriage had gone so well, your wife and daughter have not communicated with you or come to visit. What do you think?

I don't know.

You told me previously this doesn't bother you.

No.

Why not? It would bother *me*.

I understand. Our marriage is different. There must be some logical reason why they've not come.

Can you imagine what that reason might be?

No. But I'm sure there is one.

Could you take a guess?

Well, seeing me in this place might not be good for my daughter.

I can understand that. Though what about your wife?

She might not feel good about it either. I don't know.

Could it be that whatever it was that put you in here, the thing you don't want to talk about and don't remember, could have something to do with it?

Possibly. I don't know what she knows and what she doesn't know.

Would she assume you're innocent?

I don't know.

Why? Doesn't she love you?

Not to the extent that she wouldn't listen to her common sense. If she thought I did it, then that might very well be the reason. I hadn't thought of that before, but it makes sense.

Well, given the excitement with the horns, I'm going to have to cut our session short today.

Okay.

Besides, I have to see if I can find a bed.

A bed?

Yes. The storm's quite scary out there. They're not clearing the roads anymore. That means I'll have to stay here at least one more night.

One *more* night?

Yes. I slept here last night, too, if you can call it sleeping. I sat in a chair in the Administration Building. It was not very comfortable.

That's terrible.

It is. But weather is weather. We can't control it. Once in a while it gets serious enough to delay or prevent the best-laid plans.

Of mice and men.

Yes. So I'll probably see you tomorrow rather than my usual two days, since I'll be here anyway.

Fine. I'll look forward to it. But beware, the night is long that never sees the day.

Ah, thank you Joe, I needed that.

Thank you, Doctor Amador.

12

One of the guards at the Forensic Psychiatric Facility did not fully accept the idea that the warning horns blared because of a storm-related cause. Instead, he continued to search for a more sinister problem. After many hours of studying the possibilities, he discovered that the system had been designed to set off alarms for anyone escaping the compound as well as for someone illegally entering the compound— someone attempting to avoid identification and airport-style security to come inside. Those in charge had dismissed the latter idea due to the harsh weather and focused on the former one. Thus, this guard initiated a search to find potential intruders.

Good morning, Joe.

Morning, Doctor Amador.

You had another good sleep last night?

I did. And didn't dream.

Two nights in a row? Or is it now three?

Only one. Though it's happened at least three times in the last week.

Can you account for this in some way?

You mean have I been more relaxed than before?

Yes. Something like that.

No. Nothing much has changed in my life to account for it. But I don't remember anything the previous times either.

All right. Let's go on with the next line of questioning. Today I'd like to talk about Carla.

My daughter?

Yes.

Why? She's only six years old.

Seven now, I believe.

That's right. I'd forgotten I've been in here that long.

So far, that is.

Right. So far.

Since you haven't seen or heard from Carla, we'll have to speak about her and your behavior prior to when you entered this place.

I understand.

Then, let's begin with you telling me what your relationship was like with her before you were removed from her life.

Well, we loved each other.

I'd imagine that would be the case. How did you express that love?

We spent time together whenever we could.

When would that be?

After the chores were done. Remember, I had a farm to maintain and didn't have anyone to help.

Did she work with you?

Small jobs around the house. Nothing big. After all, she was six and a girl. She was more help to her mother than to me.

So you saw her only in the evenings?

Yes. She wasn't awake when I went out in the morning.

What time was that?

Around four.

Stayed out until when?

Usually seven or so. Depended on what I had to do that day.

Did you come in for lunch?

Not usually. Missy made me a sandwich the night before, and I'd brew a thermos of coffee before I left.

So when did Carla usually go to bed?

Around nine.

So your window to visit with her was about two hours a day?

Yes.

Part of that time was dinner?

Yes.

About how much time did dinner take?

Maybe an hour, more or less.

So, did you play with your daughter during the remaining hour?

Not usually.

No? What did you do instead?

I helped home school her.

Just like you had been when you were young?

Yes.

This involved what exactly?

Seeing how her homework was going. Asking her questions on her reading. Things like that.

How was she doing with those things when you last saw her?

Extremely well. She's very smart. Smarter than Missy or me, I think.

Did she ever get out and play with other kids?

I don't know, really. There were other kids in the general neighborhood. Whether she played with them or not I never asked.

You weren't concerned about her falling under the wrong influences?

Not particularly. I knew that Missy took care of such things. Besides, I don't think Carla would be interested in people like that. She never got into trouble.

Did you ever ask her to put the horses to bed?

Ah, now that's a good question. No, I never did. First, we don't have horses. Second, I wouldn't want her to face what I faced when I was young.

Did you ever punish her for anything?

Yes.

For what?

Not doing her homework.

How did you punish her?

With a strong word or two.

Never got physical?

Never.

How long did your punishments last?

You mean how long did I take giving her the strong words?

Yes.

Less than a minute. As I say, she's very bright. Didn't take her long to catch on.

Did she ever repeat her errors?

Occasionally. Who wouldn't? It's inevitable. Usually I didn't have to repeat my words though. If she'd not done whatever I'd asked her to do, it was because something had come up.

Like?

Like her mother needed her to do a job around the house or something. Nothing she could control. Thus, there was no reason to punish her more than once.

And only with harsh words?

Yes.

Did you read her stories?

Never had to much. She was reading by age three.

Before that?

No. Her mother read her some. I was usually exhausted by that time of day.

So, you never sat on the floor and played games with her or anything like that?

Not much. She didn't like to play. She wanted to learn things.

Did you kiss her goodnight?

Of course.

When she was in bed before going to sleep?

Yes. Missy and I both did. On the cheek.

That was the only time you had physical contact with her?

Not sure what you're getting at.

Just curious. Most parents like to pick up their children, toss them in the air, tickle them, and so on. Did you do any of those things?

No. Didn't seem logical.

She didn't want to do those things either?

No.

Did she laugh often?

Don't remember. She'd smile, though. Especially when I'd make a mistake, or she would.

That's a good sign.

As I say, we had a good relationship and she was a smart kid.

You said 'was.' What did you mean by that?

I *did* say 'was.' Probably because I haven't seen her in so long, I can only attest to what I knew about her then, not now. Probably should have been using 'was' all along.

I understand. That makes sense. Do you think other people would look upon you and your family and say that you exhibited strange behavior?

What?

I'm sorry. That must have sounded like it came from left field. What I meant is, your family lived alone, wasn't typically emotional, and you were happy with that. Would some people, you think, perceive that you three were a strange bunch? I'm not saying I believe that, only what others might think.

Don't know. Rarely spoke with other people. Maybe at the store, getting gas, or something like that. Why would they think of us as strange?

I'm asking *you*. You're clearly different than most people I talk to about their families.

So you think of us as strange?

Not strange. Unusual.

Because we got along and didn't mess in other people's business?

I suppose so.

Well, if that's what they think, there's not much I can do about it.

I'm not saying that's what they think. I'm suggesting that it might be what some think. There's a difference.

True. I would guess that people wouldn't have much to judge about us in the first place. How can you judge someone based on little or no knowledge?

That's just it. When you have no information about a neighbor, it could lead them to think it strange.

So be it.

Doesn't bother you?

Not at all. We were happy, are happy, and that's what counts. The farm was or is going well, and I can't imagine anything better in life.

How can you be sure the farm is going well? Especially with you gone?

I don't know. But I think Missy would have hired someone to help out by now. Only logical.

I see.

After a complete count of the population in the facility, the guard was convinced that no one had entered any of the buildings. He'd been very careful to check all those unexpected overnighters by examining the logs kept at the entrances as well as the guards and those not present because of the storm. He included patients, pharmacists, and janitors. He was sure he'd not made a mistake. No one was present that shouldn't be. So, if there had been an illegal entry, the person had somehow not entered a building yet—unlikely since the weather was so terrible—or the warning horns had indeed been an accident. Even so, the guard remained suspicious. He couldn't imagine such a state of the art system so easily going amiss.

What do you think about how our discussions have been going thus far?

You're asking *me* that? I don't understand.

You're smart. We both know that. You must have an opinion on how things are progressing.

I don't. As I see it, you're doing a job that you know how to do. That's all.

Let me put it another way. If you were me, what questions have I not asked you that you think I should have asked?

You're asking me to critique you?

Yes.

Well, I'll have to think about it. I wasn't expecting such a question.

You're a quick study.

All right then, here's a question I would have asked. Maybe early on. 'Did you do it?'

I remember asking you something to that affect and you telling me you didn't.

Maybe.

I got the idea that you *knew* you couldn't have done it.

Good. Because that's exactly how it is.

Any other questions you think I should have asked, but didn't?

Possibly something more about why I think you think I committed whatever crime I'm accused of committing.

Wow. Let me make sure I follow that. You think I think you committed the crime, and I should have asked you why you think I think that?

Yes.

I don't think you committed the crime or didn't commit the crime.

No?

Whether you did or didn't do it isn't germane to the reason I'm here. Therefore, I don't have a professional opinion about whether you committed the crime or not. I'm here to decide whether you're sane enough to stand trial. I guess I'm old fashioned, but I think someone is innocent until proven guilty.

Good answer.

Can you think of anything else I should have asked you?

Not off hand. But could I ask you a direct question?

Yes.

Why are the lights kept on all the time in here?

You asked that before. I then asked the administration why, and they wouldn't give me an answer. I told you that.

But this time I would like you to tell me what *you* think.

Oh, I see. Well, I don't have any idea.

Studies have proven that doing so can cause sleep deprivation leading to many mental problems. It would appear to me that keeping the lights on at all times would be the very *last* thing you'd want to do in a place designed to help people get mentally better. Do you see my point?

I do.

Well?

Well, I didn't design this place, and you're the first person I've met here who's asked me that question, so I'm not sure I'm the best person to guess at an answer.

Didn't it occur to you the very first day you arrived? Why the hell do they keep the lights here on all the time?

I suppose it should have, but it didn't. Not until you brought it up the first time.

And you haven't asked anyone about it since we discussed my preference for the dark?

No. I guess I don't spend much time here and have never experienced it myself.

How about the nights you were here during the storm?

I stayed in the Administration Building where you can turn the lights off and on.

I see.

Now that you've brought it directly to my attention again, though, I'd be happy to question those in the know and get back to you on it. Maybe I'll get an answer this time.

Please do that.

Have you noticed people getting worse while you've been here?

I don't deal with people in here much, so I wouldn't know.

Have you been getting worse since you've been here? Experienced insomnia, and so on?

I'm not sure. That sort of thing would slowly develop, not suddenly.

Suppose it would.

I'm sure you're familiar with circadian rhythms and how much we depend on cycles of light and darkness to insure we get our proper doses of melatonin. The sleep hormone.

I am. As I say, I'll ask about it again.

Good.

My guess is that the lights are low. That would help. And maybe the color is different enough from sunlight and the sky that that might explain it. As I remember, blue is the color of light that keeps most of us awake. It resembles daylight. Whatever you call this light, it's not blue.

Puce.

Puce?

Yes, a combination of pink and brown, I think.

Not blue?

Not that I remember.

That might be the reason. I'll find out the cause and let you know tomorrow.

I'd appreciate it. Take it that the storm isn't letting up any.

No. Another storm apparently followed the big one in and it's turning out bigger yet. Might be a couple of days before I can actually return home.

I see.

Good. I still have some things to finish that I can do by email or phone, so I'll leave you now and see you tomorrow.

All right.

Goodbye, Joe.

Bye.

13

For some reason, the guard at the Forensic Psychiatric Facility came to the conclusion that someone had entered one of the buildings, switched places with one of the inmates, and that inmate then left by the same route the illegal entrant had, thus making a clean exchange of personnel. While this guard's supervisor thought the idea strange if not impossible given the circumstances, he gave the guard latitude to continue working on the scenario in his off time. All this, of course, was done under the most stringent secrecy. No one beside the two of them could know of this suspicion.

Morning, Joe.
Morning.
Have you heard the rumor going around?
Yes I have.
What do you think?
It's impossible is what I think.
Impossible?
Yes.
How so?
Even without the storm raging outside, I don't see how anyone could get into or out of this building. As far as I can tell, no one could breach these walls, ceilings, or floors. The heating ducts are too small, and every door to the outside is carefully monitored.

It sounds like you've considered it yourself?

Might have. When I first got here.

But what if someone could compromise one of the things you mentioned?

How?

By digging a tunnel under the building and coming up in, say, a storage room or something else that may not be as secure as you think. You've never seen the insides of one of those, I presume.

Haven't. I guess it might be possible.

And this person could replace one of the inmates and the inmate could escape by the same route.

That's what they're thinking happened?

Maybe. Just hypothesizing.

This person would have to have architectural plans and figure out distances pretty carefully to make it even remotely possible. But why do it at all? One person might escape, yes, but another one would have to give up his freedom for the one who escaped. That's a lot to swallow.

Actually, the person who escaped would be free, and the person now inside would be discovered soon enough and probably go to prison for his part in it.

Makes it even *more* unlikely.

I agree. It's only a rumor anyway.

Did you find out anything about the lights this time?

Oh, yes, I did. Good you asked about that.

And?

I think the first person I asked didn't know the answer but hid that by telling me it was none of my business.

That's what he told you?

She, actually. But not important.

Why, then?

The person who ultimately told me said that apparently, unlike you, most of the inmates here tend to be at their worst in darkness. That's when the monsters come out of hiding. Therefore, to keep these monsters at bay, the administration and the designers of the building decided to keep minimal lighting on at all times. Interestingly, your feeling comfortable in the dark would add proof that you're sane. Though I would not feel comfortable in giving much credence to the professional advice provided by the administration and designers of this place.

Interesting.

Let's move on to more important things.

Like?

You.

Okay.

I know we've discussed you previously, but I have some new questions.

Like?

Do you have any other people close to you in your life?

No.

Not one?

No. Or, yes, not one.

I think I know what you're going to say, though let me ask you this anyway. Why do you think that is?

I keep to myself.

And you like it that way.

Yes.

Some official forms, like those used for borrowing money, require that you put down the name and address of someone you know for them to contact if you're unable to pay, or something were to happen to you. Things like that. Who do you put down in those spaces?

Never had to fill out such a form.

What about the loan on your farm?

Forgot about that. I put down my mother's name.

But if you had to fill out one of those forms and not put down a family member, whose name would you enter?

Probably you.

You mean you think you know me better than anyone else outside your family?

Yes.

You hardly know anything about me. Only that I'm a psychiatrist that asks you questions every couple of days or so.

I know *that*, at least.

So, being a farmer, as you are, you don't actually have any acquaintances beyond your family and me?

That's pretty much it.

But that's what I'm getting at. Your use of the words 'pretty much.' You told me earlier, for example, that you had met people in stores where you shopped, people like that.

Yes. I believe I know you better than them.

Why is that?

Because you and I have spoken about things we know, not just the price of something I want to buy.

But most of our discussions have to do with you, not me.

Doesn't matter. We actually talk about things of consequence.

The others you mentioned don't?

No.

So there's no one you could mention outside of me and your immediate family?

Well, there's George.

Who's George?

My cousin.

You haven't mentioned him to me before this.

No.

Why's that?

Because I don't know him. He's shown up a couple of times at my house, that's it.

You talked to him?

I did.

What did you talk about?

Money.

Money? He wanted to borrow money?

No, actually, he wanted me to buy something from him.

What?

His car.

He wanted you to buy his car? Why?

Because he wanted a new one and didn't think he'd get a fair shake from the dealership he was going to buy his new car from.

Did you buy his car?

No.

Why?

Didn't need a car. I had one that ran fine. I certainly didn't need two. Barely drove the one I already had.

He understood that?

Yes.

But you said you saw him more than once.

Yes. He came back.

With the same proposition?

Yes.

And?

I gave him the same answer.

You didn't need another car?

No, I didn't.

How did he take it this time?

Got a little miffed. Said we were cousins and all.

What did you do?

I told him I wouldn't change my mind. Didn't need another car and he'd have to try someone else or take the dealer's offer.

He left?

Yes.

And you never saw or heard from him again?

Right.

So you wouldn't put his name down on the form we discussed earlier because?

He might not be such a good reference.

That's an interesting word.

What? Reference?

Yes. I didn't use that word, you did.

Thought that's what you meant.

I see that. So, if you were now faced with a form requiring a reference you'd put me down?

Yes. Unless you refused to allow me to do so.

I probably wouldn't, but say I did, what name would you put down?

If I had no choice, I guess I'd put down my cousin.

So that means that in your entire extended family, you don't know anyone else well enough to act as a reference?

No I don't.

Never met your grandparents on either side?

No.

No more cousins?

Not that I know personally.

Aunts or uncles.

Not that I met.

Don't you find that rather unusual?

Have nothing to compare it with.

I get that. From my experience, though, that's unusual.

Fine.

You still don't know anyone inside the building here?

No.

Why? You've had plenty of time to get to know someone.

They're all somewhat off base.

True, but if that were not the case, from what you've told me you still wouldn't make their acquaintance.

That's right.

Because you're completely comfortable being by yourself.

I am.

This is remarkable.

How so?

Because I've met hundreds of people in my profession, and none of them could, I think, continue living as you do.

I can understand that.

What, then, makes you so different?

Don't know. You're the psychiatrist. You tell me.

Good point. Maybe before we finish, I'll be able to do that.

You can't now?

No.

Because?

Because, none of the books, classes, and degrees I've earned have given me the knowledge to account for your feelings and behavior. So far, in my experience, you're unique.

Isn't that a good thing?

In some ways, it is. In others, not so good.

The guard looking for clues to how someone might enter one of the buildings discovered one thing that no one apparently had thought of previously. Like any standard locked-down facility, there were certain entrances and exits other than doors and ducts. For example, evacuation of the toilets required pipes of a size that a person could fit through. Not that anyone would want to, of course, except it was a possibility. Up to a point. No one could actually crawl up or down through a toilet. So the tunnel would have to be breached through a hole large enough for someone to crawl through. To date, no such breach existed. Another possibility was water pipes. The ones in the rooms of inmates would not allow someone exit or entrance, but these pipes fed to larger pipes that in turn led to the outside in some way. There, again, however, these pipes would have to have been breached in order for entry or exit to have taken place. None had.

What's the not-so-good part?

Well, humans crave companionship. That's something that exists in our DNA.

DNA developed over millennia to include mutations, didn't it? And many of these mutations are good things, not bad things, even though the word itself tends to have negative connotations.

Correct. So you're saying that you could belong to a line of people who were created by such a mutation?

One way to consider it. Yes.

It's possible, I suppose.

There are other ways.

Such as?

Well, it doesn't need to occur through breeding. It could occur by experience. Nature versus nurture. For example, my family has been farmers for generations. Farmers are alone most of the time by necessity. Thus, the idea of aloneness and being all right with being alone could be passed from generation to generation by simple observation. By conditioning rather than by genomics.

That's an excellent observation, Joe. I keep forgetting how intelligent you are.

Thanks.

You enjoy our discussions, don't you?

To an extent.

What do you mean?

I mean that were I given the choice, I'd probably be as happy alone as in here with you.

But not *more* happy?

Don't know. Maybe. I don't want to hurt your feelings.

You wouldn't. I'm a professional, and part of being a professional makes me somewhat immune to what my patients do or do not think of me. In fact, this is a real necessity since many of my patients don't like me at all. If I took that personally, I'd be ready to join you in here. See my point?

I do.

Good. So don't spare my feelings when you have something to say. I'll understand and not be hurt in the slightest.

All right.

Have you held back anything else you wanted to say to me in the past because you felt it might hurt my feelings?

Probably.

Can you think of anything specific?

Yes.

Do you feel comfortable in telling me?

I do now.

Okay, tell me.

Do you really not think about whether I'm guilty or not? Because I think you *do* think about it, and that you have an opinion. And that it's coloring the questions you ask me.

Wow. That's some question.

You're not hurt?

Hurt? No. Confused? Yes. I don't have an opinion. None at all. I'm only asking you the questions that any professional would ask in my place.

So, from that I can glean that you could have sent your questions to me by email or by video?

No, of course not. I ask questions based on your answers to my previous questions. They can't be prerecorded.

Then, from what you've just said, you have to make personal decisions about what question to ask following my previous response. That your process would actually be different than anyone else's would.

To a degree, I suppose. In reality, the basic ideas and processes would be the same.

So, if I were to tell you I now remembered the crime I'm charged with committing and am completely guilty of committing it, your next question would be fundamentally the same as another psychiatrist's question?

Yes.

And what would that question be?

Why?

That's it? You're absolutely sure that any other professional in your situation would ask the same question?

Yes.

What if I told you I don't believe you? That you have unique emotions and experiences, and that your question might very well be quite different than someone else's. Another psychiatrist's questions.

I'd say you were wrong.

To you, I'm nothing but an object you're studying? Like a bug under a microscope?

No, of course not. What I'm saying is that I'm the bug under the microscope. I'm responding to your answers in ways that have proven to get results. I'm following a plan laid out by thousands of psychiatrists who've gone before me. *I'm* the bug, not you.

Then why do I feel like *I'm* the bug?

Good question. Maybe one I should ask.

Are you asking me?

Yes.

Nice turn around.

What do you mean?

I asked you a question, and you turn it back toward me. Like a Ping-Pong ball.

Doing my job.

Like you said you were.

Yes.

So, as the bottom line here, and to make sure I've got this right, you're telling me that you're following a course of action with me that itself follows courses of actions set roughly in stone by thousands of others before you. I'm the subject of your study. Nothing more. Not a person. And you're also telling me that you're the subject of my study. You're the bug. Even though I'm answering your questions to the best of my ability, without having thousands of others before me answering as I am.

You're an incredible debater, Joe. You know that?

Yes. I do.

That's what you were just doing, wasn't it?

Not intentionally, though yes, I suppose I was.

Do you like debating?

I don't like it or not like it. But you changed the subject nicely again. You're a good psychiatrist.

My God, now you're trying to manipulate me.

You asked for it.

I did?

Yes. You asked me if I had any questions that I'd not asked for fear they might hurt you. I did, and now we're at this point.

Except they didn't hurt me.

Maybe not on the outside. But since you diverted our debate at two points, it seems you're emotionally different in terms of your views of me now than you were before.

Possibly. Now I have a question to ask you. Did you ever debate with your parents or your wife?

Ah, there you go again.

There I go again, what?

Turning everything around toward me.

That's my job.

So it is.

Well this has been a great exchange, Joe, I've enjoyed it.

Believe me, so have I.

So I'll see you tomorrow?

I'm not going anywhere.

14

The curious guard at the Forensic Psychiatric Facility, whose name was Matthew Brady and nicknamed Matt, had pretty much exhausted his potential avenues for entrance and exit into and out of the various buildings in the compound. If someone had accomplished either of these feats, he was at a loss as to how they'd done it.

Yet he remained convinced that something had occurred to make the horns sound. So, while he didn't know exactly how to proceed, he'd not given up. At almost precisely the second he'd decided this, the very same horns again jumped to life, nearly deafening him and the rest of the occupants in the facility. They blared for a good two minutes before coming to an end. When they did, all the guards on duty, including Matt, immediately busied themselves counting inmates and other personnel to make sure no one was missing. Because the weather had not improved significantly, the towers outside and the gate in the outer fence were not manned, and so no one could actually tell much about what was occurring beyond the walls.

Good morning, Joe.

Not so sure it's such a good morning.

I know what you mean. Or maybe I hear what you mean. It wake you up as well?

Yes. I didn't get back to sleep. Any idea what happened?

According to my sources, which aren't that high up, it was another glitch in the system. No one apparently knows how to fix it. And the storm is blocking anyone who knows how to fix anything from getting here.

So it may go off again? At any time?

Don't know. I would presume that's true.

Crazy way to run a business.

I agree. Shall we get started anyway?

Yes.

Today, I'd like to discuss your future.

Besides living in here for the rest of my life?

Yes.

Right.

Beginning with what you'd like to accomplish with the gift you have.

Gift?

Your abilities at math, reading, and so on.

I'm not setting goals while I'm in here.

Why not?

Feeling too good. The meds are great.

What if I took you off the meds?

Don't do that.

Why?

I wouldn't feel so good.

It's that simple?

Yes.

So, that means you didn't feel good before you came here? Before I prescribed them for you?

Yes. I didn't feel as good.

Why?

How would you feel if someone charged you with a crime you didn't commit?

Terrible.

That's how I felt before the meds.

But you *still* don't remember what the crime was that you're charged with.

True.

Maybe if I told you, it wouldn't be so bad.

I doubt that. After all, as you've pointed out, my wife, child, and my mother haven't come to see me since I was admitted. And, I doubt if being sent here forever would be on account of a misdemeanor.

Can't argue that. From another perspective, however, how do you know you didn't commit the crime if you don't know what the crime is?

Because I wouldn't commit a crime of the magnitude that has sent me here. I wouldn't do that. I'm not capable of doing that.

Maybe we'll discover that you went temporarily insane.

I won't buy that.

You still won't let me tell you about it?

No. I'm sure it would make me sad. The meds you're giving me make me happy. It's as simple as that.

What if I told you I thought you were guilty?

Are you telling me that?

No.

Then what's the point?

Right you are.

So maybe this is a fruitless line of reasoning to pursue.

For now, at least, it is.

When would that change?

I don't know that it would. But I agree, now is certainly not the time to pursue it.

Good.

Should we try another tack?

Whatever you think is best.

That's good to hear.

My pleasure.

I've only seen you when you've been on the meds I prescribed for you.

Yes.

Could you tell me in what ways you were different before you began taking the meds?

I was sad.

No. I mean before this whole thing began. Before you were charged with the crime you don't remember.

I was a farmer. Someone who took care of business and acted as logically as I possibly could.

You must have felt happy, sad, something?

I felt satisfied. I had a great daughter, a wonderful wife, a good farm, a good job, and I just, well, felt satisfied. That's the only way I can describe it.

Not sad. Not happy. Not jealous. Just satisfied?

Well, satisfied usually means happy. So, the best word you've used would be happy.

Not happy like you are now under the meds I've prescribed?

No. I had purpose. Something to do. Something that made me feel satisfied. So I was probably happier then.

What was that something?

I was helping feed others including my family. That I worked hard doing something I liked doing. Those kinds of things.

Good. That helps me understand.

And, I think I felt wanted and needed.

Now that makes it even clearer. Those are important things in your opinion?

Absolutely.

So. Satisfied, wanted, and needed.

Helping and working rather than sitting around.

Yet you're basically sitting around here. Does that make you happy?

I waste time, and now doth time waste me?

A good quote. Your answer?

No, of course not. The meds make me happy. If I were to work here, it most likely wouldn't be to help others, it would be something to keep me busy. Not something to feel proud of.

I see. That makes sense.

Good. Besides, being on the meds as I am I wouldn't be able to work very hard anyway.

Because they make you feel light headed?

Among other things.

Like?

Like lacking in energy, lacking in purpose, lacking in direction. Those kinds of things.

Then, what if I took you off the meds and put you to work. Would that make things better?

No. I'd still know my work wouldn't accomplish anything for anybody as I said before. I'd only be working because you asked me to work.

So we're right back where we started?

I think so.

You still feel you'd like to get out of here and face trial?

Yes. Prove my innocence.

But you'd learn of the charges brought against you.

You're right. I hadn't thought of that.

Now that you have, does it make a difference?

I'd have to think about it.

Think about it.

I guess I'd rather stay here.

A quick change of mind. Particularly on a matter of such importance.

I suppose it is. I hadn't thought about the effect of my learning of the crime on my staying here or leaving.

So, given these new circumstances, you'd rather remain here?

I like this place and could willingly waste my time in it.

Please answer my question.

Wouldn't you?

Don't know. This isn't about me. It's about you.

Well, I'd a lot rather be happy than be torn apart in a court of law with people telling me I'd done something I hadn't done and risking my life over it.

What if I told you the court is asking me to make a decision based on your sanity at this very moment. And my tendency at this point is to tell them that as far as I can tell, excepting your lack of memory about what you would be tried for, you're sane as far as I'm concerned. Capable of standing trial.

That would make me unhappy.

Even if I kept you on the meds?

Yes.

Because I mentioned you'd discover the cause of your being charged?

Yes. I don't want to face that.

Even if you're not guilty?

I'm *not* guilty. I cannot remember, and I know there's a good reason for that. Don't you think so?

Probably. Hiding from it won't do you any good, though. Remember, cowards die many times.

Yes. But I'm happy now. Knowing would make me unhappy. I'd rather remain here.

Forever?

If that's what it takes? Yes.

Well, my question would then be, what have you told me during our many conversations to suggest that you're not capable of standing trial?

That's for you to decide. I've been as honest as I can with you. I don't have any idea if I'm sane or not. I'm hoping you can keep me here and declare me unfit to face trial. If that's not to be, than it's not to be.

You're okay with that if it were my decision?

No. But I don't see what I can do about it.

You could stand up and crow like a rooster.

I couldn't. I'm a rational man. A genius according to you. I won't change myself to fit some stereotype that you and the court have in mind for me.

You see the fix that puts me in?

No.

I either make you sad by telling the court what I think, or lie and tell them you're unfit and let you remain here as a happy man. And that would make me sad.

Maybe another possibility would be to tell them you haven't enough information yet to decide, and must wait until you do.

Is that true?

Yes.

Meaning?

You haven't asked me the right questions yet.

That's interesting, I thought I had. What questions are you referring to?

Am I allowed to plant questions for you to ask me in order for me to answer them correctly and make myself unfit to stand trial, at least for the moment?

If I follow your question, I think you are. After all, this is literally your life we're talking about. You have to be given the chance to tell your whole story. I remind you that I cannot divulge what you've told me to anyone. I will gain an opinion, but the stranger you make yourself sound, the guiltier you might make yourself appear.

Then it's a risk?

Yes.

I think it's worth taking.

You do?

Yes.

Then we'd better get down to brass tacks. What questions should I ask you to get a better picture of who you are?

Matt had discovered a little-known way to climb to the roof of the building he was charged with guarding. Now that the storm had subsided, he followed it. Once up there, he looked around for telltale signs that someone had been there before him. Nothing he could see. No footprints in the snow. Nothing particularly unusual as far as he knew, not having been up there before.

He did notice, though, that each of the buildings had several large smokestack-type protrusions maybe five-by-five feet square, and that on his building, the top of one of those protrusions had its lid removed. This interested him. He couldn't see much else at this distance, but clearly the upper section was not attached as the rest were. Either that, or all the others had been attached when they shouldn't be, and he doubted that.

The sky had cleared somewhat, and no longer snowing. This helped visibility and he wished he'd brought along a pair of binoculars.

Why not ask me more about my daughter?

Carla? What should I ask?

Maybe something about how she came about.

Came about?

How she was conceived.

All right. How was she conceived?

Normal way, I suspect.

This's getting us nowhere. What's this all about, Joe?

Well, let me take it further on my own.

Okay.

When my father was diagnosed with terminal cancer, he sort of went nuts.

How so?

He did things without regard to how they might affect other people.

For instance?

Well, take my mother for example. He treated her as if she wasn't actually there. Wasn't his wife, I mean.

Like?

He started to more than look at other women.

All right. How did that turn out?

Not good. Working the farm had not treated him well, and he looked much older than he actually was. Plus, he wasn't a worldly man, and the women he attempted to sleep with were not willing to go as far as he wanted.

What did he do?

First, he discovered the brothels in the nearest towns and made deals with prostitutes.

How did you discover this? He must have attempted to hide it from your mother and you.

That's just it. He didn't. While he wouldn't actually boast of it, he did nothing to hide his adventures either.

How did your mother take this?

She didn't like it. But what could she do? He was dying and she figured, I guess, that he was taking a shot at what he'd apparently missed all those years. Divorcing him would have taken longer than he had time left in the world. I imagine she didn't enjoy it much or give him any time with her in bed. Beyond that, she took it on the chin and fed him his meds.

A very strong woman.

She was that. Anyway, he kept at it for a time, as long as he could that is.

Not a very admirable choice on his part, but I've never been told I have terminal cancer either, so I guess I can't be too harsh a judge.

That was my feeling at the time.

You still lived on your own farm with your family?

I did. Though it wasn't a family yet. Carla hadn't arrived, or been a gleam in our eyes at the time.

I see. And this helps me how?

Wait. I'm far from through.

Sorry.

No problem. Well, sometime before he became bedridden, he made a choice that might change your mind about what he did.

Excuse me. What type of cancer did he have?

Prostate. It had spread to everywhere in his body. Everything was a mess. Not sure which organ failed him in the end, but it was all prostate cancer.

Understood.

Anyway, this choice had to do with something he'd dreamed about since he'd met my wife to be.

Oh my, don't tell me.

I must. It will help you understand me better.

Go ahead.

Well, he tried to get Missy to, well, couple with him.

His own daughter-in-law?

Yes.

What happened?

Of course this didn't make her any too happy.

Right. Did she rebuke him?

Rebuke him she did.

And?

That made him mad. Extremely mad.

In the sanity definition of mad? Or angry?

Both.

He was sick at the time, right?

Yes, though he was still a large man.

Are you telling me he raped your wife?

That's what eventually happened. Yes.

Oh, my God. That's incredible. Did you know about this?

Not at the time, no. Missy was very upset about something, but she wouldn't tell me why.

Did he beat her?

Not so you'd notice. But she wouldn't bed down with me. *That* I noticed.

So, what happened?

Getting there. Not too long after that, maybe a month or so, Missy announced she was pregnant with our first child.

How did that make you feel?

Great. But a little confused as well. Not only was it unexpected, it was impossible. I asked her about that, and she told me I'd miscounted. That she was further along in her pregnancy than I realized. Everything was going along fine.

You bought it?

Sure. Why not? I knew she wasn't the fooling-around type. She'd been faithful to me. So I let it be.

And Carla was born.

Carla was born. And my father died. In great pain, I should add, for drugs never had much effect on him.

How did you take his death?

I took it okay. I mean we knew it was coming. I was never close to him, so it wasn't something that stopped me from working, for example.

Carla's birth?

Went fine. She even looked a bit like me.

Not surprising.

No.

Then how did you find out?

As Matt made his way across the roof of the building toward the unattached smokestack-type protrusion, he found footsteps slightly imprinted in the ice-covered snow. While these prints could have been made by someone attempting to fix the protrusion, it was unlikely that anyone would attempt that during a heavy snowstorm. So he thought he had something. The reason for the horns sounding.

He took photos with a digital camera he'd brought along for gathering evidence, and surveyed the area around the unattached section to see what else he could find. All this time, he kept away from the footprints that were there when he'd arrived. As he took pictures, he noticed four randomly placed small holes in the snow. When he dug around one of these holes to see what had caused it, he found a large screw, one he felt surely belonged to a corner of the detached section. The footprints and the screw confirmed for him that this had not been an accident caused by the wind during the storms that had passed, but a manmade attempt to enter or exit the flue or whatever it was that this large smokestack-type protrusion belonged to.

Then he looked down into the aperture to see where it went.

Unfortunately, being daytime, he'd forgotten to bring his flashlight. All he found there was darkness.

She told me.

How?

When Carla was small, maybe two months old, I asked Missy again when she'd been conceived. After all, I can add and subtract pretty well, and I'd done the math many times. At no point did it make any sense. Carla was not premature. The doctor said she was a perfectly normal child born at the right time. So, I was curious how this had happened. Had I forgotten the night?

So she told you?

Not at first. It took a while as you can imagine. She finally did. After all, the logic was there and she couldn't deny it.

Was your father dead by then?

Yes. He never saw his daughter. First too sick, and then dead.

How did Missy tell you?

Well, there was a lot of uncharacteristic crying and it took quite a long time. In fact, the whole night. But she eventually got the story out in all its ugly details.

How did you feel when she finished?

Like I wanted to kill my father.

But he was already dead.

Yes.

One pain is lessened by another's anguish?

So true.

What did you feel like, besides killing him?

As if I'd been deprived of a very important duty.

To kill your father for what he'd done?

Yes.

Missy?

She felt relieved to have it out in the open. Except she felt like me. That some retribution was in order to repay my father for his horrible crime.

That was impossible.

Yes.

You must have gone crazy.

As in 'pardon the expression?'

Yes. Sorry.

I did. I was a virtual gun ready to be fired, but with no one to fire at. It was terrible. I hated my father, but couldn't tell him of my hate.

So you bottled it up.

Sort of.

Sort of?

I went outside and took my emotions out on anything nearby I could find.

The animals?

No. I wouldn't do that. They were blameless. I kicked sacks of grain. Beat my fists against the barn's walls until my hands were bloody. Things like that.

In other words, you mostly hurt yourself.

Suppose so. That way I could feel what I wanted my father to feel if he weren't dead.

Completely understandable. What happened next?

I thought it over and made plans. First I had to decide who I was.

Who you *were*?

Yes. Was I Carla's stepfather? Carla's half-brother? Or what?

And?

I decided on the what part.

Meaning?

I was her father. I'd try to forget the mess we had going and be the best father I could be.

Shakespeare says that there are three people in yourself—who *people* think you are, who *you* think you are, and who you *really* are. Seems to fit here.

He was never so right.

So you and Missy never spoke about it again?

Absolutely not. We tried to ignore what had happened and get on with our lives. After all, Carla had no responsibility in this, and neither did Missy or I. So we got on with our lives.

Your mother didn't know?

Absolutely not. She had no idea.

So let me get this straight. Carla was your half-sister because you shared the same father?

Right.

But she was also your stepdaughter because she was your wife's child by another man?

Yes.

You were everything except her *real* father, and that's what you decided to become? In a very real sense by acting the part?

Right.

My God, what a story.

What do you make of it?

Psychiatrically speaking?

Yes.

I'm not sure. There have to be case studies of such things in the literature. I must admit, however, that I've never come across one that I remember. Of course, they fall into a general category of such things.

And?

Well, the immediate catastrophe that occurs in both the mother's and, in this case, the stepfather's minds, would be intense distrust. Of everyone and everything. Since your father, the culprit, was dead, you'd both continue to see him in your stepchild's looks and actions as she grew older.

Less so because she was female and not male?

Yes. But you'd likely at least perceive her actions as resembling your father's at times. So you would be mentally crippled no matter whether you were aware of it or not. You can't think something like that away, you understand. It would be with you for the rest of your life.

I see. And therein lies the rub.

Yes. Will you let me think on this overnight? I want to see what I can read on the subject and try to understand it better, so I won't give you a simple Reader's Digest version of my analysis.

I appreciate that.

The weather's clearing and the snowplows are out. So I'll be able to sleep at home tonight for a change. That will be good for me.

I hope so.

I'll see you in two days?

Yes.

Goodbye.

Bye.

Oh, and thank you for telling me this. It changes everything.

I thought it might.

Goodbye, Joe.

See you soon.

15

Matt studied blueprints of the Forensic Psychiatric Facility and discovered that the flues he'd discovered on the roofs of the compound's buildings had been added since the architectural drawings were first submitted. Apparently the architect had forgotten that the heating and cooling systems for each building required ventilation. Not of hot or cold air, only the byproducts from the making of hot and cold air. Heating, the type of process used during winter as now, required venting the carbon dioxide from the burning of natural gas. Not venting this byproduct could cause suffocation for those inside. When Matt looked down the flue with his high-powered flashlight then, he wasn't at all surprised by what he saw. A larger flue. But as he looked, he couldn't figure out how someone could climb down inside this flue and then find a way into the building.

Morning, Joe.

Doctor Amador.

No good morning?

Good morning.

Thanks. Anything bothering you today?

No. Why should it?

Nothing actually. You seem to have an edge to your voice, that's all.

Had a bad dream last night.

Wish to talk about it?

Yes. That's what you're here for, right?

Partly, yes.

I was caught inside a tunnel of some kind and had gotten stuck going headfirst. I could see light far in the distance, but couldn't reach the entrance or exit, didn't matter which as far as I was concerned.

Are you claustrophobic?

Isn't everyone?

To a degree. But some are *really* claustrophobic. Which are you?

I'm normal. Somewhat claustrophobic, though not so bad I'd go crazy in that situation.

Go on.

That's pretty much it. I couldn't get out. My arms were pinned to my sides by the walls of the tunnel so I couldn't go forward or backward.

Were you fearing something in this dream?

Yes.

What were your worries?

That something would enter the end I could see and kill me.

Kill you?

Maybe eat me. Whatever.

What about something coming from behind you? Water maybe. Might that not have pushed you out the end of the pipe you could see?

Glass half full?

That's the idea.

Never occurred to me in my dream.

Not even when you woke up?

No.

Why, I wonder?

Don't know. I was preoccupied with what would occur *to* me rather than what might occur *for* me.

Why do you suppose that is?

Just the way it was.

Interpreting dreams is what I'm supposed to help you with here, so let's try to figure out why the glass half full scenario didn't occur to you. Have any ideas?

I've been thinking about what I told you the last time we met.

The story about your being a half-brother to your daughter and a stepfather to her as well? Did I get that right?

Yes. I suppose that could be part of my dream.

You felt, maybe, that you were stuck with a problem you couldn't solve. The fact that your father raped your wife, your child was his and not yours, and you had no way to rectify the matter, only make it worse.

That's a reasonable explanation. Yes.

Not the only one?

No.

Can you give me another possibility?

I can try.

Go ahead.

It could be that what I told you was just a story. Not the truth. That I made it up to give you something to work on. To help me remain here and happy. And there was no other reasonable way to guide you to this conclusion. That's why I only had one way out of the tunnel. Tell you and wait for something to happen. That something, no matter how I worked it, wasn't going to be good. Lie and stay here, or tell the truth and leave. Both unacceptable.

Well, I hadn't expected you to say that. I guess I have to ask you, then, was it only a story? Or did it happen?

You *sure* you want to know?

I think I *have* to know in order to continue being your psychiatrist.

And continue prescribing my meds.

Yes.

It was only a story.

Is this the truth?

Yes. Why?

Because once you lie, I'm going to have difficulty believing you again. Our mutual friend the playwright says, 'Don't trust the person who has broken faith once.' Now, I'll have to rethink everything you've told me so far and decide whether to believe it or not. That was a very convincing tale you told. Extremely convincing. I could think of not much else since I left you last time. Now you tell me it was a story. That's hard to believe. Do you see what I mean?

I'm sorry.

Do you see, though, how that won't cut it?

Yes. I've lied and can no longer be trusted.

Not only that, but since I now know you've lied, I have to wonder

144

whether *anything* you've told me has been the truth. It may be that I'll have to resign from your case and have someone else take it starting from the beginning with the knowledge that you are not to be trusted.

As I say, I was stuck in the tunnel and saw no good way it was going to end.

I would say that's a perfect metaphor for what we're facing now.

Understood.

How does it make you feel when I tell you I might quit and have another person take over from the beginning?

Both good and bad.

Good?

Yes, because that person would probably take as much time as you did to discover who I was, and during that time the meds would continue and I'd be happy. Bad, because that person would probably not be as intelligent and perceptive as you've been. I'm comfortable with you, Doctor Amador, and that means a lot to me.

That's kind of you to say, Joe. Except if that's the case, why did you lie to me?

To keep you here and prescribing my meds.

I'm not sure I understand.

Simple. You were about to go to the court and tell them I was fit to stand trial. I don't want that. By fabricating the story, I hoped I'd convince you that your decision couldn't be made yet. That you'd have to keep visiting me. And *that* I would appreciate.

Interesting. Did you come to the decision to tell me the story in advance of my visit the other day?

No. I improvised it as I went along.

So, it was because I told you that I might be ready to tell the court you were ready to stand trial that you abruptly created this situation with your family so I would change my mind? On the spot.

All correct.

Now, could you tell me if anything you told me before that created story about your father and wife was similarly made up?

I can. I made up nothing else at all. My first lie, the one I told you last time, was the first and the last one I will tell. I can promise you that. I even felt guilty telling you as I was telling you. It wasn't a good feeling. I've felt remorse ever since. I knew it would come out eventually, and also knew that I'd have to tell you the truth. And I have. Though I didn't think it would come out so quickly.

That's good to know, Joe. I'm going to have to give this situation some serious thought before we meet next time.

Before you go, though, I'd like to give you a question to ask me for which I will give you an entirely truthful answer. Are you willing to hear my question?

I'm not sure. You see how difficult the problem you've given me has made my decision? On one hand, it's made me suspicious of you for the future things you'll say. Interestingly, it also makes me feel that I shouldn't give the court the go ahead on your being able to stand trial. After all, if they put you on the stand you might do nothing except tell lies. Lying, you see, is an indication of mental illness, especially when taking it to the extreme as you did in telling me that story.

I understand.

Fine. We have the time, so why not tell me the question you want me to ask and see where that leads us.

Matt had spent nearly an hour attempting to figure out how to make his way down into the chimney-like flue using a rope he'd brought along to lower him into it. He had trouble initially finding a place to tie his rope but, surprisingly, the location he found was right in front of his eyes. The removed screen that apparently protected the flue from snow was extremely heavy and gave plenty of support for the rope.

As Matt climbed down with the flashlight he'd brought along to find his way, he wondered offhandedly how, whoever it was that had preceded him down here, could have removed that screen in the first place. After all, he'd seen only one pair of footprints, and he was sure that no single person could possibly lift that much weight. But, he would have to figure that out at a later time. It *had* been removed, and now he would hopefully discover *why* it had.

Can you ask me which parts of the story I told you were the truth?
Consider it asked.
Almost all of it.
Almost? Are you telling me the truth this time?
I am.

Which parts?

Everything except the part about my father raping Missy.

So, you *are* the father of your child?

No, I am not.

But your wife wasn't raped by your father?

No, she wasn't.

I guess I'm not understanding what you're saying.

My wife was artificially inseminated.

You're incapable of fathering a child?

I am. We were going to adopt one, but Sissy wanted to give birth and so we decided to go that route.

So the parts of the story about your father seeing prostitutes, and so on, are all true?

Absolutely. You could check them by asking my mother.

Your father didn't try to rape your wife?

He did, actually.

I thought you said he didn't rape her.

He didn't. She fought him off. Though she be but little, she is fierce.

Yes, I see that. So everything you said was true except the rape itself?

That and, of course, my daughter being my half-sister and me being her stepfather.

Of course. So, you didn't lie that much, you extended one aspect of the story in a false way.

Yes.

Well I'm glad we had this discussion. As far as I can tell, much of my first reaction is still true. Though the rape consummation part, the centerpiece we should call it, is different, all the rest still stands. As such, you still went through a major crises in your life that could easily have changed your personality. Made you act in irrational ways.

I imagine so. Of course, while I wouldn't have killed my father for what he did to my wife, it was traumatic enough for her that I still hold immense anger towards him. Or at least I would if he had lived to the point when she'd told me about his attempts.

Understood. You've had quite an experience here, even in the amended version. As before, though, I'm going to have to give this situation some serious thought before we meet again.

I understand. Sorry I lied to you.

I am, too. On the other hand, this new revelation may help me construct some further directions to take our discussions.

Good to hear.

Must go now, Joe. See you tomorrow or the next day.

Goodbye.

16

When Matt reached the bottom of the flue, he found something unusual. The inner screen, also used as a filter-ventilator to release
gases from the heating duct, had also been removed, and the flue
metal was split in such a way as to create a hole capable of admitting
someone the size of an average human being.

Inside the hole as he looked, Matt could see that it was large
enough to allow someone to move around within it. So he climbed
inside. Since the ceiling of the room below still separated him from the
inside of the building, it seemed unlikely that anyone could enter that
room from above and gain access to the occupants. But, from the way
the sides of the flue had been bent from the weight of knees, hands,
and other body parts, it was obvious that indeed at least one person had
entered the flue and basically created the hole and entered it.

How someone could compromise as large a heating unit as this
one confused him. However, no use in quitting now. He'd discovered
a good deal in his quest to find out why the warning horns might have
sounded, and now was no time to stop.

Good morning, Joe.

Morning, Doctor Amador.

I've given our last exchange a lot of thought.

And?

I've come to the conclusion that, though you did lie, you did so for reasons you thought necessary. As well, it may have been a good thing. After all, every one of us enhances the stories we tell. Maybe you'll be more cautious in the future about doing that. Interestingly, in a way, you didn't *actually* lie. You *exaggerated*. Therefore, I'll continue with our sessions as your psychiatrist, and, because you confessed, I think I'll believe this and the other possible accounts you may yet reveal. Thus, I will not at this time advise the court you're prepared to stand trial.

Thank you very much. I appreciate the vote of confidence.

Okay, now let's get started. You mentioned other past experiences you've had that might reveal things about yourself that I wouldn't otherwise know.

I did.

Would you like to expand on one of those experiences at this point?

Sure. Ask me a question.

I can't. You'll have to give me something to go on. Like last time. And, of course, unlike last time, keep your embellishments to the lowest possible level.

Understood. Why not ask me a question about my mother.

What can you tell me about your mother?

My mother did not like Missy very much.

Why not?

Missy's from Atlanta. A big city. My mother felt from the beginning that Missy would eventually get lonely from living the farmer's life and leave me.

But she didn't. So, did you mother change her mind about Missy?

Not at all. In fact, her feelings worsened.

In what way?

When I first got married, Missy and she would talk occasionally, especially when we came to visit her on weekends. We stopped after a few weeks.

You mean you stopped visiting?

No. They stopped talking.

For what reason?

My mother claimed that Missy was using her education to look down upon her. Condescendingly.

Was that true?

Have no idea. Missy was well educated. I could keep up with her, no problem. My mother, though, might have felt overwhelmed. After all, my mother came from a relatively uneducated family and wasn't well schooled. I think Missy assumed that because I was smart, my whole family would be smart as well.

But your father liked Missy. Obviously.

Yes, though not because he thought she was smart or that he could keep up with her. Only because he liked her looks.

Did you know that from the beginning?

To an extent, yes. My father didn't keep things to himself. I figured it was a natural proclivity of his. Gave it no serious thought at the time.

So, what did it mean to you that Missy and your mother stopped talking?

At first, nothing.

After that?

Missy didn't want to come with me to visit my parents.

That pose problems?

It did. At first I went alone and gave excuses for her. After a time, though, it became obvious that Missy had visited for the last time. As well, I was getting tired of talking to my father. We had nothing much to say to one another, and so it was *I* who spoke to my mother. Unfortunately, that didn't work either, since we both knew about Missy's absence and why.

So?

I stopped going there as well.

That must have been awkward.

It was. But it became a habit and we forgot about it. Until my father was diagnosed, that is.

Then what happened?

Well, we visited, of course, though what could we say? He was dying. He knew it. We knew it. But we couldn't sit around and talk about that. And we couldn't sit around and talk about much of anything else either. So we stopped visiting again. That, of course, made my mother unhappy with me as well as with Missy. She hadn't minded it when we'd not come when my father was well. But now that he was dying, she considered our not coming as an insult. She no longer forgave either one of us.

I can see both sides of that issue.

You can?

Yes.

Well, that's when it started.

What?

My father's appetite for other women.

You think your lack of visits caused that?

Have no idea. That's when it began, so I have to assume the two issues are related in some way.

I see. What happened next?

As I told you earlier, at first he tried to date other women. That didn't work, so he visited prostitutes. Of course he wasn't rich, and that had to stop. Besides he was getting sicker and sicker and wasn't so much up to it, if you'll pardon the expression.

That's when he attacked Missy?

Around that time, yes.

So now you're telling me you think that somehow your not visiting your parents is somehow connected with his attack?

No. I'm *not* telling you that. It's that Missy believed that. In some way, she felt responsible for him coming on to her.

Now that's very interesting.

Why?

Forgive me. I don't mean that I'm not understanding her feelings, only that from a psychiatrist's perspective, it's full of subtleties.

Okay.

You're telling me that Missy, feeling grief for your father since he was dying, not having visited him and your mother for some time and feeling guilty for it, and you, lest we forget, not being able to impregnate Missy for the child she'd like to have and now approached by your father for the purposes of fathering her child, felt *guilty* for turning him down?

That's *exactly* what I'm saying. And you should add to that the fact that I knew nothing about this at the time. It was only later that I found out.

Yes. Did your father initially attack her, or attack her after she said no?

The latter.

152

So he came by your house, struck up a conversation with her, posed the question, she said no, and then he tried to rape her?

Yes and no.

Please explain.

When she told me about this, she was obviously conflicted. She knew I wasn't close to my father. At the same time, she knew that fathers are special to their children, and in some ways very special to their only sons. So she couldn't assume I'd take her side of what she was about to tell me.

I understand that.

So what she told me was probably tame compared to what actually happened.

Go on.

She told me that he came on to her in a gentle way.

Physically?

At first? No. He tried to sweet talk her into it first, she said. They spoke for a time and he told her how beautiful she was and how he'd wanted her from the beginning. And how, now that he was dying, he could no longer resist telling her these things. How much he hoped she would understand and forgive him.

Did he know you were incapable of impregnating her?

Yes.

So he suggested that since you and he both had the same genes, that him impregnating her was as natural as could be,

Almost exactly what he said.

So his approach was, if you can't carry on the family genes, the only thing she could possibly do was to carry the family genes from him?

Right.

This is truly unbelievable. Maybe more unbelievable than the first version.

Unbelievable? You think I'm lying?

Not at all. I'm referring to how incredible it is. Except that wouldn't have been a better word either. I'm hunting for the right word.

Understandable?

I suppose. Certainly, however, what he was proposing was not understandable from any rational perspective.

Yes, but from his perspective it makes a certain kind of sense. From hers it could be—given the moment—right in a way.

That's what I meant to say. The word I wanted to say was 'unthinkable.'

That might work. However, I would say that no word actually covers it.

Yes. I understand that.

All right. From Missy's point of view, it's completely wound up with her emotional attachment to wanting to have a baby. My baby. Not anyone's baby, *my* baby.

I get that.

So we have him giving her a way to have the closest thing to my baby, her wanting that but not wanting that either since that would be something I've never even heard of.

I don't think there's a name. The Bible tells of Judah who had twins with his daughter-in-law and, interestingly, these twins were in the ultimate lineage of Jesus.

Holy crap, I didn't know that.

Forget I said anything. Let's get back to Missy.

Well, as my father made his proposal to her, as she tells it, she hesitated and gave it some thought. After all, it was weirdly tempting to her. She wasn't, after all, in the family, and the ramifications that would bring about. So it might work. But she eventually told him no. That slight pause while she gave it serious thought, though, made him think, in her eyes at least, that she inspired his rape attempt. In fact, when she first told me, she actually didn't use the word 'rape.' She only told me that he refused to accept no for an answer. That's exactly how she put it. He refused to take no for an answer.

My God, what a story.

Yes, and it isn't over.

There's more?

Yes. There was a tussle.

A tussle?

They fought one another. Physically.

She must have won.

She did. She wasn't strong, but he was severely weakened by the cancer. He left, completely deflated.

154

And?

She felt from then on that she'd hastened his lack of will to live. That he could have survived much longer than he did if she'd given in. Maybe even lived to see his child.

God. How awful. Is that it?

I don't think it will ever be 'it.' She's felt extreme guilt ever since, and that's most likely why she doesn't visit me here. Feels she doesn't deserve me. She doesn't bring Carla because Carla's not mine or my father's child. Not related to my family in any way.

But you treated her like one of your own when you were home.

Yes. Only I think you don't understand the depth of her guilt.

I see. How does this make you feel?

Logically, I'd like to see them both and hope she'll get over it. Though she obviously hasn't. I can understand that.

That's an incredibly mature view of the situation.

It's not meant to be. The whole thing's a mess. All beginning with simple visits to my parents' house and exacerbated by my inability to father children.

You don't blame yourself, do you?

Partly. I can't blame myself for the way I am physically. But I am at least partially guilty of not working out a solution to the problems between my mother and Missy.

I can see why you might feel that way, except those problems shouldn't necessarily lead to what, in this case, they led to.

Likely true.

Did you or Missy consider using your father's sperm for artificial insemination?

I certainly didn't. By the time I discovered what had happened, my father was dead, and she was far too humiliated from the experience to think clearly.

Matt played his flashlight around and saw dust everywhere along with cobwebs and evidence of spiders here and there. In some places, there were unmistakable signs of footprints leading in and out of the hole.

He moved forward onto what he could now see was a ceiling joist of the room below and, trying not to step on the prints put their previously, followed them, bending over to avoid hitting his head on the roof above him. He immediately found an area in the room in which someone had recently established a camp of sorts. Here he discovered candy-bar wrappers, empty pop cans, a dirty handkerchief, and a mysterious coil of wire, as if someone were planning to return and use it for something. Even more interesting, however, he could hear voices from the room below when he bent over while standing. He couldn't understand what the voices said because they were too soft. But they were clearly voices.

So, if I understand correctly, all of you share some kind of guilt, with you having the least of it.

I suppose. Remember, though, I told the story. My mother or Missy would, I'm sure, give you other versions. Somewhere between them would no doubt be the truth.

So your mother knew of this as well?

She did.

I can't imagine what she must of felt when hearing the story.

Me either.

You've never spoken about it with her?

No.

Missy?

No.

Then how do you know she knows?

My father told her.

Your father? I'm getting lost here. Help me out. If you've not heard from your mother, how do you know he told her?

He told Missy.

What? *He* told Missy?

Yes.

Why?

To punish her, I think. Make her feel worse about the whole situation than she already did. Maybe enough to get her to change her mind.

She didn't?

No.

Wow, it sure turned into a mess.

Yes it did.

Is that all there is to tell?

Guess so. At least all of what I have to say on the matter.

I should ask you then, is that the *complete* background you referred to when you asked me to ask more questions?

No. There's more.

As complex as the story you just told me?

Some of it even more complex. Some not so much.

Unfortunately, I'm going to have to stop us here for today though our time is not up. I have to think this over. It's fundamentally the same story you told me in the first place but without the rape, though there are many subtle aspects to it that require time for me to digest. I'll see you again in a couple of days.

All right. Goodbye.

Bye, Joe.

17

Matt Brady waited for at least an hour before he realized that hearing the voices from below was all he was going to discover about the hiding place he'd entered. So, he retraced his steps, climbed back to the rooftop, and looked around in case there was anything he'd missed.

It was then that he noticed something especially interesting. The footprints he'd seen in the snow that were not his own did not approach his position, but only moved away from it. This meant that the person who'd come here had not only left, but did so a significant time after arriving, since no prints approaching the flue were visible. The falling snow had filled them in. Over time.

On one hand, this could have given the person time to create the entrance hole he'd discovered in the duct. On the other hand, it could mean that something had been placed here during the visit that he hadn't yet discovered. He realized this second bit of imagining on his part could be just that. But it was also a distinct possibility. So, for him at least, the mystery widened.

Good morning, Joe.

Morning.

Sleep well?

Yes, actually. Didn't dream.

Interesting. Maybe telling me the story you did cleared something from your mind. Let you sleep better.

Could be. Or count myself a king of infinite space, were it not that I have bad dreams.

So true. Shakespeare definitely had a way with words. Anything new you want to tell me?

Happening inside the prison, you mean?

Well that, though it's not really a prison. A medical facility with patients. Maybe you could tell me another one of those stories you promised me.

Why not ask me about me?

Okay, do you have something you wish to tell me about yourself?

Yes. I love magic.

Magic, eh? Good. I like magic as well. At least watching it. I don't know many magic tricks myself, though would be happy to learn.

Great. I rarely have an audience to play to, and you can tell me how good I am.

Is this going to clarify something about you?

I believe so.

All right. Let's see.

I'll start with an easy one to warm up, and move on from there to more difficult ones. For me to create, and you to understand.

Good.

Now, I have a straw here that I brought from the cafeteria.

I see that.

I'm going to pull off the paper wrapper and put the straw aside. So far so good?

I hope there's more to it than this.

There is. Watch now as I rip this long straw wrapper into several pieces. Take a good look to make sure I'm actually doing what I say.

You are.

Now, I'm going to take these separate pieces of which there are maybe twelve, jam them together into a single ball, compact that ball into as small a wad as I can, and place it in the palm of my right hand. See it there?

I do.

Watch carefully now, as I whisper magic words over my hand, close it up tight, open it, and slowly unwrap the ball.

Whoa, that's good. It's back in one piece.

Yes, it is. And I have no sleeves up which I could have pulled out the non-ripped one. Here's my open hand showing no sign of trickery there either. One straw blanket, as I like to call them, first torn to shreds, and then magically restored to its original form, albeit a bit more wrinkly one than previous.

I see that.

Magic?

We both know there's no such thing as true magic.

Don't tell that to magicians. It hurts their feelings.

Right. I take it back. At the same time, I'll ask you what this reveals about you.

First let me tell you how it's done.

I'm not sure I want to know.

Good. I prefer it that way too. So we both agree. It's magic.

So what does it reveal?

Magic, that is *real* magic, not the simple trick I just showed you, is a matter of deception. Deception is not actually lying, it's diverting an audience's attention away from what you're actually doing. And to show you what I mean, I'm going to do a more advanced form of magic now, one you might want to understand when I'm done. Let's agree that I won't tell you though, all right?

Okay.

Now, along with the straw, I took an apple from the cafeteria as well. Here it is. I'm going to give it to you to make sure it's what I say it is. Here.

Got it.

Is it a real apple?

Yes.

You're sure?

Yes.

Why not take a bite out of it to make absolutely sure.

I don't need to do that, I believe you.

You shouldn't. Not when I'm doing magic, at least. Take a finger-nail and peel off a bit of it to be positive.

It's an apple.

Now, I'll take it back and pick up the straw I didn't use in the last trick. You'll want to take a look at it as well to make sure it's what I say it is.

160

I can see that it is.

Make sure by feeling it. That's important because it might be metal.

Metal?

Check it to make sure it's a standard straw.

It is.

Good. Now, here's the trick. I'm going to take this straw and push it completely through the apple without it even bending.

Hmm.

That's what I would say were I in your shoes. It doesn't seem possible, does it?

No.

Well, a few magic words and here goes.

Wow.

Take a look at the straw. Same one?

Looks like it.

Is it really all the way through the apple?

Yes. I can see bits of apple in the end of the straw where it went through.

Quite a trick, no?

Yes. How did you do it?

Whoops. We promised ourselves I wouldn't tell you, remember?

Yes. Again, though, I ask, what does this tell me about you?

Magic is deception. There's something you don't know, and when I perform the magic and use that thing you don't know, it allows me to make you see something that appears magical. It's always some kind of deception. Whether it's a card trick or a guy with three cups and a peanut. All variations on the same thing. Deception. Not a lie. Do you understand?

I think so. Are you telling me that what you've described to me about your father and your wife so far was a deception?

No. That was prior to this demonstration. I lied the first time about the rape. The second time I told you the truth. That stands.

Are you telling me that from now on everything you tell me will be a deception? That you're telling me the truth, but not always the complete truth?

Good question, isn't it?

Are you going to answer it?

No. I'm going to let you be a psychiatrist. Let you discover my deceptions. What I've done this morning is tell you the truth up front. Watch out. I'm not ever going to lie to you again. Though I may use deception.

But why do it this way? Why not continue to tell me the truth?

Good question.

You're not going to answer that one either?

I will, but only partially.

Well?

No one ever tells the complete truth.

Why?

They're not capable of doing so. That's because our minds hide things from us. We're not deceiving on purpose, only by lack of consciously knowing the complete truth ourselves.

That's very perceptive. Something I might have said.

It's an honor to hear you say that. The wise man knows himself to be a fool.

So you're being extremely honest in telling me what you've told me?

One way to put it.

The deceiving you do will not be on purpose, at least from your conscious point of view.

Correct. I'm most likely leaving something out.

What am I to think?

I will tell you this. Do you remember the test you had me take?

Of course I do.

Remember I got all the answers wrong because I misunderstood the proper boxes for the answers?

Yes.

Do you think I did that on purpose?

No. You couldn't have faked your reaction to my telling you that you got zero percent right.

Good. So why did I do it wrong?

Because you misunderstood.

No.

Why?

162

Because my alter ego, something I'm sure you're familiar with, deceived me.

Thought we'd decided you read the boxes wrong?

I did. But I'm pretty smart, as you know. I could have figured it out. I wasn't paying attention, and my deceiving brain did that to me. Let me give you another example. My memory. I can't remember what I'm supposed to have done that got me into this mess, right?

Yes.

Why do you suppose that is?

Same thing?

To me, yes. My alter ego has a mind of its own. It never ceases to amaze me. So I'm telling you I am not going to intentionally deceive you. I'm also telling you, however, that I will most likely deceive you unintentionally. Do you understand?

I do now.

So you've got to be careful with me. Like the tricks I presented, my mind is a deceiving bastard. It deceives even me. I'm not always in control. I can be fooled as well as you. So we both must be watchful. Deception, as my magic was intended to demonstrate, can be a very powerful thing. And with human minds, and particularly mine, I won't actually know when it's happening. From now on, please help me rein it in, will you?

I will.

Good.

Matt visited his supervisor and advised him of the discoveries he'd made on the roof of Building J. His supervisor listened carefully, asked a few questions, and then told Matt he could continue his search for unknown visitors in his off time but needed him to continue working his full regular shift due to some of the guards who had called in sick with the flu. Matt understood, requested that his written reports be entered into the facility's log, and returned to work. This entering into the log was important since, now that the storms had passed, he didn't want someone seeing him on the roof and reporting his strange behavior without having clear authorization to do so.

I'd like to know more about your teen years.

Makes sense. Maybe you'd like me to tell you about the dead girl?

Dead girl? You never mentioned anything about a dead girl before.

You never asked. I have lots of memories. You can't expect me to pick ones you might think important but I don't.

Tell me about the dead girl.

This has to do with Bradley something.

Bradley something?

His first name was Bradley. I never knew his last name.

Go on.

I met Bradley around the time high school began.

Thought you didn't attend high school.

I didn't. He did. He told me he was beginning high school.

All right. You also told me you didn't have any friends except for the girl that accompanied her father when she visited your father occasionally.

I did tell you that. It's still true. Just let me tell the story and you'll understand.

Sorry.

Well, I was out in the fields plowing the stalks of our crops under for that year. You know, preparing for the winter. So I was in this tractor.

Excuse me a second. If you were fourteen, as would be the case if you were high school age, how could you be driving a tractor?

I see my warning you was worth it. You're asking more questions now than you did before.

I am.

We lived in the country as you can imagine. Even there, it's illegal for fourteen-year-olds to drive cars, no less tractors. My father, and most other fathers who were farmers, didn't give a damn about such laws. After all, it was his property, his tractor, and his kid. He didn't have time to do all the plowing, so he had me do some of it. I was quite capable. I'd watched him run things like that for most likely ten or more years by then. I knew how to do it well. Maybe better than he did. The police didn't have time to patrol the fields of farmers, so that was that.

Okay.

So I was plowing away when this kid ran in front of me. I jammed on the brakes and yelled at him to move. He gave me a big smile and just stood there. Fearless.

This was Bradley?

Yes. I didn't know his name then, of course, I found that out later. So I got down from my high perch and asked him what the hell he was doing.

What did he say?

He didn't say anything. He ran around the tractor with a feverish grin on his face. I tried to catch him, after all I had a job to do, but I couldn't get near him. Boy was he fast. I'd never seen anyone before or since who could run straight and then turn on a dime at right angles like he did. Really something.

So, what happened?

I sat down on a mound of dirt, and watched him run circles around me. Once I tried to talk to him, but he'd have nothing to do with me. Truly insane. Except I knew he'd run out of steam eventually, so I waited him out.

When he ran out of steam, what did you say?

That's when we both started laughing.

About what?

You know. Just one of those things. He'd run maybe a hundred circles around me and I'd just sat there watching him do it. Strange. We both knew it, and somehow it seemed funny. So we laughed until we cried. I haven't laughed like that since. Or likely before as well. It was great.

Then he told you his name?

Yes. Only his first name. Bradley. And I told him mine. He lived behind us somewhere. He didn't say exactly where, and I couldn't gauge how far away since with his energy he could have run miles before he'd stopped in front of my tractor.

He told you?

Told me what?

About the dead girl?

No. That was later. We talked then. About his farm and my father's farm.

You know, it's occurred to me that you never call you father 'dad.'

My father was a 'father,' not a 'dad.' Not in any way a 'dad.'

Understood.

165

So after we talked for a while, I asked him if he'd ever driven a tractor. He said he hadn't, so I asked him if he'd like to drive it. He said yes, so we got up on Bessie.

Bessie?

I name things. The tractor's name was Bessie. Remember Teddy?

Yes, I see.

So, once we were up on Bessie, I drove and plowed in straight lines and showed him how. He was a quick study, and before long I let him do a couple of things related to the process. You know, like turn the steering wheel or brake when the time came. Things like that. He did fine. In fact, so fine that I accused him of lying to me. That he *did* know how to drive a tractor. He didn't get mad, just asked for more information. He was quite something. Anyway, I let him drive. Greatest mistake I'd made to that point in my life.

Why? What'd he do?

He drove in circles. Wildly. Pushed the accelerator pedal down hard and off we went. And when I say circles, I don't mean round and round in a single circle, I mean circles. Plural. All over the place. So wildly, I couldn't get the steering wheel away from him. Except I had to, see, because he was making a mess of what I had so carefully done previously. It was nuts. All this time he was laughing like he was possessed or something.

How did you stop him?

That was difficult. I finally opened my mouth and screamed in his ear for as long as I could hold it. As loud as I could. Eventually, he couldn't take it any longer and rammed on the brakes. I took the key out of the ignition, something I should have done in the first place but, now that I think of it, couldn't because I was always off balance from his driving. That shut down the engine and there we sat. Him laughing insanely, and me mad as a hornet and about to punch him in the face.

Did you?

No. I was too exhausted from what he'd put me through.

Then what happened?

Well I told him off real good. I won't go into the details here, though he certainly got an earful.

What did he say?

Nothing. Just laughed. I couldn't figure the guy out. Now, of course,

166

because I'm smarter, I know he must have been a manic-depressive or what some now call bipolar. There was nothing else to explain it.

All right. Then what?

Well, I pulled him out of the driver's seat that I should never have allowed him to sit in in the first place, took the seat myself, looked at the mess he'd created, and plowed it over again, figuring that there went my lunch hour. And it took until well after noon to make the field look as it had before he'd made it a mess.

He sat there the whole time?

Oh no. He laughed and tried to fight me for control of the tractor. And he'd jump off while we were moving, things like that. I had a hell of a time. But I did it.

So, you were right back where you'd been when you'd first seen him standing in front of you.

Approximately, yes.

Then?

I pushed him away from the tractor. He was thin as a rail. I must have outweighed him two to one. So it didn't take much effort to shove him to the ground.

Was he hurt?

Not so's you'd notice. He jumped to his feet and ran around the tractor in circles again. He had no end of energy. Amazing thing.

He must have stopped sometime.

He did. Right about the time I'd finished my quick bite to eat and was preparing to get back to plowing again. I didn't want to disappoint my father.

What did Bradley do after that?

Well Bradley was Bradley. That I'd understood from the beginning. I knew I couldn't control him and that once I started the tractor he'd probably stand in front of it again until I let him drive. So I grabbed him and held him still for a second and told him if he didn't stop his strange behavior I was going to tie him to a tree. I even pointed at one. You know, we had windbreaks so the summer storms wouldn't tear down the corn stalks.

I've seen windbreaks before.

Well, when he heard me tell him that, he changed completely. He stopped trying to get away, stopped laughing, stopped everything. I figured he'd had some of that medicine previously, probably from his father, and didn't like it. So, I walked him over to a downed tree trunk, sat him down, reluctantly let him go, and told him to stay put until I finished my plowing.

Did he do it?

I'm getting to that. He sat there for a moment looking as sad as my dog did when he was alive, and began talking. Talking, talking, and more talking. Just like running, he couldn't stop. He told me about things I couldn't repeat here, even among adults.

Like what? I mean you don't have to be specific, just in general.

Mostly about stupid things like outhouses. You know, shit and piss and anything he could think of that was banned from polite talk.

You couldn't get a word in edgewise?

Not at first, no. He was clearly mad as a hatter. He jumped from one subject to another right in the middle of a sentence. Actually, it was as if he wasn't thinking at all, just letting his mind wander out loud. Strangest thing I've ever encountered. Eventually, of course, he wore himself out and stopped and stared at me. I'll never forget that stare. It was as if he was seeing me for the first time. As if he couldn't remember what had happened while he was in the field.

What did you do?

I didn't know what to do. He'd talked so much and about so many different subjects I had no idea where to begin. So I told him I had to get back to work. That my father would whip me if I didn't. He would have, too.

And?

He seemed to understand. At least nodded as if he did. At this point he was almost contrite, though I'm probably reading things into his behavior rather than actually analyzing it correctly. Anyway, he sat there looking over the field and apparently thinking about something. Then he stared at me and asked if I wanted to see something strange. I told him I didn't have time for that. I had to get back to work. He argued that this thing he wanted to show me was really unusual. That I'd *want* to see it. That it wasn't far away. He knew right where it was and once I saw it he would leave me alone and let me get back to plowing the fields. That was very tempting. If, of course, I could believe him.

And you did?

I did, yes. Anything to get rid of him at that point. I mean he'd become a very large pain in the ass, costing me many hours of my normal work time. I'd have done almost anything to get him to leave me alone. Including, by the way, tying him to that tree for the rest of the afternoon.

Did you have something to tie him up with?

Yeah, sure I did. Tractors have toolboxes, or at least that one did, and it had twine, ropes, wires, chains, and many things to do it with. Would have been a cinch. I almost pulled them out to show him, but I didn't need to. The threat of it calmed him down.

What happened next?

Well, he got up and walked toward the forest at the edge of the field, one of those small copses of trees that often separate the fields of one farmer from the next, and in we went. He actually walked at a reasonable pace. Hard for me to believe.

So he showed you the dead girl then?

Not then, no. He showed me something else first. Something that scared the bejabbers out of me.

What?

He walked a few paces into the trees, far enough that we couldn't see out of there very well and, presumably, no one could see in very well either, and pointed to something in the mess of leaves and limbs that had fallen down in the wind. I followed his pointing finger, and there it was.

What?

A shovel.

Just a shovel?

No, not 'just' a shovel, a large farm implement covered in blood. Or at least red and black stuff that looked like blood to me. I suppose it could have been something else, but I took it for blood. Lots of it, too. I didn't know what to think.

What did he say?

Nothing at all. He pointed and stared at it. As if I could glean from the thing what had caused it to look that way.

What did you think?

That something bad had happened to something alive. That's all I could figure at the moment. It was grisly to say the least. My imagination went haywire. I mean I was guessing a cow, a dear, maybe a pig, or something, had run into foul play. Maybe a homeless person had gotten hungry and killed an animal to eat and left the shovel behind. I was scared. Farmers don't like their animals killed and eaten by strangers. There was going to be hell to pay for someone. I knew I'd have to tell my father about it, and being the bearer of bad news I knew that whether I deserved it or not I'd probably bear the brunt of his anger. That sort of thing.

All this from a shovel?

You didn't see that shovel. It was very bloody. And there were things attached to it.

Things?

Like parts of skin and hair or fur. It looked like whatever had been killed hadn't liked it much, and had not gone down easily. Again, my imagination made it worse. Like in a movie I saw once, I think the only movie I saw when I was a kid. They showed only the victim of the violence, not the thing that did it. It scared the audience more than seeing the thing that caused its death. You know what I mean?

I do.

So we both sat down in front of the shovel and stared at it. I figured this was the thing he wanted to show me and I could take a second to figure out what to do. You know, like tell someone or keep it a secret. I got the idea he was doing the same thing.

At his first opportunity, Matt made his way to the rear of Building J, climbed to the roof, walked to the flue that could be seen in its entirety now since most of the snow had melted, repelled down to the secret room he'd found, and looked the place over again.

Matt immediately noticed that the coil of wire he'd seen before was now gone. Someone had returned, either needed the wire or determined that its presence might give away the intrusion, removed it, and left. He looked the place over again. More carefully this time. Trying to notice every detail he could see. No other entrances or exits anywhere. No other way to leave except back the way he'd come. He found this strange. After all, why would someone come down here just to be here, maybe listen to some voices from below without being able to understand what they were saying, grab a coil of wire, and leave? It didn't make any sense.

Then what?

Well, after a few minutes of staring at the shovel, Bradley got up and told me to follow him.

That's when he showed you the dead girl?

Yes. She was lying in a hole about three feet deep. She couldn't have been older than us. Except that wasn't the thing.

She was still alive?

No. What made you think that?

I don't know. Hope maybe?

No hope to have. It wasn't only a dead girl, it was a mutilated dead girl. I mean there was no chance of her being alive. She'd been clubbed and clubbed until she was barely recognizable as human. One of her legs had been severed. She'd bled profusely due to the assault on her body. Everything but her face was a complete mess. I thought I'd vomit.

Except for her face?

Yes. Strangest thing. Her face hadn't been the target. While it had a few scratches here and there, from the head up she looked like she could have still been alive. Lovely thing. Long blond hair splayed out like she'd been posed. At least her head. The rest of her was mangled beyond description. I couldn't imagine why someone would have done that to anyone. Angry or not. A young girl? Didn't make any sense.

What did you do?

Nothing at first. I stood there as Bradley did. It was beyond incredible. I'll never forget myself imagining what she'd gone through before dying.

How did Bradley look?

I don't know. Forgot he was there. It was only me and this poor dead girl lying in the bottom of the hole. My mind raced through the possibilities of what could have happened during her murder.

I understand that. Though you must have wondered who did it.

No. I couldn't imagine anyone doing it. So I forgot about that, for the moment at least. I stared at her face and hair and thought over who she could be. She was so young.

What about the hole?

It looked like someone had wanted to bury her, but had been interrupted, run, and dropped the shovel along the way.

In what direction had the murderer run?

Not sure. Though the placement of the shovel from the body was, strangely enough, in the direction of my father's house.

Your father's house?

Yes.

Not *your* house?

Well, yes, my house because I was his son. But my father always referred to it as his house, and I always thought of it as his.

So what did you do?

I asked Bradley about when he'd discovered the body.

What did he say?

That he'd found it just before he saw me driving my tractor. He'd then run away from the sight of the dead body.

Did he say why he'd not mentioned it to you when he first saw you on the tractor?

No. I never asked. It was clear he'd gone berserk at that point.

Did your seeing the body remind you of anything?

No. Should it have?

Yes. Mutt.

Mutt? Why Mutt?

Didn't you tell me Mutt was mutilated in much the same way? Everything ripped to shreds except his head?

Yes, but an owl killed him.

Or so your father told you.

You think my father lied?

I have no idea. So what did you *do*?

I asked Bradley if he knew who'd done this thing.

What'd he say?

Nothing. He shook his head back and forth indicating, I suppose, that he had no idea. That he'd found the girl, the shovel, and gone crazy.

What then?

We sat there for a time, not knowing what to do. Finally, I told him I was going to get my father. He'd know what to do next.

And?

That's what I did. Told my father the entire story.

172

What happened then?

He called the local police, followed me to the scene, and saw the girl.

Did he say anything?

No. I think it made him sick as well. He didn't say anything until the cops arrived and we told them what we knew. By then Bradley had gone home, or at least left the scene.

You mentioned him to your father?

Sure.

And?

The cops let us be, an ambulance came and, I presume, took the girl away and we left. Went home and ate dinner.

Did your father talk about this at all?

No. In fact, he didn't say a word after I showed him the girl. At least nothing to me. He talked to the police in that way he had.

What way was that?

Short bursts of sentences.

Then?

Then, nothing. That was the end of it as far as I know. I imagined the cops searched for the murderer and found him, but maybe not. My father took over the field where I'd been plowing, and I took his plowing duties in another field far from the crime scene. And that was that. The subject was never mentioned again.

How about newspapers, television, radio, and so on?

We had none of those during my childhood. We were virtually shut off from the outside world. The cops never returned and I figured it had been taken care of in some way. That's everything I know.

Curiosity being what it is, didn't you try to find out what happened to the little girl after you'd grown up?

No. Many other things had happened by then and, farms being what they were in those days with no Internet, computers, or electronic record-keeping like we have now, I figured whatever had occurred was history. Not much I could do about it. She was dead. By then for many years. What good would my searching do? Couldn't save her.

If the murderer hadn't been found, maybe you could find him.

I was a farmer like my father and didn't have the time. You're not a farmer. You have no idea what a day in the fields can do to your curiosity. Dead tired means exactly that. You work, eat, and sleep. That's about it.

I understand.

Not really, I don't think, but you get the idea. It wasn't possible.

Surely you didn't forget about the experience.

No, of course not. I could think of nothing but her for weeks after that.

What about Bradley?

Well I haven't gone into that yet.

Will you now?

If you want.

I do.

Well that one day was all I ever saw of Bradley. Maybe for an hour or so, all in all.

That's the end of the story?

No. About a week later I heard that Bradley had hung himself.

What?

Yes. That's what I heard at least.

From whom?

My father, I think.

You think?

I'm not sure exactly, but I'm pretty sure he told me.

You sound more than dubious.

Don't mean to. Anyway, it was all the information I got and I was still in shock. As I say, my father was a man of few words. He didn't tell me why, where, or when except, of course, I knew it had been some time since I'd last seen Bradley.

What did you think?

I didn't think. Don't now know anything more about it. Remember, I worked all day, even on weekends, and didn't have any friends. I had only my father's word on it.

Do you doubt that word?

No. Never seemed to me my father lied. He did lots of things, but he hadn't lied that I could remember. However, he was my only source. My mother talked less, so she was no help.

Do you wonder about it now?

Sure. I went from imagining that the murderer had come back

174

and killed Bradley making it look like suicide, or that his bipolar mental problems had driven him to depression and he'd had enough of it. All that mixed in with seeing the dead girl was a heavy burden for a young man my age to endure.

Did you imagine that Bradley killed the little girl, and he couldn't take his guilt any longer?

That, and a thousand other things. Except, as time wore on, even that moved to the back of my mind. And like with the little girl's death, I had no way to get further information from anyone until it was too late to matter.

That's quite a story.

It made *me* feel guilty.

Why that? You had nothing to do with it.

Not that I could figure out. But it happened so close to my father's property. In fact, with the small amount of forest between farms, it would have probably been difficult to actually determine on whose property the murder actually took place. It could very easily have been on my father's farm, which made the whole thing worse, and me feel guiltier.

I guess I can understand that.

For a few minutes there I imagined my father might have done it.

Whoa. That's very interesting.

Yes. While I didn't see anyone running from the scene or anything, he would know that area as well as anyone. I imagined him doing it, being interrupted by Bradley, and running away.

Did Bradley mention seeing anyone?

No. He told me he hadn't as a matter of fact.

He could have been lying.

I suppose. Didn't know him at all.

And no one told you about any motive for the crime?

I couldn't imagine a motive existing. She was young. As I say, about my age at the time. What kind of motive could anyone have for killing her? Especially in that manner?

Sometimes people do things like that to hurt other people, *not* the one that's murdered.

I'm aware of that. It occurred to me as a possibility. But I didn't know enough people to have any idea who that might be.

Thus, your father as a suspect.

I suppose.

Listen, I'm late for my next appointment. We're going to have to continue this discussion next time. This has been quite interesting. Please attempt between now and when I see you next to think of anything else you remember about this episode, will you?

Yes.

Goodbye, Joe.

18

M att Brady spent much of the previous afternoon searching the room in which he now found himself. Then he worked a full night's shift, and after that returned to what he now called the secret room to further investigate his discovery. Thus, he was nearly twenty-four hours without sleep. It was no wonder that once there, he shut his eyes and fell immediately into deep sleep.

Sometime after that, another person quietly entered the room, successfully negotiated around Matt, fiddled with something on the upper part of the ceiling of the room below, and left. Fortunately or unfortunately, depending on your point of view, this visitor caught a piece of his or her clothing on a ragged edge of the entrance cut into the side of the flue and suddenly woke Matt from his nap. He immediately noticed the vanishing shoes of the person who'd come down, grabbed for them, missed, and struggled to get a look at the visitor but failed.

By the time Matt had fully wakened, the person had vanished and Matt was left with a piece of cloth and the memory of seeing the person's shoes. Not much to go on except for the fact that Matt was now certain that the visitor, given the cloth he'd found and the type of shoes worn, was a woman.

Hello, Joe.
Doctor Amador.
It's good to see you. How have you been?

Fine. Happy as usual.

Glad to hear it. Did you get a chance to think over the story you told me last time we spoke to see if any other details emerged?

I did.

Were you successful?

Somewhat. I remembered a few things that might make for interesting discussion.

Great. Let's get right to them.

The first detail I forgot to mention and that might have been a deception my alter ego played on me, was that the murdered girl was naked.

My God. Are you sure?

I think so, yes. While I stared at her face more than her body, I remember that it struck me odd that I couldn't see anything resembling a dress or any other piece of clothing in or around her body. It seemed strange then, and it still seems strange now.

To me, too. Why do you think that is?

Why do we think it's strange?

No. Why she didn't have any clothes on.

Well, it could suggest some kind of sexual activity.

You mean you think the girl was raped?

I don't know. It could have been consensual. Or no sex at all.

Both good points.

So I didn't hang onto that memory as much as my others. Now it makes me wonder.

About?

The murderer. He could have been sexually obsessed and stripped off her clothes to get a look at her. Maybe sodomy, something like that. He killed her to keep her quiet. Mutilated her body afterward to make it seem like he did it for another reason.

Such as?

No idea. It's strange to me, that's all.

I agree. I'm sure the police were aware of that.

Don't see how they couldn't have been. It was quite obvious.

Anything else?

Yes.

What?

Her blonde hair had a pretty red bow tied in it. And, like her face, this bow was completely intact. Like it might have been placed there by the murderer *after* he killed and mutilated her.

Like he was posing the body or something?

Yes.

Did the police ask you any questions about this?

No. I didn't volunteer information both because they could see those things for themselves and because I was too obsessed with what I'd seen to talk much. I guess you could say I was in a state of shock.

I can certainly understand that. Anything else?

Yes.

Still more?

Yes. There was something black at the far rim of the hole in which the girl lay.

Like what?

I can only remember that it looked like a dark piece of cloth that had been torn from something. Seemed out of place since the dirt in that area had been freshly dug and was light brown by comparison. So it was hard to miss.

Could it have been a part of the girl's clothing? And the murderer had taken the rest?

I suppose, but it didn't look like a color a girl her age would wear.

That's it? Nothing else lying around you could see?

Nothing except the shovel I told you about last time.

So, this dark piece of cloth was lying on freshly dug earth, and therefore looked like it was part of the crime scene?

Absolutely. It was clean as far as I could see. No dirt on it at all. Like somebody might have left it behind as a memento or something, or it had been torn off in the struggle.

I see. The struggle between the girl and her attacker?

Yes. But, remember, this is a current supposition on my part not something I thought about then.

Understood. Anything further?

No. I think that's it. Naked, ribbon, and near-black fragment of cloth. That's it.

Wow. You've given this quite a bit of thought since we last met.

Hard not to. Remembering it in the first place has kept me from sleeping much. Almost like it just happened though it was a long time ago.

Any new ideas who might have done it?

Not a one. Remember, I didn't know anyone much at the time. I've already given you the people who I thought might be possibilities. But I don't think they did it. Bradley was nuts, and my father far too busy to do something like that.

Interesting that you didn't pronounce their innocence for any other reason than their mental state and being busy.

Well, of course, I didn't know Bradley at the time and my father, well, you know a lot about him already so you can understand my reluctance to admit his innocence based on my understanding of him which was nearly zero.

Yes.

The fact that his visitor wore women's shoes and the cloth seemed light and airy like a woman's dress confused Matt. The Forensic Psychiatric Facility contained only men. While there were certainly women working in the pharmacy and the Administration Building, they weren't likely candidates for illegally entering one of the buildings in the inmate's compound. Though he was acutely aware that the horns had gone off signaling a possible entry or exit from outside the facility during the storm, he doubted anyone could have made it this far at that time, no less a woman. Certainly not one wearing the kind of shoes he'd seen, nor the frilly material he'd found that resembled part of a skirt or blouse. It didn't seem possible. So, the more he investigated the situation, the more confused he became. Not the way things should work.

So do any other experiences you've had come to mind?

Jar my memory.

All right, I'd like to hear more detail about your first meeting with your wife Missy.

Are you sure? Not very interesting.

Let me determine that.

Well, I've already mentioned we met at Niagara Falls and that we were both with someone else at the time. One thing led to another, we fell in love, and got married.

I remember that. But let's investigate the relationships that both Missy and you had prior to, during, and after you met.

That's complicated. I can only tell you about it from my perspective.

Of course. And that's the perspective I'm most interested in.

Well, as I told you before, we met at the Falls one day when we each had someone else along. That made things quite difficult.

Immediately?

No, certainly not then. I had no idea a new relationship was beginning. I saw someone who I thought was attractive, and who looked at me like she was interested. That's it. A fleeting glance.

That's all it took?

Yes. For me at least. I had one of those queasy feelings in my stomach that told me she was the one.

I understand. I've had one of those as well.

About your wife?

Let's not get into my personal life.

Sorry.

Don't be. Just not pertinent.

That was it at first. Only a look. I'm sure she noticed I was with someone else and she in the same boat.

Obviously it escalated from there.

Yes. We met by accident outside our rooms the next morning and struck up a conversation.

Who started it?

The conversation? Don't remember exactly. I think we both did. That is, we both talked at the same time, apologized, and then did it again.

Like in the movies?

Wouldn't know. Haven't seen many of those. I think it probably happens to a lot of people who are interested in one another but not yet comfortable. Nervous, you know? So I eventually let her talk, and we fell into a conversation with no trouble at all.

Natural.

Absolutely. She was easy to talk to. She listened to me as I listened to what she had to say. That's the secret isn't it?

Listening as well as talking?

Yes.

Absolutely.

Once we began talking, there was no stopping us. I loved looking into her eyes and hearing about the things she liked to do. I loved everything about her from the first moment on.

Do you remember what you talked about?

A little. She spoke mostly about her love of books. Reading. She liked many kinds of books. Fiction, non-fiction, poetry. Everything. Couldn't get enough of them. Like an addiction.

Did you tell her about your experiences with books?

That I could read them fast without seeing separate words?

Yes.

No, actually, I didn't. I figured that might intimidate her, so I left that part out.

So you sub-consciously didn't tell her? Like your alter ego doesn't tell you some things?

Maybe. But actually I don't think that was it. Mine was definitely a conscious decision. I wanted to impress her, though not so much that she felt our conversation was one sided. You know what I mean?

Sure. I only wanted to point out the similarities. Maybe what you think is your alter ego isn't your alter ego at all. Maybe it's your subconscious trying to protect you from something it thinks might not be in your best interest.

Now that I think of it, that might be an excellent point. More likely what I'm calling my alter ego is really a mixture of my subconscious and conscious minds.

Possibly.

Good.

Now. Tell me more.

Anyway, there's not much a farmer can talk about to someone of the opposite gender who's not been on a farm. Describing what a tractor does or how it works is completely uninteresting, even to me.

So what did you talk about?

By then I'd read a few books including the dictionary I mentioned, and I knew what every word she used meant, and she used plenty of long ones. We talked about Steinbeck, Hemmingway, and so on. She had a lot of good ideas about what the authors might have intended to say in those books.

Beyond the words they used?

Yes.

So what did your girlfriend-soon-to-be-ex-girlfriend have to say about this?

Plenty. She immediately guessed what was going on between Missy and me. I don't know how, but she did. And she let me have it. Said I'd brought her there to spend time with her, not so I could meet someone else. That I should pay more attention to her, rather than some tart I'd seen on the boardwalk overlooking the falls. She was incredibly pissed.

Just because you spoke to another woman?

Yes. I have to admit, though, while nothing physical was going on, I think it was pretty obvious to anyone that something had happened between Missy and me.

All right. So what then?

Missy's boyfriend showed up. After I got through explaining to him there was nothing to it, the two of them wandered off. After that, I paid more attention to my girlfriend. The one I brought along. We talked through it and, for a time, I thought we might make it together. After all, I'd not gotten Missy's name at that point, or her phone number, or any real information about her. Though for the short time we'd talked I thought we might see one another again, it then didn't seem likely. So I pretty much gave up on it.

Until?

Until I *did* see her again.

Outside your room like the previous time?

Yes, and in almost exactly the same spot. Like Kismet or something. We both knew it and knew the other knew it. All we had to do was smile, and it came clear.

So what did you do?

I suggested we go see the falls again. And we did. You know, it's very misty out there on that boardwalk overlooking the water, and I figured we wouldn't be so conspicuous there.

So what did you talk about this time?

That's just it, we didn't talk about anything. We couldn't talk, actually, for the water going over the falls was much too loud for that.

So what did you do?

We looked at one another.

Did your respective partners catch you this time?

No. We were pretty well hidden. I suppose if they would have come out to the falls they could have seen us, but from where we were seen the last time it was impossible.

What had you told your girlfriend you were doing when you left her in the room?

Going for a walk.

So she had no need to come out and look for you?

No.

So how did your vacation end?

Well, Missy left me her name, phone number, and address, and I left her mine.

Were you still living with your father at the time?

No. I was farming on my own by then. On a plot not too far from his. I didn't actually own the farm, but it was my place and I didn't have to explain my behavior to him or anyone else.

How long before Missy called?

I called her. Just about the time I walked in the door from vacation.

And things took off from there?

Well, we had to break off with our partners at the time first.

That a mess?

Yes. At least in my case. My girlfriend apparently thought we'd had plans that I didn't actually know anything about.

For marriage?

More for engagement, I think. Anyway, she took it very hard. Claimed I'd misled her all along and had taken advantage of her love for me.

So, it got ugly?

Very. She'd call me often and get angry when my phone machine picked up. I tried to explain something she already knew. I was a farmer and had to work for a living. The crops couldn't plant themselves, fertilize themselves, harvest themselves, and so on, ad infinitum. That, of course, wasn't what was bothering her. She was angry with me because

184

in her mind she'd wasted a big part of her life on me, and I'd turned out to be what she called a rotten tomato.

How long had you dated her?

We'd been going out for slightly more than a year when I met Missy.

That's a long time in a young person's life.

I knew that. But I hadn't made a single commitment to her. We'd never discussed marriage or engagement. She was fun to be around, and I liked her. We just weren't meant for one another. Not like Missy and I.

You told her that?

Not in so many words, no. She and I had fun. That's all it was. Fun. With Missy it was something else.

But she didn't think that way?

Not at all.

How long did this end-of-relationship business last?

Couple of months.

Did it get violent?

Violent? No. Well, she slapped me a couple of times, but I didn't slap her back.

Did you feel like it?

Sure. Who wouldn't? But it wasn't logical. So I talked her down from her emotional highs. See, that's what confused me about the whole thing. I'd be logical and she'd be emotional. It could never have worked in the long run.

I wish I had a dollar for every time I've heard those words.

Now you've heard them again.

Don't shoot the messenger.

Sorry.

She must have finally seen the light.

I think she got tired is all.

Realized it wasn't going to change? Rather, that *you* weren't going to change?

Right.

Were you seeing Missy while this was happening?

No. She didn't live nearby, so that was pretty much out of the question.

That obviously changed.

Yes, except long after I broke up with Nancy.

That's interesting.

What?

That's the first time you've mentioned her name. Nancy. Why do you suppose that is?

Trying to get her out of my mind, I suppose.

Well let's finish with Nancy before we continue with Missy. When did you last see her and how did that go?

About two months after the incident with Missy at Niagara Falls. It went badly.

Can you elucidate?

Yes. She called me a few names, told me I'd wasted a year of her life, and said I'd go to hell for it.

That's definite.

It was clearly over at that point.

How did you feel by then?

Confused. I'd never promised her anything. Somehow, emotionally I guess, she felt by my actions that I had. I didn't understand that.

Had you slept with her?

Yes, but by mutual consent. I didn't force myself upon her if that's what you mean.

No. I only wanted to know how far the relationship had gone.

Well, it had gone that far. Though again, no promises.

So she could have felt, as many people do, that in a way sleeping with her suggested more than a casual acquaintance. It meant you were serious, though you had never said those words.

I can understand that, I suppose. It seems illogical to me, but what can I say?

Did she make any threats before she left?'

Beyond telling me I was going to hell?

Yes.

Not that I can remember.

Is that because of your alter ego, your subconscious, or your conscious self?

Have no idea.

Because Matt worked as a guard at the institution he could access its records. And he did. He found exactly thirteen women employed by the Forensic Psychiatric Facility. All of these women worked in administration, a separate unit from the rest of the buildings. While the women and men who worked there had fewer security requirements than those entering the buildings containing inmates, he knew that the chances of any of them bringing coils of wire into the flue on the roof of Building J were not high. But, of course, any of them could find wire in the building to use if they wished to. So he decided his next course of action was to read each of these women's personnel files to see if any looked good for the part of entering Building J and setting up some kind of stakeout or other illegal activity.

So you and Nancy parted ways. Did you ever hear from her again?
Yes. Unfortunately.
In what way?
She'd write me postcards every now and again.
Even though she lived close by?
No. She moved to New York City not long after we split up.
What did she say in the postcards? And how many did you get?
About twenty in all. Something like that. She'd mostly tell me how great life without me was. Something about her newest conquest. About how everything had been my fault.
She had really made the separation?
No.
How long did this keep up?
For about a year, I guess.
She was obsessed with you.
I would say so. Love is merely madness, they say.
Or maybe she was only obsessed with the failed relationship?
You're the psychiatrist.
So I am.
What do *you* think?
I don't know.
There we are.
What about Missy? When did you two get together?
She visited me on the farm one day.

That must have been something. Her coming to you.

Why?

Usually it's the other way around.

I suppose so.

How did it go?

Incredible.

Was Nancy still sending you postcards at that time?

Maybe. I've forgotten the exact order of events. By then I didn't actually care. It was Missy or nothing as far as I was concerned. And when she came to visit, my dreams came true. Literally.

Sounds wonderful.

It was. She stayed for three days, and for those three days we didn't leave the house.

Did you invite her, or did she just show up?

Arrived unannounced one evening about dinnertime. She stayed, as I say, for three days after that.

Spend your time together mostly in the bedroom?

No. Not even close to that. In fact, we slept apart. It wasn't *lust*, it was *love*. We talked about everything under the sun. It was great to see her. We covered everything we could. Had a lot in common. But even when we discussed something we didn't have in common, we didn't argue. If we had different ideas about things, we agreed to disagree. It was absolutely wonderful.

What happened when she left?

By the time she left, I'd asked her to be my wife. She agreed. And we began making plans for her to move to my farm.

Fast.

Yes, though not fast enough for me. I missed her between the time she left and when she arrived with all her stuff. It was only a week or so, but it was far too long not to have her around.

Matt found one possible candidate from the thirteen women in the Administration Building. Her name was Nancy Buffet. She'd worked there only a month or two, and her background was strange for a woman as far as he was concerned. She'd grown up on a farm and had worked there until she graduated high school. She'd gone to college and majored in agriculture. She knew how to run farm equipment as well as repair heavy machinery. She'd certainly know how to use a coil of wire. Her working hours at the facility were unusual in that she worked halftime seven days a week, mornings or afternoons at her own discretion. This made it possible for her to work half a day and spend the other half doing the kinds of things Matt thought she might be doing. The only question for him was why she was doing them.

Before I leave, I'd like to ask a question that may seem like it's from left field.

Okay.

I remember an earlier time in our meetings when you said you noticed the young daughter of a neighbor of yours when she came with her father to speak with your father. She had blond hair if I remember correctly, and you liked her.

It wasn't that I liked her so much as she looked interesting and likeable to me.

Would it be possible that the girl you saw mangled in the hole that day was the same girl? After all, she was blond and lived nearby.

Never occurred to me.

Wouldn't they have been roughly the same age?

Yes, I think so. They could have been about the same age. But I think I would have made the connection before this, since the dead girl's face was not damaged. I remember that face to this day. Angelic, especially with the red ribbon in her hair. She didn't look that much like the little blond girl I'd seen many years before.

Are you positive about that?

Mostly.

What does *that* mean?

It means 'mostly.' I can't be positive either way.

Do you think your memory might be deceiving you?

I can't be sure about that either.

Well, give it some thought, will you? I'll see you in a couple of days.

Yes. Goodbye, Doctor Amador.

Bye, Joe.

19

Matt took his findings about Nancy Buffet to his supervisor at the Forensic Psychiatric Facility. His supervisor told him that Matt's thoughts on the matter were still inconclusive. However, the supervisor again allowed Matt to continue working on the case in his off time. A relatively patient guy, Matt still found these roadblocks—or at least they appeared that way to him—unnecessarily prudent. He had many incriminating facts. Why wouldn't his supervisor allow him to continue working on this case on company time rather than punishing him by making him do it on his own dime?

But, so was the way of institutions, especially ones on a tight budget. Thus, without arguing the point, Matt continued to study Buffet, keeping an eye on her activities during his off time, and trying not to fall asleep on the job. So far, she showed no interest in Building J.

Morning, Joe.
Good morning, Doctor.
How did you sleep?
Better than the last time we talked.
No dreams of the dead girl?
No. And no dreams of Nancy either, thank God.
Glad to hear it. No dreams at all?
Nothing you'd be interested in.
Try me.

Well I did have one about Missy.

And?

She was teasing me about being in here. Like she knew I was innocent but figured I wanted to stay here so as not to spend time with her.

That doesn't make much sense. She's the one not visiting you. She knows you can't visit her.

It doesn't make any sense to me either. It was short and sweet and, like I said, she was teasing me, not dressing me down.

Sounds innocent enough. What I think we should talk more about today is a statement you made to me last time we met. Something like, 'It wasn't lust, it was love.' You said it in regard to the time that Missy came to visit you at the farm, when you said you spent three days together in your farmhouse and asked her to marry you.

I remember.

You told me you didn't sleep together during that time.

Yes.

Did she know about your inability to impregnate her?

No. Even I didn't know that at the time. It only surfaced after we were married and we tried to have a child. Then we both visited our doctors and I was told the bad news.

How did she take it?

She was, of course, saddened by it. She very much wanted a child, maybe more than one, so it was quite a shock. After all, she and I both assumed we'd be able to make it happen.

Was she angry?

Absolutely not. She was great, actually. She was sad and told me so, though there was never any regret about her marrying me, or anything like that.

Good to hear. You discussed the possibility of adopting?

Yes, but she had her mind set on actually having the baby herself.

That's when the discussions of artificial insemination began.

Around that time, yes.

How did you feel about that?

I was sad, of course, mostly that I couldn't pull my weight, but agreed that the best course of action was artificial insemination. After all, we could make love as often as we liked, and the child would be hers to have. Except for having the genes of her natural father, our child was my child too. I treated her that way. From the very first day, I literally forgot the process and concentrated on Missy and my baby. That's what I called her, my baby.

That's great. I wish more people in your situation could think like you did.

You mean other couples with the same problem end up with different views?

Oh yes they do. I'd say roughly a quarter or more of them end up getting divorced at least in part because of the feelings the father has about the child. That it's someone else's. For fear that one day that child, after it's grown and discovers the secret, will eventually search out the real parent, the one whose sperm was a source of the child's life, and then bond with that person. And the father who raised the child gets second shrift.

I had no idea.

Yes. Even most of those who don't get divorced have similar thoughts that lead to problems. Did the issue ever come up with Missy after Carla was born?

Never.

I know you worked a lot of the time. Did that thought ever cross *your* mind?

It might have, once or twice, though I never brought it up with Missy.

Why not? Wouldn't it be good to get it out in the open while Carla was still young?

Because I didn't feel that way.

So how will you feel if Carla eventually searches for her sperm-donor father?

I hear that information is sealed.

It is. Completely unobtainable supposedly. I also know that there are ways, expensive ways mind you, but ways nonetheless that people in that situation can get around the law and find their birth parent. Or rather, in your case, their donor parent.

I see. Didn't know that. I don't think it would change matters much. I love Carla without reservations. If she were able to unite with her donor father, I wouldn't mind. If she decided to call him father rather than me, I would of course be disappointed, though I'd certainly not blame Missy for that. It would be illogical, you see. What did Missy have to do with that? I would still love Carla as well. My love is not restricted to those who love me back. Do you see?

I do. Again, it's quite mature of you to think that way.

Thanks.

Matt spent a week following the movements of Nancy Buffet, but got nowhere. Most of the time she spent on the grounds of the Forensic Psychiatric Facility she was working. When she arrived, left, or took a break, she gave no indication she was up to anything. In fact, as far as he could tell, she never glanced at Building J, or at any of the other buildings in the complex.

He marveled at the precise timing of her actions, both to and from the Administration Building. No wasted movements. Her dedication amazed him. And, as he watched her go about her business, he also kept a lookout for anyone else on the roof of Building J. No action there. Either Nancy was aware of him watching her, or she'd had nothing to do with the break-in. As time wore on, he began to think the latter was more likely than not.

You know, psychiatry is an interesting business.

I imagine it is.

There are two ways to proceed. You can trace a person's life from the beginning as you would, say, play a chess game. Or, you can begin from the end and work your way backward.

Which do you prefer?

Actually, I prefer the backward approach. Beginning from the endgame—checkmate—and working my way back to the beginning. You look perplexed.

I'm trying to see it from the chess perspective. Beginning with the end of a game and trying to play it in reverse. Seems like a hopeless task.

Well it would be if you had to replay it exactly as the original game was played. All that's required in my view, though, is that you understand the basic principles of how the original game was played.

And, following the chess model, the winner of the backwards

game would be the player who got his pieces in the beginning alignment first.

Right.

How do you add pieces back on the board?

It was a metaphor, Joe, not an exact model.

I know, though it would make an interesting actual game to play. Maybe each time you got one piece back in its original position you could add a piece or something.

You play chess, Joe?

I do.

Here?

No.

Why not?

No one to play with. No chess sets around. Things like that.

Do you miss playing the game?

Not really. I fooled with it when I got bored. It's a great game.

It is. I imagine you were very good at it.

Couldn't tell. I never lost, if that's what you mean.

That tells me you were very good.

Not necessarily. After all, it's the quality of the opponents that tell the true story.

You didn't play good opponents?

I didn't play *any* opponents. I played myself.

Interesting. How did that work?

I'd make a move, block my rationale for making that move from my mind, and then turn to the other color. Kept doing that until one of me won.

Interesting. You could actually block yourself from remembering your reasons for making a certain move and remember that move after you played the other side's piece?

I got pretty good at it after a while.

When did you find the time to play? You mentioned you were always so busy on the farm?

Late at night, when everyone else was sleeping.

Therefore you always won.

Yes.

Could you play a game backward?

Have no idea. I'm curious, though, why you're analyzing me forward rather than backward if you'd rather do it the other way?

Because, Joe, you don't remember what you've been charged with and won't let me tell you.

I see that.

I respect your desires, and beginning a little way before what you're charged with committing might reveal the crime itself.

Ah. Thank you. I appreciate you're taking me the long way around. Sorry for making you change your natural approach.

No reason to apologize. It's good experience for me. In actuality, I should be using a mix of approaches rather than exclusively one or the other.

I can understand that.

Good, now let's get back to where we were.

Right.

Have you ever imagined if Carla was grown now and she wished to find her donor father what he might be like?

No. Never occurred to me to imagine that.

Will you imagine it now?

By the way she looks? Resemblance?

That, but more in the way she acts. You know that recent studies suggest that DNA can actually determine many personality traits as well as physical ones.

Yes, I've heard that.

Does she appear different in looks or in the way she acts than what you might consider natural for her if she were your own child? Both yours and Missy's child?

Having never considered her anything except my own child, I haven't thought about that much. I'll think it through now though.

Good. Doing so will help give me insights into your behavior.

My behavior?

The fact that you can't remember the crime.

My supposed crime has to do with Carla?

See, I was afraid this would happen if I took us to now rather than stayed with my forward approach. But no, I'm very cognizant of the fact that I'm treading close to the edge here. So don't take this centering on Carla business as anything except curiosity. In no way am I suggesting she has anything to do with your current situation. I've thought this through carefully and, believe me, my taking our conversation in this direction shouldn't be telling you anything about the case, only that I'm interested in your answers.

Good. I'm relieved.

I'm sorry for scaring you like that. But, after considerable thought, it seemed like the advantages of asking this question outweighed the disadvantages.

Now that I think of it, Carla strangely resembles *both* me and her mother. I guess I knew that before, though never thought it was anything other than wishful thinking. You know, like how older couples come to look like one another? That she does many of the things we do, not doing the things we don't do. Things like that.

Does she *really* look anything like you both or as individuals?

What are you getting at?

I'll tell you after you've answered me.

Because I'm not allowed to have pictures in this place, I'll have to rely on my memory.

Understood.

Then I would have to say that she looks like her mother mostly.

Is that strange?

I wouldn't say that. She has the same color eyes, same color hair, things like that. After all, Missy is her mother.

Anything unusual about the comparison?

Not that I can think of. Maybe her smile, though I wouldn't think a smile would be inherited. More experiential, wouldn't you say?

Yes. Children learn by mimicking their parents, and as such even physical attributes can be considered environmental. Like I may have mentioned previously, nature or nurture. Anything else come to mind?

Not immediately.

Now, let's take the opposite approach. Does she remind you of anybody you've ever seen before?

This is weird. What are you getting at?

Absolutely nothing, Joe. It's a standard line of questioning in matters such as this. You can feel free to answer truthfully, without in any way giving me a notion of what it might mean. I'm simply asking questions.

All right. But remember I don't know many people. If you're suggesting I might actually know the father, or have seen him someplace, it's highly unlikely.

I understand.

Does she remind me of anybody other than Missy and me?

Yes. That's my question.

I'm giving it some thought. My first answer is 'no.' On the other hand, being truthful, she probably looks like a composite of all the people I've ever seen. A slightly bent nose from one, a mole from another, a body type from another. That kind of thing.

Interesting.

How so.

Well, it's a good answer. I think I'll take it a step further. Is there any one of those people you know that she shares more than one trait with?

You're getting specific here. I'm not sure I like where this is going.

I didn't figure you would. On the other hand, we both want to discover the truth don't we?

Yes. I'm thinking that because you're asking the questions the way you are, you already know the answer and trying to lead me to it without telling me.

Cagey, Joe. I wish I were that smart, but I'm not. I don't have any idea of the answers to my questions. Believe me, I'm not leading you anywhere on purpose. I'm only asking what I feel are important questions, and putting your answers into a large salad bowl full of them and attempting to figure out what they mean.

Now I have the feeling you're talking to give me time to think.

That's right. Exactly what I'm doing. The 'salad bowl' metaphor was ridiculous. I was improvising. Something I'm not very good at.

All right. My answer to your question would be 'yes.' I don't like that answer, but it is what it is.

What's that answer mean?

She has two traits in common with my father.

Does that bother you?

It does now.

It didn't before?

Had never occurred to me before.

What are those traits?

Well, she has bigger ears than normal. Something that I have as well. It makes her look clownish sometimes. And she wears her hair long so they'll be covered all the time. I think that's why I hadn't remembered it.

What else?

She has a mole on her neck. Almost unnoticeable unless you're looking for it. My father also had such a mole, though in a different place on his neck. I remember that because he proudly showed it to me once as evidence of his own father's similar one.

Does your daughter hide that with her hair as well?

I think it's more her mother that's doing that. While combing Carla's hair. I'm fairly sure Carla doesn't know it's there. It's on the back of her neck where it's difficult to see without a mirror. Now, with her hair so long, she'd probably never find it.

Any thoughts?

Aside from the obvious, I would suggest that these kinds of things happen all the time. They could be inherited from millions of other people that have them. They could be natural mutations as well. On one hand, they suggest something, but on the other they suggest nothing at all except an accident of fate.

What do they suggest, Joe? Besides an accident of fate?

That Missy lied to me. That my father *is* Carla's father as well.

Do you believe that?

No.

Why not?

Because Missy is a logical person. And it would have been harder for her to tell me that my father forced himself on her and she resisted than it would have been to tell me they had sex and that Carla is my stepchild and my half-sister. Why would she have taken the harder way out of the situation?

I don't know. As you, I doubt there's much to be made of it.

Then why'd you ask the question?

Because that's what I do, Joe. I ask as many questions as I can to get to the truth of things.

You're right.

I am right. I've been doing this a long time. Getting to the heart of the matter, however unpleasant it may be for those I'm questioning. It has to be done if I'm to come to conclusions about how to help.

You're right. Sorry to put you on the spot.

No reason to be sorry. It's your right to do that. I would hope you'd always feel free to do it. Again, I don't take anything personally. After all, this is not about *my* life, it's about *yours*.

Matt had nearly given up his suspicions about Nancy Buffet, when one day she unexpectedly left her desk in the Administration Building and exited it. He knew of her flexible schedule, so in some ways it was quite ordinary. Except, of course, for the fact that she hadn't done it previously before completing a shift. He watched her walk toward Building J.

Unmistakably.

He was on to something.

She continued walking until she got to the far end of the building and disappeared from Matt's view. A few minutes passed before he saw her again. And when he did, he knew he'd hit pay dirt.

Nancy was on the roof of Building J. Walking directly toward the open flue.

How she'd gotten up there was beyond him at the moment, but he'd found the person he was looking for.

All this happened so quickly he had no idea what to do. Follow her and confront her? Wait where he was and continue watching, time her inside, and after that follow her to see what she did then? It had occurred so quickly, he was caught flatfooted.

I'm not sorry we're investigating this line of thought.

Good, Joe, then let me take it a step further. Did you know that you could, without Missy's permission, use DNA samples from Carla and have them checked against a possible donor's medical records? Then you'd know for sure whether or not some particular person was the father or not?

I suppose I knew that from my readings, though it never occurred to me to do it.

Why not?

I trust Missy. Beside that, I'd have to get the DNA sample from the person and that would require permission or deception that I wouldn't be willing to undertake.

I see your point. But wouldn't you like to know? Just to be sure? Missy would never have to find out, and your father's dead.

So, you think my father's the father?

Quite a mouthful. I guess my assumption is that we were speaking in terms of that. Yes.

Okay. I would know that I tried. And my knowing I didn't trust Missy would make our relationship different from then on. I couldn't risk that.

So now, after you realize you could do it, you still wouldn't try?

No.

That ends that particular line of questioning, I guess.

Good. Besides, I'm quite positive Missy didn't lie about it.

How?

My father had advanced prostate cancer. I don't know everything there is to know about such things, though I can't imagine that in the state his prostate was in he could father a child.

I see. Then you have considered this before?

No. It just occurred to me.

Fine. Let's change the subject.

Good idea.

Matt decided to stay put. He timed Nancy's visit down the flue to see not only how long she stayed there but, by inference, what she could be doing. She'd not taken her purse or anything else he could see. She also surprised him: not only was her visit short—ten minutes by his watch—she looked the same when she exited as when she'd entered. Her dress was unwrinkled and she wasn't carrying anything. By the time she disappeared around the opposite side of the building, he couldn't begin to guess what she'd been doing down there. He watched as she reappeared, walked normally back to the Administration Building, and nonchalantly found her way back to her desk. There, he supposed, she returned to her work as if nothing out of the ordinary had occurred. And that was that.

Now I'd like to investigate a completely different line of questioning than we've taken previously.

I'm game.

Good. It will take us back to the chess metaphor I mentioned earlier. That is, as difficult as it may sound, work backward rather than forward.

To a degree you've already been doing that, haven't you?

Maybe. But this will be more drastic.

Now I'm curious.

Good. Given that you don't remember what crime you've been accused of committing, this may seem impossible, but here's what I'm thinking. Let's both assume that what you've been charged with is catastrophic. Not in the sense of blowing up the world, but catastrophic in the sense that more than one person is involved, and that there have been casualties. Plural.

Is that the case?

I'm not saying anything of the sort. I'm telling you that, for the sake of this line of questioning, we make that assumption. Are you all right with that?

Yes.

Given the vague and more than likely incorrect version of the crime of which you claim innocence I just gave you, who do you think could have committed it other than you?

Wow. How do you come up with these questions?

My job. Usually I don't need to figure things out exactly like this because the person I'm talking to knows what they're charged with committing. This time I had to do some creative thinking.

I'd say.

Well, give it some thought, no matter how ridiculous it may appear to you.

I'll try. What you're actually asking me, in a roundabout way, is who do I know that's capable of committing a horrific crime? Right?

I suppose. However, you've got a stake in this way of looking at it. In other words, normally the question I ask can be answered objectively. Here, you've got a subjective interest in answering the way you do.

I get it. So who do I know that might have perpetrated something as terrible as you've vaguely described?

Yes.

Well, my first reaction is my father. From all the whippings he gave me and the way he generally worked me to hell and back when I was young, it certainly seems he'd be my first choice. But he's dead. He couldn't have done it.

Couldn't, that is, if he's *actually* dead.

You doubt that?

No, I'm asking if you know that to be a fact. After all, he could have manufactured his illness in order to take himself out of the equation.

No, he couldn't. I watched him waste away before my eyes.

I asked you that to assure you we were thinking outside the box.

Well, that's certainly the case.

Who else?

Well, Nancy I suppose.

Why her?

You remember how I described our breakup. She could have been so angry about it that she decided to commit some grisly crime against my family to get even with me.

Wouldn't she be more likely to do something directly to you?

No. That's not like Nancy. She'd punish me by punishing those I loved, knowing full well I'd get charged with the crime and, well, here I am.

So Nancy would be a perfect candidate?

Yes. On the other hand I don't think she's that nuts. Strange, yes, though not completely crazy. After all, a long time has passed since our relationship ended. People, even her, get over these things eventually. She must have a life beyond me by now. She'd have to.

Who else?

Don't know.

What about Missy's previous boyfriend?

Hell, I don't even know his name.

Didn't she ever talk about him?

When we first met she did. But less and less over the ensuing months and eventually nothing. As far as I know, he found someone else and that was that.

Could she have kept it a secret from you?

Not likely. We shared everything. Though, given your scenario, anything's possible.

Anyone else come to mind?

No.

How about Missy's family? We haven't mentioned them at all in our conversations.

No, I guess we haven't. Compared to my family they were the most normal people I've ever met. They were very nice, especially to me, and thought our wedding plans were fantastic. They even paid for the whole business which, I suppose and according to tradition, is the bride's parents' responsibility.

Did your parents attend the wedding?

No. My father probably knew about his cancer by then though he hadn't told me, and my mother couldn't leave him by himself. She apologized, but it couldn't be helped. Everyone understood.

So both sets of parents would be out.

Yes.

Now think carefully. Anyone else?

You act as if you know of someone, and are prodding me to say a name. A *particular* name.

I don't know of anyone. I'm only trying to be thorough, that's all.

Well, I suppose I couldn't count out my mother.

Your mother?

Understand, I don't believe there's any way she could be responsible for whatever I'm charged with committing, though you asked me to think out of the box.

That I did. But what made you bring her into the picture?

The last person I can think of that I know anything about. She's the only one left on my list of possibilities.

Are you sure?

I'm never sure of anything. You again sound as if I shouldn't be sure. As if you know someone that should be on my list. That bothers me.

Don't let it. I don't know of anyone. I'm only prodding away at my job as a psychiatrist.

All right. Let me think.

Matt's first consideration about what he'd seen Nancy do was to report it to his supervisor. After giving it some thought, though, he decided to revisit Building J's roof and go down the flue to see if anything had changed. He was very curious. So he crossed over to Building J, climbed the ladder he'd secretly stored there from his previous visits, and walked across the roof and descended the passageway as he'd begun to think of it.

When he got to the secret room, Matt discovered nothing at all. It looked the same as it had the first and last time he'd been there. No coil of wire, and nothing else changed. It even seemed like the dust hadn't been disturbed by Nancy's visit.

Had he missed something along the way?

Was this secret hideaway just a ruse to get him to believe that the action was here when it was actually somewhere else?

He gave that serious thought.

Anyone come to mind?

No.

Well, let me spark your memory. What about Bradley?

Bradley? My God, Bradley's dead. He's been dead most of my life.

How do you know this?

My father told me.

Did you see his body?

No way. My parents wouldn't let me see that.

Was there a funeral?

Don't know. Didn't hear of one.

So your father is your only source of information on this?

Yes.

Well, what if his father lied to your father? What if Bradley's father created the suicide story so Bradley would be kept out of jail for killing the girl? Maybe Bradley has spent his life hiding somewhere. Possibly committing other atrocities we know nothing about.

You have quite an imagination, Doctor.

I'm not trying to put words in your mouth, but could this be possible?

Of course it could. Except it isn't. Why would Bradley pick on someone I knew to commit this terrible crime?

How do you know you knew the person or persons he committed the crimes against?

I just assumed.

Shouldn't do that, Joe. Don't assume anything.

Then I suppose it's possible. But I don't know, it sounds crazy.

I agree, it sounds crazy to me, too. But you agree it's a possibility?

So is my suddenly getting released from this place because they found the person who actually committed the crime. But possible doesn't make it true.

You're completely right.

Was that your big revelation?

It wasn't meant to be a revelation. It was meant to be a stab in the dark. A way to get you to consider all the possibilities. Now that I've done that, do any other names surface in your mind?

Let me think for a minute.

Take your time, Joe, my next appointment cancelled, so I'm not in a hurry to finish today.

Fine.

I'm going to think back through our previous conversations to see if you've mentioned anyone else I could test.

Well, *I* didn't do it. Missy didn't do it. Carla certainly didn't do it. I'm afraid, with the exception of people I've briefly met over the years, that's pretty much our cast of characters.

Are you sure?

Again, you're asking me that in a way that makes me believe there are such people, though I can't think of them at the moment.

What about me?

What about *you*?

Could I have done it?

Are you kidding? We didn't meet until I'd been in here for a year. I don't know anything about you. Why would you be involved? You're my psychiatrist for God's sake. What would your motive be?

I can't answer any of those questions for you, but I'm out of the box. No?

Very out of the box. That's for sure.

Well consider it. I know a lot about you at this point. Why would I want to know these things if I wasn't involved in some way?

Well you are involved in some way. You've been hired by the court to report on my sanity, my ability to stand trial. I don't know anything else about you.

Why do you think that's true?

Because, as you said, this is about me, not about you.

Isn't that convenient?

No, it's what you've been taught. What are you doing, trying to make me feel insane so you can help me remain happy and not go to trial? If that's it, you're doing a good job.

I'm not trying to do anything of the sort, Joe. I'm attempting to get you to examine everything, not only the obvious things. Can you see that?

Yes, I suppose I can.

Then work with me here. Is there anyone, anyone at all, you haven't thought of? Maybe a guard in here, or another inmate?

No. I pretty much keep to myself. I told you that. Besides, most of the people in here are crazy.

Exactly, Joe. Crazy enough to commit the crime. The crime you're accused of committing.

I say hello to the people in here once in a while. That's all.

Even when you're eating?

I have special permission to eat in my room. Alone.

Who gave you that permission?

Don't know.

Do you know why they allow that?

No. I suppose it could be because I tend to be by myself even when I'm in the cafeteria.

Did other inmates come sit with you when you were still eating in the cafeteria?

They tried to.

What did you do?

I told them to go away.

Maybe that's why?

I suppose so.

How about we play a game now?

Where did that come from? Kindergarten?

Just an idea. I'm sorry it sounded like that. Didn't mean it to.

What's the game?

I ask you what crime you think you've been charged with, and you give me your best guesses as to what it is.

I'd rather not.

Why?

It would make me both sad and mad to consider such things.

Except it's logical, right? You like logical things.

I do. But maybe this is logical for you, not me.

Bear with me, though. I'm not attempting to trap you. And I won't give the crime away if you agree to play and accidentally guess it. I promise that.

Okay.

Okay to play the game, or that I won't give away the crime you're charged with?

Both.

Go ahead.

State what I think I've been charged with?

Yes.

I don't know.

Work with me here, Joe, will you?

All right. Maybe the cops have reopened the case of the dead girl in the hole those years ago.

Why would they think you had anything to do with that?

Don't know. Maybe they discovered some incriminating evidence they think implicates me.

What kind of evidence?

Have no idea. I couldn't have left any evidence since I didn't kill her in the first place.

You brought the evidence bit up yourself.

I did, though you asked me to tell you why they'd think I did it. Had to come up with something.

Well, you were there after the fact and could have accidentally left something.

But I didn't. At least I don't think I did.

That's a reasonable assumption. But you were in shock, and you might not remember. You're now thinking logically and that's what I want you to do. What else?

What other reason they'd believe I killed her?

No. What other crimes might you think you're charged with committing?

Nancy.

Nancy what?

Maybe they think I murdered her?

How do you know she's dead?

I don't. Supposing, that's all. And you're giving the crime away now, aren't you?

No. I'm playing the game as well. Nancy may very well be dead. Or she may not. Let's decide she *is* dead. Why would they think you did it?

Because we have a history, she and I. Because she thought we had something we didn't have and hounded me for years. Maybe they think I'd finally had it with that stuff and murdered her.

Would that be a likely possibility?

Could be from their viewpoint. I wouldn't do it. Didn't do it.

I understand.

Do you?

Yes. What other crimes might you have committed?

Maybe they think I set fire to my farm.

Why would you do that?

To collect the insurance?

Do you think that's a big enough crime to have them put the state to the expense of keeping you in here? Possibly for life?

No.

What then?

Maybe the fire accidently killed Missy and Carla?

That would certainly escalate their interest in you being convicted and sent to prison for a long time.

Or execute me.

Possibly. What else?

Where are we going with this?

I'm attempting to see how your mind works, and whether you do or do not come close to the crime you're actually accused of committing.

If I do, wouldn't you stop at that point and thus give the crime away?

Not anymore I wouldn't.

I'll give you one more guess, and that's it with this game.

Good. What?

I murdered my mother.

Why would you do that?

Don't know.

Then why did you bring up the possibility?

Because I'm playing the game.

Give me a reason, even if you have to make one up. Why did you kill your mother?

She was driving me nuts about Missy. Because she was convinced that Missy and my father had consummated the act. That Carla was his daughter and not the result of artificial insemination. That Missy had lied about the whole thing. He did rape her. Or my mother thought she'd come on to my father and raped *him*. She might have been driving me crazy with some of these possibilities. I love Missy and couldn't take it anymore. So I shut her up. For good.

Now that was some bit of fantasizing, Joe.

It was, wasn't it? I think I'm getting too good at this game.

You are. Want to continue?

No. I've had it. Did you learn anything about me?

Yes.

What?

One man in his time plays many parts.

Shakespeare again.

Maybe the game wasn't such a good idea?

Maybe not.

Well, Joe, I do have to go now. I hope I've given you something to think about while I'm gone.

You have.

Then goodbye for now.

Bye.

20

As Matt worked his way slowly out of the secret room and back up to the roof, he stopped several times to see if he could find any other passageway that Nancy Buffet could have taken while down there. He didn't find anything.

Matt was beginning to think he'd struck out, when something occurred to him. While he couldn't turn around in his current position, he could when he got to the roof and come back down again. So he finished climbing out, roped himself to a large bolt, and crawled his way down to the secret room again. Maybe he'd missed something there. Something so obvious it would seem like a normal part of the building's structure. If Nancy had come here, as he knew she had, there must have been a reason. And it was clear that this reason was nowhere else but in the secret room he'd discovered when he'd first found the passageway.

Morning, Joe.

Doctor.

How are things?

Well, I've been dreaming a lot since our last session.

Good dreams? Nightmares?

Crazy dreams, mostly.

Can you remember any that you'd like to tell me?

Sure. The one I had last night is particularly relevant to what we've been discussing.

I'd like to hear it.

Well, you were the villain in this one. You'd committed the crime to punish me for something you thought I'd done to you.

What was that?

You secretly loved Missy. Had loved her your entire life. You'd been angry with her previous boyfriend, and when I married her you were actually mad at me.

What did I do in the dream?

I don't know, except it made me damn angry as well, though I'd never met you. At least in the dream.

What happened?

You weaseled your way into an advantageous position using lawyer tricks to drive me crazy by making me think out of the box.

Whoa. That hits pretty close to home.

It does. I think I was angry with you for putting me on the spot last time. That's why I dreamt it.

I see. Any other dreams relevant to what we've been talking about?

No. The rest were about the usual.

The usual?

Yes. Wet dreams, thoughts about suicide, and so on.

Wait. Hold on a second. You've never mentioned you have dreams about committing suicide.

That's not what I meant. These dreams are about *others* committing suicide, not me.

Like Bradley?

Yes. I think he's the primary source for those dreams, though the persons killing themselves in my dreams are usually not him.

Who?

No one I know. I hear about them.

How does that make you feel?

Sad, I suppose. To me, though, suicide is illogical and therefore stupid. So I don't take those dreams very seriously.

I understand. Have you thought about our previous out of the box processes?

I have.

Come up with any other names we should consider as candidates for committing the crime you're accused of?

Yes. Three names, as a matter of fact.

Great. Let me hear them.

Well, I warn you they're far out of the box.

Doesn't matter.

The first, and I guess the most in-the-box name I came up with is me.

You? Are you telling me you're actually considering the possibility that you did commit the crime?

No. I'm only saying that we hadn't discussed that possibility seriously because I know I didn't do it. But I've told you I couldn't remember what the crime was because of my deceitful alter ego, so I'm now suggesting that same alter ego could be the one that's making me forget I actually did commit the crime.

You're now admitting that it's possible?

No, I'm not. I firmly stand my ground. I'm just putting me on the table with the rest of them, because to leave me off the table would be ridiculous given where I'm staying at the moment and why.

All right, I get that. Do you have any additional information about your possible involvement that would help us find the real culprit?

No. Just adding my name to our list.

Who else?

Remember, out of the box, right?

Yes.

Then I suggest that the blond girl—the dead one in the hole and who I might've met before when her father brought someone like her to my father's house—could be a hoax.

A hoax?

Yes. Both Bradley and I saw the shovel with all the apparent blood and hair on it and, when I saw the body in the hole, I put two and two together. The body could, after all, have been a dummy covered in cow's blood or something, rigged there by someone else, maybe even the little girl herself for some reason. She might have actually been in love with Bradley, he'd rebuked her, and she did this to get even with him.

How old did you say this girl was?

Well, she would have been roughly our age, that being somewhere around fourteen, I guess. Ready to enter high school.

That's old enough. And she would have committed the crime now implicating you because?

Well maybe I was her murder target. Maybe she liked me. I hadn't rebuked her, but I'd not followed up on seeing her again.

That's slim, Joe.

Isn't it? But it belongs on the table with the others. That Bradley's on the table isn't any weirder than her being there, is it?

I suppose not. You said there were three names?

Yes.

Who's the third?

This one's actually someone I've not considered before. As far as I'm concerned, he's the least one possible for the list, but here goes anyway. Missy has a brother. We had dinner a couple of times with him and his partner.

I assume by 'partner' you're indicating he's gay?

Yes. One of the nicest guys I've ever met. And so is his partner. I don't want to sound PC, here, but they really are great.

What did he think about your marrying Missy? His sister?

He seemed grateful for my marrying her.

Grateful?

Yes. He mentioned some of the other boyfriends she'd had previously and told me I was not only his favorite, but someone he thought was the perfect match for her.

The perfect match, huh?

Those were his exact words.

Missy got along with him as well?

Absolutely. She told me so, he told me so, and with no reason to lie about it.

At least that you know of.

Of course.

Matt looked around the secret room in the roof of Building J for anything that might give away what Nancy had done in there. To make sure he didn't miss anything, he also ran his fingers over every surface he could find in order to check all possibilities. But his search was in vain. No coil of wire. Nothing. He was truly stumped. Had he thought Nancy innocent of any serious wrongdoing, he might suspect her for smoking in here or something else not permitted on the grounds. But there were no signs of a cigarette, a telltale smell, or anything else.

Then, just before he left, he played his flashlight toward a corner of the room that seemed illogical to check earlier. This corner was where the ceiling and the roof joined together at an angle that left absolutely no room for anything to be hidden. Except what he found there was not something hidden, but something missing. A small part of a beam was missing, creating a small hole.

Now, I suggest we once again turn things around and begin at the beginning with me asking you a simple straightforward question. Of the people we've discussed so far, which one of them, no matter how in or out of the box he or she might be, do you feel most capable of committing the kind of crime I creatively described to you the last time we spoke?

Wow. Didn't see that coming.

I didn't suppose you could. It's part of my tactics. Make sure you don't work your answers out in advance of our meeting. That some of them come about right here when you're on the spot.

I'll need a minute to think through the names we've discussed.

Take your time. No hurry.

Unfortunately, the hole he saw was not large enough or did the arrangement of beams allow him to move over and look inside. However, he could reach out and put his hand in it. That gave him pause. He had no idea what might be inside. On the one hand, it could be the exact thing he was looking for, the reason for Nancy's visits. On the other hand, though, it could be a trap. He had no idea what kind of trap, but he remembered his mother placing a mousetrap in the cookie jar to keep him from sneaking cookies out when she wasn't looking. He'd never done *that* again, and he wasn't about to do it now. At the same time, he couldn't let the idea go either. His curiosity was much too intense to resist at this point.

Matt eventually decided to take off one of his shoelaces, make a slipknot at one end, and lower it down into the hole in hopes he might snare something useful and pull it back up. And that's exactly what he did.

I think I have a best guess.

Good. What is it?

Me.

So you think of all the people involved in the crime of which you know nothing, that you're the one most likely to have committed it?

Yes and no.

Same reservation as before?

Yes. I know I didn't do it. But, from the perspective of the people and scenarios we've discussed and attempting to see it from everyone else's point of view, I can see that I'm the most obvious candidate to have done it.

Therefore the decision to officially accuse you of the crime.

Yes.

Your candor, obvious intelligence, and maturity tell me that you're fit to stand trial, Joe. I don't see an alternative. On the other hand, these same attributes tell me you didn't do it. So I'm conflicted. This is the second time this has happened since we started our sessions. I've never had this problem before.

I'm sorry to cause it now. Maybe I can once again come to your rescue.

You can?

Yes. As before, there are questions you still haven't asked me that might shed some light on my innocence or guilt.

My job here isn't to determine your innocence or guilt, Joe, it's your fitness to stand trial.

Even though you've just told me you're conflicted because of my innocence?

Yes, even though that.

Strange.

Psychiatry is a strange business. But your telling me yet more stories seems like you're stalling.

I know that. But in my relating these stories, you might discover my true fitness. After all, you most likely held a different opinion before and after I told you of the murder of the girl.

Yes, I did.

That's what I'm getting at.

I'm willing to give it a try, Joe, though I must warn you that the judge's patience is wearing thin. I believe he's thinking that I'm delaying my verdict so I can wrestle more money out of the county. I've got to give him something tangible, or else come to a decision. And that decision may very well be to the contrary of what you want.

I understand.

Can you give me something?

Yes.

What?

You'll need to prod my memory.

This is game playing.

No it isn't. It's the way my brain works. You've been doing a great job so far, but we need more prodding to get my insane alter ego to give it up. I promise you, it's worth our time.

How can you *promise* me that?

I don't exactly *know* how, except something will occur to me. Somehow I know it will.

Then where should we begin?

Ask me a question about my youth again.

Something in particular?

Yes.

Random?

No, based on what you know about me from our discussions.

Give me a few seconds.

Sure.

Matt was lucky. His shoelace went down into the opening like a fishing line through a hole in the ice on a frozen lake. He dangled it ever downward. And he felt something there. About two inches down. Now if he could only get the noose around it and bring it up through the hole. Try as he might, though, that didn't seem possible. Each time he thought he had it, his shoelace came up empty. Then, on what was to be his last try, the shoelace caught and he had his fish. Or whatever it was. He brought it up. Slowly, so he wouldn't lose it. And there it was. Probably what he least expected, but what he should have most suspected. The coil of wire he'd seen when he'd first descended into the secret room. It looked exactly the same as it had before. Not attached to anything. Just a coil of wire.

Okay, I have something.

Go ahead.

You mentioned some time ago that your father was not particularly religious. Maybe you mentioned your mother as well, but I don't remember her in that conversation.

All right.

You also mentioned you never went to church.

We didn't.

Did the church come to you?

How do you mean? How does a church come to me?

Maybe the preacher, minister, priest, Rabbi, whatever, came visiting one day.

No, I don't remember anything like that.

Maybe one of your parents had a Bible in the house?

Bingo.

You mean I got it?

Not 'it' so much as one of those memories I have that we've not investigated yet.

Is this a dead end?

That depends on you. Several areas we've discussed seemed pointless at first. Yet they turned out to be valuable insights into my past. This may be the same thing.

Tell me about this Bible.

It was the largest book I've ever seen, except that it didn't dawn on me at the time that it was a book.

Why?

The damn thing was as big as a watermelon. Maybe because I was small when I first saw it, but I don't think so. I grew up with it, and later it still was huge.

A family heirloom?

Maybe. Not sure. There was an inscription inside the front cover except it was unreadable, so I couldn't tell.

Date?

I once knew that, not anymore. Nineteenth-century, I'm pretty sure.

Probably worth a fortune now.

Maybe.

How long before you read it clear through?

Never did. I started, but when I got to the created in six days part, I considered that, and gave it up.

Then what role did it play in your family?

Not much of any role. My father ignored it. I'd occasionally catch my mother reading it when I returned from the fields before my father did.

Was religion in their backgrounds?

Have no idea. There was never a mention of either set of grandparents.

Never?

Not a word. As if my parents had been born out of thin air.

That must have been strange, every other kid having grandparents.

Not at all. I didn't see other kids very often. Of course, I imagined that my parents had parents, but it never came up.

All right, so continue on about the Bible. That can't be the whole story.

No, it isn't. You see, my mother would occasionally read parts of it to me.

The Bible?

Yes.

What parts?

I think the first one was the Ten Commandments.

Pretty good choice.

I suppose. But once through them, she got stuck on number ten.

Stuck? Which one is that?

'Thou shall not covet thy neighbor's wife.' I remember it well, because she told it to me so many times. That's often all she'd say, 'Thou shall not covet thy neighbor's wife.' Kind of strange, huh?

Yes. What did you make of it?

Nothing at first. Hell, I was five years old or so. Later, I realized I didn't know what the word 'covet' meant. That may be the reason I picked up the dictionary and read it straight through.

In one sitting?

I think so. Hard to remember exactly. It didn't take long.

What did covet mean according to that dictionary?

It meant 'take,' mostly. So I guessed that the tenth commandment meant don't take your neighbor's wife. Seemed like a good principle to me. Too gender specific, but I got the idea.

By gender specific, do you mean it should have included women taking other women's husbands as well?

Yes. I guess in those days things were male dominated.

Probably still are. So what did this mean to you after you learned what 'covet' meant?

I tried to put two and two together as best I could. I suppose the first thing that came to mind was that she worried about my father coveting our neighbor's wife.

Was she the wife of the neighbor who came over with the little blonde girl you told me about?

I think so, though I never met or saw his wife.

What was the second thing that occurred to you?

That maybe something in her background had occurred that made that particular commandment special.

Such as?

Maybe her father had coveted some other man's wife.

Though you had no basis for this in fact?

I had no basis for anything in fact. It was just strange.

Matt took the coil of wire to his supervisor as evidence that something was going on in the secret room. After all, he'd seen Nancy enter the flue after she'd climbed on the roof. For the first time, his supervisor took Matt's report seriously. He told him he would definitely look into this. He'd interview Nancy Buffet and see what was what. After all, while she was not specifically banned from climbing on a roof, she was definitely banned from entering any building other than the one in which she worked. Her security clearance was not high enough to give her any right to enter Building J. Once inside the flue she was clearly in violation of the agreed-to restrictions.

In the meantime, Matt should continue his watch and would now be paid for his efforts. He still had to work during his off hours and wouldn't get a bonus, but he would certainly get overtime.

So that's the end of your story?

If you want it to be.

What does that mean?

It means that if you stop asking questions, it's over. If you have more to ask, go ahead. I don't actually know what's left to say on the matter. What I've said so far was provoked by your questioning.

All right, let me ask you this, besides finding her constantly quoting this one commandment from the Bible, did anything else seem strange about this Bible and who used it?

Good question.

Thanks. What's the answer?

My father *hated* the thing. Every so often, he'd scream about it still being in the house. For my mother to get rid of it.

Why didn't he get rid of it?

I don't know. I think it intimidated him. I never saw him even touch it.

What do you think that meant?

That he'd had a bad experience in his youth with religion maybe. Or he'd broken the tenth commandment and it made him feel suspicious about it. I prefer the latter version, though I have no proof. Suspicion always haunts the guilty mind.

All this information, whether supposition or not, *is* important. It tells me a lot about you. And it's relevant to the impact it may have had on you and how you lived your life. Then and now.

I understand.

Anything else?

Yes.

What?

My mother had another favorite story from the Bible that she told me more than once.

Was this from the Old Testament as well?

Yes.

And?

It was about Rebekah.

I don't remember the story, so you'll have to tell me.

Don't remember it very well myself, despite my so-called photographic memory. My mind may photograph things I see, but not things I hear.

Understood.

Well, the version I remember is that Rebecca, spelled R-E-B-E-K-A-H in those days, was married to Isaac, and she had twins named Esau and Jacob. She apparently favored Jacob over Esau. Isaac, who had gone blind by that time, wanted to bless Esau, not Jacob. Apparently, Esau had a lot of hair on his body, so Rebekah dressed Jacob in goat fur and told Isaac he was Esau. Blind Isaac then blessed Jacob instead. Something like that.

What did that mean to you?

Nothing at all. There were no twins around, so I accepted my mother telling me these things for reasons I would eventually figure out on my own.

So you thought both of these things—covet your neighbor's wife and Rebekah's story about Jacob—as something more than your mother's favorite biblical stories, but having some hidden message for you. *Specifically* for you.

I didn't at first, though eventually it seemed that way.

Remember, though, the devil can cite scripture for his own purpose.

I hardly think my mother a devil.

So what do you make of it?

Good question.

Do you have a good answer?

Maybe.

Well, will you tell me?

Yes.

When exactly?

Now.

Well?

First, my mother was no dummy. She'd married a farmer, for good or bad, and that was it. She'd gotten what she deserved for not having understood him as he was. So, I think my father was coveting our neighbor's wife and thus the reason for a visit from the husband, the farmer next door. Whether the little blond girl was my father's or not, I have no idea, nor could I guess the truth. I think my mother told me that commandment because she didn't want me to turn out like him. She used it because she was a kind woman at heart, and didn't want to tell me directly what he was up to.

Actually that's a pretty good interpretation. No proof, mind you, though I can easily see your point of view. Particularly in light of your father's actions in relation to Missy.

Good.

And the second story?

I think that also had something to do with my father.

How so?

In the story I read in full later on, Rebekah was initially barren. She couldn't have children. Her husband prayed to God, and that's when the twins were born. Although it's a bit different, I think our neighbor's wife was in the same situation as Missy was with me. Her husband couldn't impregnate her. In those days, the only way to have babies in that situation was to have someone else provide the sperm. I think my father, with or without the permission of the woman's husband, got our neighbor's wife pregnant. And, instead of having one baby she had two. Since the neighbor who came to visit those days with the little blond girl didn't appear particularly angry, I have a feeling he was either paying my father for services rendered, or asking him questions about the impossible situation he was enduring.

That's some interpretation.

Wait, I'm remembering more as I go along.

What?

If the neighbor had two children, two daughters, twins, then there were two little blond girls. One of whom might have been murdered for some reason, and one who's still walking around out there someplace. Maybe she knew about my father's role in her being conceived. Maybe she's angry as hell, and we should put her on the table.

Whoa. I was with you up until that last part. Imagining this wild twin out there trying to get even with you because of something that happened with your father is pretty wild and, frankly, unbelievable.

I'd agree with you, if it weren't for something my mother also once told me.

What was that? For that matter, *when* was that?

This was right after my father died, and she was no longer intimidated by him possibly overhearing her and me talking to one another.

What did she tell you?

To watch out for something that happened when I was young that might come back to haunt me.

That's how she put it?

Yes, I remember it clearly now. That's pretty much exactly how she put it.

Anything else she said?

No.

You asked her to explain?

I did. We were at a gathering of some sort, I'm not sure where. Anyway, that's all the time we had before being interrupted.

Was you mother a soothsayer?

A fortuneteller? No. I didn't take her warning as that. I think she knew something that would put my father in a bad light and didn't want it to distort my feelings about him. That's why she led me by using parables. Though her last statement to me, you're right, was more like a prediction than a metaphorical quotation from the Bible.

All this reminds me of something we discussed a while back.

What?

Judah who had twins with his daughter in law.

Right. I'd forgotten about that. What's past is prologue, huh?

This really is something. And important. You've led an incredibly complex life.

I don't think so. If people are willing to notice things and think about them carefully, everyone could discover lots of things about their lives and themselves they couldn't have imagined beforehand.

That sounds like a lecture from a psychiatry professor.

After leaving his supervisor, Matt felt very good about his progress in the case. Very good, that is, except for the fact that he still had no idea what Nancy Buffet had been doing in her not so secret room in Building J. With that in mind, he returned there and once again made a thorough search of the room. Unfortunately, he found nothing new. No incriminating evidence. No giveaways about her visits. No new wire coils. He'd gotten somewhere with the case, though not far enough to justify the amount of time he'd spent watching, waiting, and observing.

That's all I remember about religion in my family.

I understand. You do know, of course, that there are many websites you could visit on the Internet that describe family histories, don't you?

Remember, though, I hadn't given this angle much thought until you asked me those questions just now. Genealogy is not something I would ordinarily think of prior to my being in here. Equally confusing would be that I doubt such things as those we've discussed would ever find their way into a genealogy.

True. But still worth a try. I have a computer at home and can look up your family tree to see what's what.

That's good. I'd appreciate that. And you'll tell me?

Of course. That wouldn't be privileged information. I'll need more information about your family, though.

Like?

Like what your mother's maiden name is and anything else you can tell me about what you remember of both your parents in terms of family history.

Her maiden name was Reno Torosino, and I know next to nothing beyond that.

Torosino? Your mother was Italian?

Guess so. She never spoke about it or her family. As I said previously, neither of them mentioned their parents—my grandparents—ever.

That's interesting. Italian families are generally close knit. Family is a very important part of their tradition. It would seem that your mother didn't inherit that aspect of Italian culture.

Or else something occurred on her branch of the family that made her want to forget all about it.

Yes. Now, anything else you can remember?

Nothing. Except the Bible, of course.

Was the inscription in that Bible you couldn't read possibly written in Italian?

Suppose so. Though I wouldn't have known that at the time.

Does she have that Bible still?

Probably. I haven't seen her in a while.

Would she still live on your father's farm?

Don't know that either. On one hand, I don't know where else she'd go. On the other hand, though, she wouldn't know the slightest thing about farming, and couldn't keep the place up by herself. Maybe she hired someone to do it for her.

Do you remember the address there?

Never knew it.

Your parents get mail there?

Yes. Certainly that.

So, what was your father's first name?

Now that's something.

What?

I actually never knew that. He was just 'father' to me. That's it.

Never told you?

Nope.

You're absolutely sure about that?

He could have and I've forgotten, though I doubt it. He didn't talk much. A thing like that I would have remembered.

I would think so, too. Okay, I have enough information to find the Bible, or at least find out where your mother lives at the moment. Not sure where that will get me, but it's worth a shot. After all, speaking with her, even on the phone, could be useful in ferreting out some potentially important information. Of course, I'll need your permission first.

You have it. Thanks for doing this. Maybe discovering these things will jar some other memories for me.

Good. Well I won't waste any time on this. I'll leave you now and see you here again tomorrow.

Goodbye Doctor. And thanks again for doing this.

Not a problem. Bye.

21

Matt thought long and hard about his lack of discoveries. It then occurred to him that he hadn't ever attempted to reach his hand down into the hole to find what might be there. After all, at the time he'd discovered the hole, he was afraid of getting caught in a trap of some kind. A mousetrap to be exact. So, he worked his way back into the corner and, with some serious trepidation, reached down into the hole as far as he could to scratch around and see if it contained any more coils of wire, or anything else of value.

At first, nothing.

Then, however, he touched something that initially felt like his shoelace. But that couldn't be it. He'd retrieved his shoelace the day he'd found the coil of wire. Then, he realized he'd touched a wire, a straight one, not coiled. He gave it a tug, but it resisted in both directions. Tightly secured on both ends.

After moving his hand down the wire, he felt a knot of some kind. A place in the wire that appeared to have been tied together. As if the wire had once been much longer, but some loose part had been removed and then the connection reattached. His mind raced with possibilities. That, of course, could be the origins of the coil of wire he'd originally found. A removed section of the wire.

Matt now felt he was getting someplace again. All he had to do was find a wiring diagram of the building and discover where this particular one connected, and he'd at least have more information. Possibly even have the answer to his puzzle.

Good morning, Joe.

Morning, Doc.

Doc?

Felt like calling you that. Is it not appropriate? After all, I feel like you've become a friend as well as my psychiatrist.

I hate to sound rude, Joe, but I think you'd better continue calling me Doctor Amador. Otherwise, we might have to call it quits.

Why?

The last thing in the world I can be is your friend. It's the kiss of death for psychiatrists. I'm doing what I'm doing on the basis that I'm your doctor, and these things I'm doing might reveal a part of you that neither of us could know otherwise. I can't be your friend and your psychiatrist, too. Do you understand?

I do. I'm sorry.

Nothing to be sorry about, Joe. It's a common mistake for patients to make. I completely understand your making it. Except we can't go that route.

Right, Doctor Amador.

Good. Perfect, in fact.

Now, what have you discovered?

Not a great deal, I'm afraid. I can tell you that your mother is still alive and living on the same farm you both lived on for so many years. And she still owns the Bible that you remember.

You spoke with her?

I did.

That must have been interesting.

In some ways, yes, in other ways, no.

Tell me about it.

Well, she seems in good health, though as we talked it became clear that she's not quite together mentally.

What do you mean?

She wanders all over the place with her answers, and never wants to stop talking.

That's not her characteristic style.

Maybe she changed after your father died.

Could be.

Anyway, she told me she still had the Bible and that indeed it was a family heirloom as we suspected. *Her* family's Bible, not his. We both could have guessed that.

True. What about my grandparents?

That's where she became reticent. Like she couldn't remember much about them. Or that she was suspicious of me for like you, she'd forgotten the crime you're accused of committing. She did say that her folks—your grandparents—came over as immigrants to America when she was very young and became first farmhands and then, after saving money most of their lives, farmers themselves. In fact, according to her at least, the farmhouse where you grew up had been theirs, and your father and her inherited it from her parents. That was quite a revelation, I think.

Interesting. I suppose that explains the Bible in a way.

Meaning?

It was so big and weighty. It came along with the house rather than having to be moved there.

My goodness, you did think this thing was *really* big, didn't you? To imagine that your mother would stay there in order to not have to move the Bible.

I didn't mean it that way. It just made a certain amount of sense, that's all.

She didn't tell me much of anything I could understand about your grandparents, their role in her life, or whether anything strange went on about twins being born, and so on.

Understood. Did you discover anything about my father's family?

No. At least I don't think so. There are quite a few families with the last name Barnum in that region of upstate New York. And there were too many stories for me to figure out which one of them might be related to you given I didn't know your father's first name. I could take guesses, of course, though most of them were farmers and most had wives. None of them, though, had wives named Reno Torosino. That would certainly have jumped out at me.

I wonder how that could be?

Don't know. They must have somehow escaped the census. Maybe they used false names for some reason. No clue.

Interesting. Was the Torosino family described anywhere? That might shed some light on things.

I wish it had, but nothing. Only the grandparents were listed. And, strangely, no mention of a daughter name Reno. Could she have changed her name?

No idea. It's a mystery to me. So that's all you discovered?

Not entirely.

What else?

Matt finally got access to the wiring diagrams of Building J. Actually, since all the buildings were identical except for Business Administration, he could have used any one of them to get the information he needed. Only one of the electrical wires in the building ran through the area where Matt had found the wire that interested him, and what the diagram told him answered one of the mysteries he'd wondered about for so long. This wire ran from the manual alarm console directly to the electric warning system that set off the horns. He'd discovered the reason for the horns sounding during the recent snowstorms. Apparently someone, Nancy presumably, had found the wire which at that point must have been slack, pulled it out of the hole, cut the line setting off the horns, figured out a way to remove the slack from the line and hence the coil of wire he'd found, and reconnected the line in the hole by tying the bare ends together. Why she'd taken out part of the line was still a mystery, but other than that, problem solved. Actually, he did have two more questions. Why set off the alarms in the first place? An accident? Probably. And how did she avoid electrocution in the process? Low amperage? Probably. These questions aside, however, Matt felt satisfied for having the wits to figure out at least part of the puzzle that had dogged him for so long.

I checked several phone books for the area and discovered a woman whose last name was Torosino. I called her, and discovered she had a sister who she'd lost touch with named Reno.

Hey, that's great. My Aunt. What did she have to say?

Not much. Her sister and her had grown distant after they'd both graduated from high school.

Too bad.

There was something she said that did interest me, though.

What's that?

Reno was not only her sister, she was her *twin* sister.

Jeez. Now that's fascinating.

Yes, I think it is. How does that fit with what your mother told you about Rebekah?

I'm not sure, except that given Rebekah suddenly got pregnant when she'd previously been fallow might mean that she hadn't been fallow in the first place. Her husband was incapable, and she'd been impregnated by someone other than him. My mother's knowledge and apparent acceptance of that might explain her obsession with that passage in the Bible.

And?

My grandfather might not be her father at all.

Or?

I might not be my father's son either.

What? That doesn't necessarily follow, though it certainly is consistent with the situations we've been describing.

That everyone's been screwing everyone else in order to have kids?

Something like that.

I don't buy it.

Got a better explanation?

Not at the moment. But I haven't had much time to consider it. Give me some time, and I might. After all, the best possible explanation is that we're making something out of nothing. She may have liked the story. That's it.

True. The twins part's real enough, though. So it sure makes one wonder about the rest.

I suppose you're right. Let me give it some thought.

Things get more complicated as we go along.

Let's make sure that we're not the ones making them complicated.

I agree.

Prudent is the word.

When Matt returned to his supervisor, he told him about the wire connected to the horns. His supervisor listened carefully and told him it sure seemed suspicious. But why did she do it in the first place? No one had escaped. As far as he could determine, other than being an annoyance, the horns going off during the snowstorm had no ill effects whatsoever on the state of life in the compound. So he asked Matt to continue his investigation.

While Matt was there, his supervisor also told him he'd had a few words with Nancy Buffet about her being seen entering Building J through the roof portal. She told him that she'd never done any such thing. That whoever had seen her was lying or had seen someone else do it. His supervisor then told Matt that he'd talked with others in the building who might have seen Nancy leave, but none of them could remember for sure. Therefore, it was her word against his, and while he tended to believe Matt's story over Nancy's, he didn't have enough proof to fire her. After all, he too had supervisors who would ask questions about his decision, and possibly revoke it without more substantiation. He had to have more proof. He then returned the coil of wire to Matt until such time as he might need it to build a case against Nancy.

Matt understood the way these things worked, and determined to find a way to prove Nancy had lied. At the same time, he attempted to figure out what she'd actually been doing in Building J roof's secret room. After all, while setting off the alarms was a criminal activity, it didn't actually seem that serious. Something more was occurring that he'd not yet discovered.

So, where does that leave us?
More questions.
From me to you?
Yes.
About what?
You decide.
How can I?
Think about it.
Give me a hint.
All right. How about more than one?
More than one what?
More than one person. We've talked a lot about individuals com-

mitting the crime, but rarely have we considered plots by more than one person.

Why don't you tell me about the relationships of the people on the table, as you call it?

Such as?

How about Missy and your mother, for example. Could they have concocted a plan to do the crime you've forgotten?

Missy and my mother?

Well, we've discovered that they have something in common.

What?

They both might have been fathered or have mothered children not by their respective husbands.

Yes, that's right. Good first try. Missy with my father or a sperm donor and what you've uncovered, that my mother might have been conceived by someone other than her father or me the same. That about right?

Yes.

Well, they might have something in common then. That might make them a logical pair.

And from that deduce they somehow not only committed a horrendous crime, but set you up as the criminal who committed it.

Doesn't make much sense, does it?

No. Well, now it's your turn to try.

Fine. How about Nancy and Missy doing the same thing?

Do you think that works?

Not really. They don't have anything in common except me. I don't think Missy hated Nancy. I can tell you, though, that the last time I heard from Nancy, she sure as hell didn't have friendly feelings for Missy.

Any other pairs of people?

Well, I suppose that some more unlikely candidates come to mind.

Such as?

Bradley and his father. Bradley and Nancy. Other groups with Bradley in them.

Do any of those make sense?

No. Bradley was too young, too crazy, and most likely too dead to be of any use to his father or Nancy. Besides, how would Nancy know he existed? I never told her the story of the dead girl in the hole.

232

Now that's interesting.

What?

What about groups of people that know each other and have common knowledge of particular events.

Isn't that what we've been talking about?

I suppose we intuited that. But making it clear will keep ridiculous possibilities from arising.

Matt returned to the roof and found his way to the secret room he'd already visited many times. What he expected to find eluded him, though another look wouldn't hurt. After all, he'd discovered the wire that connected the alarm control the last time he visited. Maybe there was yet more to find.

After sitting on the main joist in the room for almost an hour, investigated once again the hole with his hand, and looked over every detail his eyes could see, he became nearly despondent. All this time spent, and so little return. He'd missed the most important and likely most obvious thing about this case, and had no real clue how to proceed.

What about my father, the neighbor who might have fathered the two little blond girls, and Bradley's father being connected in some way? I don't think I'm guessing when I say all three knew about the murder of the blond girl, they knew about Bradley and his manic behavior, and maybe they knew about the problems various people had in conceiving children. While that's a larger group of people, it seems to me they fit perfectly with the conditions you just described.

Wow, now that had certainly not occurred to me. Why would they set you up like that for some terrible crime? What had you done to each of them that would cause them to hate you so?

Maybe they didn't hate me at all. Maybe it was a tough decision to make and I turned out to be the obvious choice. It was either them or me. I think I could imagine my father giving me up. If it were me or him. Especially if he was dying at the time.

So this plot must have been hatched before he died?

Well, yes, I think that would have to be a condition of the scenario I proposed.

How sharper than a serpent's tooth it is to have a thankless child?

Good quote. Likely the opposite, but still a good one. This plan would have to have been in play for quite a while and carried out a long time before we assume it was. Say before Missy and I were married. Are you inferring that such may be the case? Without, of course, telling me anything else about my memory loss?

I can't answer that question for I'd be giving you a hint about the crime itself.

Then let's leave my father out of the equation, and consider the two farmers who maybe were the fathers of their children both of whom may have died. Bradley by suicide, and the girl next door by murder, possibility committed by Bradley himself.

Now you're talking. This has possibilities. Maybe you should take this further.

Such as?

What crime they might have a common motive for carrying out, and how they could have implicated you instead of them.

Well, possibly they figured I committed both the murder of the girl and Bradley to keep him quiet. That would make both the parents plenty mad if they thought it so, and they plotted a way to get even with me.

Why wouldn't they turn you in?

They didn't have enough proof. Or couldn't convince the cops. Maybe my father gave me an alibi for both events, or at least for Bradley's suicide. He concocted one because I was his son. They knew that and had to settle the score.

So they bided their time, did their ugly deed, and set you up for it?

Exactly.

Now there's a scenario that has legs.

Legs?

Figure of speech.

Never heard it before. But it makes sense.

As Matt sat there desperately trying to think of anything he'd missed, he imagined what he would have done if he were up here. Among the many possibilities he considered was that of planting a tape recorder to record what was being discussed on the floor below where he now sat. Why anyone would want to hear anything from down there didn't make much sense, especially since he couldn't understand what was being said, but he thought it his best bet.

So, back into the hole his hand went. Searching ever further until the pain from his bent wrist forced him to withdraw. Empty. He tried again and again. Each time attempting to stretch his hand a bit further. Still no luck. Finally, with both his wrists complaining bitterly about what he'd put them through, he gave up. A tape recorder, while one would certainly fit in that space, would require Nancy to replace tapes or disks or whatever they used these days. Her hands and wrists might be slimmer than his, but he didn't think her accomplishing the act was conceivably possible. Especially since his fingers were most likely longer than hers.

So, the two fathers were mad at you. In their minds, you'd killed one of each of their children. And in relatively ghastly ways. Thus, they had a perfect reason to get even. That makes sense.

Then we've gotten somewhere, haven't we? From nowhere to somewhere by you jogging my memory a bit. And, of course, my ability to think on my feet.

Yes, we have. So what?

What do you mean?

Well, there's that lost memory of yours. Without that information, we can't tie them to the crime. I mean, I could on my own, except that leaves you out of the picture.

Not entirely. From your perspective, does our discovery today make any sense at all? Can you tell me that much?

It makes as much sense as any of the other scenarios that one person did it.

Well, that has to be good enough for me. Don't we have an argument to make to the district attorney?

Not my job, Joe. I don't imagine he'd listen to me anyway. My job is to determine whether you're mentally fit to stand trial. Providing alternate arguments for why someone else might have committed the crime is well beyond the scope of my assignment. In fact, it's so far beyond that scope they might remove me from your case.

Why?

Because I would sound like I was on the defense team when I am supposed to be unbiased.

Do you see that?

Sure I do. But, since I don't have access to a computer in here, do you think you could research the possibilities?

Not knowing the names of either father, how do you suggest I go about doing that?

Maybe you could call my mother back and ask her?

Well, that's certainly an idea. Hadn't thought of that.

Will you do it?

Yes. But I've got to go now.

Thank you, Doctor Amador. I very much appreciate it.

Sure. Goodbye, Joe.

Bye.

22

However he felt about the possibilities, Matt reconsidered his focus on taping conversations from above the ceiling as a viable option. Thus, he took it to his supervisor. His supervisor listened to him carefully, and then pointed out to Matt that the room directly below the secret hideaway was the kitchen for the cafeteria. It made no sense that anyone would find anything interesting by recording the conversations of the cooks and bottle-washers there. And for that, Matt could not disagree. Unless, he pointed out, one of those people was passing messages from one of the inmates to the person checking the tapes in the room above.

Matt asked his supervisor if he would check the personnel files of those people working in the kitchen to see if any of them had backgrounds that might suggest such activity. While his supervisor suspected it would be a waste of time, he told Matt he would do his best when time permitted.

Good morning, Joe.

Morning, Doctor. Contact my mother as we discussed?

I did, but she wasn't much help. Didn't know the fathers' names. Actually, she was more out of it than the time I called before. Not sure I could trust any information she gave me.

Sorry to hear that.

Me too. Did you have a good night?

Yes. And I had another very interesting dream.

Well, as always, dreams are of interest to me. We are such stuff as dreams are made of. What was this one about?

It's long, so I hope you'll have patience with me as I tell it.

Go ahead.

I dreamt that the situation I'm in wasn't over yet.

Well, it isn't.

I don't mean the trial. I mean that whoever is attempting to get even with me for something I didn't do is still trying to finish me off. The way things stand, I'm in heaven and they somehow know it. I'm alone, well fed, and have meds to keep me happy. Do you see what I'm saying?

I do.

The dream begins like a science fiction film. I'm in some kind of rocket ship flying through space. I'm all alone, but know that the ship can fly itself. This ship's similar to the ones you read about in early science fiction novels. You know, the ones with the lurid covers? In any event, the ship had windows, plenty of room, and several other passengers.

I thought you said you were alone?

I was. The passengers were in some kind of stasis. The kind where they put you to sleep for hundreds of years and you don't age? You must have read about such things.

Not actually. Though I did see the film 2001.

2001?

The movie. I guess you haven't seen many films. Anyway, I know what you mean.

So I'm alone in space except for these sleeping passengers and taking them someplace. Now that's the interesting part. I have no idea where I'm taking them. As I said, I'm relying on the automatic pilot or whatever. I don't seem worried about not getting there, or that I don't know how to fly the damn thing. I'm sitting in the pilot's seat, or at least a seat with a view out the window. I'm watching Saturn pass by. It's quite beautiful, and I'm thrilled at seeing it up so close. Then the dream starts getting interesting.

How so.

Well, the ship is floating along, and it abruptly stops dead in its tracks. Like it's struck something I can't see. Everything in the cockpit where I presume I am at the time rattles around, and there we are, dead in space with the pilot—me I assume—not having any idea what's going on.

Sounds like your current situation.

Yes. But it gets better. Or worse, depending on your point of view. There I am, locked in orbit around Saturn, and I see something in the distance approaching the ship.

Another ship?

Don't know, it's too far away. But I can tell it's moving fast and that I'll soon know.

How are your passengers faring through this?

That's the thing, they've disappeared. Gone. Just like that. Somehow, whatever stopped the ship made them vanish. Only me left on board. And here comes something I don't understand approaching me from Saturn.

Interesting.

I thought you'd enjoy hearing this.

You're not deceiving me now, are you?

Not a chance. I have a logical mind. This would never occur to me when I'm awake.

Go on.

The ship closes in on my position and I see that I was right. It's another spaceship, though it doesn't look like my ship at all. At least I don't think so since I've never seen the outside of the ship I'm in. Anyway, the damn thing is constructed wrong. Like maybe a madman built it. Aerodynamically ridiculous. Protrusions all over it. Things like antennas, bulbous globes of various sizes, stairs or ladders I can't tell which, strange holes in the fuselage. I mean it's a mess.

Like it had been in many battles?

No, like it had been designed that way from the outset.

Go on.

It stops right alongside my ship and I hear the two bulkheads clang together. Really loud. I'm not sure what to do and don't know enough about the cockpit to find weapons or anything to defend myself. I'm a sitting duck. So, what the hell, like an idiot, I wait for them to come and get me.

Do they?

Absolutely. I hear them coming through the door inside the ship below my deck. They don't make any attempt to hide their entrance at all. They know I know they're coming. Doesn't bother them. I think maybe their numbers are so large that I wouldn't have a chance regardless of my having a weapon.

What happens next?

That's just it. Nothing.

The dream ends?

No. Everything becomes silent. I know they're there. They know I know they're there. And so on. That's it. Like they're waiting for me to come down to see who's come aboard. I can no longer see Saturn. The big ugly ship is blocking the view out the window. The silence is unbearable and I know I have to do something.

And?

I look down at the floor beneath me and discover there's no door there. No way for me to get down to them, and no way for them to get up to me. I'm sealed in the cabin.

Where did the passengers go then? You said they disappeared.

Hell, I don't know. It's a *dream*. All I care about is those things in the cargo bay, or whatever it is beneath me.

So, what do you do?

I don't have any idea what to do. I look around the cockpit and discover there's some kind of wrench there.

A wrench?

Yes. I didn't see it before, but do now. I also see a series of nuts sticking to the floor.

Nuts?

Not *those* kind of nuts. *Lug* nuts. The kind that fit on bolts.

So you now have a way to go down and face them.

Apparently so. But do I? I'm safe up there in the cockpit. Why commit suicide by going down below where they're waiting for me?

Makes sense.

Yes. Then I see one of the bolts slowly turning. Silently. Someone below has figured out the connection as I had, and is now attempting to climb up through the floor. It's as if I'd gotten bored in my dream and invented the damn lug-nut scheme to liven things up a bit.

So you're now aware that you're dreaming?

No. Only that I hadn't seen those nuts before now. Seemed strange.

Was there a door there, too? You said before that there wasn't.

Not that I could see. Just the nuts and bolt-ends.

So, what do they gain by unscrewing them?

No idea. At that moment in the dream, all I could see were the bolts turning, bolt ends suddenly disappearing, and my life going up in smoke.

Was more than one bolt turning?

Yes, they were all turning now. Silently. Truly a nightmare.

So what happened?

I waited. Nothing else to do. I wasn't about to make their job easier by helping them turn the bolts.

Matt couldn't resist returning to the secret room he now knew was situated above Building J's kitchen. When he got there, he was surprised to find the hole in the corner of the room had been covered by a piece of cardboard of some kind. For no reason he could figure out.

He crawled over and removed it. Nothing special about it he could see or feel. Just a piece of cardboard. No markings. No nothing to iden-tify it in any way. Even the edges had been manufactured that way. No scissor marks. Nothing to indicate that it had any particular purpose.

Nancy Buffet had obviously risked him seeing her again by re-en-tering her hiding place and putting the cardboard over the hole. Why?

So what did you finally do?

I sat back and relaxed.

Relaxed? When what might be monsters were about to attack you?

What else could I do? I didn't have a spacesuit, and I couldn't exit the ship through a window or anything anyway. I still couldn't see an actual door in the floor that would allow them entrance. All I could see were these meaningless bolts turning and losing their nuts on the floor of the cabin.

What happened next?

The nuts and bolts all finally disconnected and I could hear the bolts clang on the floor below and saw the nuts rolling around on my floor as I watched. And still no door. Just some meaningless nuts and holes for bolts placed there by whoever had built the ship I was in. That's it.

What happened then?

Well, here comes the strange part.

The strange part? Hell, what would you call what you've been telling me?

This is stranger, believe me.

Okay.

The floor I'm on falls down.

What do you mean, 'falls down?'

It's like the nuts and bolts had held it up in some way. It drops down to the floor beneath and I fall along with it while sitting in the captain's chair. Then I hear this screaming underneath my feet.

What kind of screaming?

Horrific sounds. As if whatever kind of life had entered the ship had been squashed when they'd unscrewed the nuts and bolts. It was terrible. I couldn't believe the sounds. While I somehow knew these beings were monsters and would like to have killed me, now they'd unknowingly committed suicide. I pitied them. The screams were that compelling. And real sounding.

That's it?

That's it.

What do you think it means?

Good God, Doctor Amador, that's your department. I have no idea what it means.

Matt suddenly had the idea that Nancy had come here to this place again, put something in the hole, and covered it with this cardboard for some reason. To hide something from him? Not a chance. She would know by now that he'd see it when he returned, as he knew she would know he would.

Why?

'Of course,' he thought to himself, 'she planted a trap for me.'

She had come up here for the express purpose of punishing him for turning her in to his supervisor.

And so, in that hole she'd placed something that would get even with him. A mousetrap maybe. Just like his mother had used to stop him from eating her cookies without permission.

On the other hand, of course, she could be toying with him. Guessing that he was thinking she'd set a trap, so instead of putting one there, she'd placed whatever she'd wanted to place there knowing he wouldn't try putting his hand in the hole.

With those alternatives, what was he to do?

So you're suggesting I analyze your dream?

Yes. Maybe not this minute, but sometime after you have time to think about it. It certainly seems riddled with suspicious clues as to what my subconscious is up to. Or my alter ego. Whatever. Monsters. Suicide. Missing people. I could go on and on. Of course, most of it doesn't make any sense at all. That's what makes it a dream.

Yes. You're right, of course.

Matt had a decision to make. Put his hand in the hole or not put his hand in the hole. Of course, he remembered his last dilemma like this when he'd used his shoelace to avoid getting trapped. So he pulled up one of his pants legs, untied and unlaced one of his shoes, tied a slipknot similar to the one he'd tied before in his shoelace, and sent it down into the hole exactly as he had the last time this situation had occurred.

He wiggled it around several times.

And it landed on something he knew had not been there before.

Something fairly large.

Something that would have surely been difficult to get down into the hole, for it was almost as wide as the hole itself. And nothing had happened as a result of him probing the area.

Of course, many mousetraps were not that sensitive. It might still be down there waiting for him and not be tripped by his shoelace.

So he kept at it, trying to find someplace to catch it and bring it up through the hole.

Any preliminary ideas?

Yes. Most of them along the lines you've already suggested. You are obviously the pilot. I think that's certain.

Right.

The monsters are likely the people in your life we've placed on the table that we think might be involved with putting you into this place.

Logical.

The notion that these people are so stupid as to commit mass suicide seems quite interesting as well.

Assuming that's what they were doing. Might just be stupid. So intent on getting back at me, they hadn't thought things through.

Good point. So these monsters may be enemies that you, at least in your subconscious, believe have made mistakes that will cause whatever they've designed to backfire.

Yes. Of course, how could I, confined in this place as I am, have any knowledge of such things?

You wouldn't. Others could. I thought that might have been the reason you brought up the idea that more than one person might be responsible for the situation in which you now find yourself.

Good thinking.

The most interesting point of the dream to me is that it suggests that by doing nothing, you'll eventually be saved. I wonder why you'd think that?

No idea. Except, of course, that when I'm in here, I can do nothing.

True.

Matt eventually gave up on the shoelace and replaced it on his shoe. Then he stared at the hole, the cardboard, and the room. Nancy was a smart one. She'd given him a tantalizing puzzle to solve by placing a piece of cardboard over the hole, realizing it would confuse and put him in the maze in which he now found himself. Should he take a chance, or not? Could he convince someone else to stick a hand in the hole? Probably not. Any way he looked at the problem, it was his and his alone.

So you think the dream means something?

Yes. Dreams always mean something. It's *what* they mean that's the problem.

I see your point. And this one is particularly difficult?

Right. Or maybe it's too simple. Often I find dream analysis can be over-analyzed. Sometimes, as they say, a cigar is just a cigar.

Maybe this one is a simple fear scenario, indicating nothing of particular importance.

Could be, though I doubt it. The various symbols appear pretty real to me. On the other hand, they're so obvious that, as you say, your alter ego may be at work.

This psychiatric stuff is certainly a quagmire of mixed signals.

That's precisely what it is. I like the way you put it.

Thanks.

Matt made his decision. He stayed where he was because he'd already worked his way toward that end of the room as far as he could manage. He reached out his hand and gently lowered it into the hole. What happened as a result startled him as much as it hurt. Something snapped, and up his hand came, reflexively, with his fingers locked in an ordinary mousetrap. He'd been had.

Matt ripped the thing off as quickly as he could, trying not to scream. As he did, he knew his doing so would compromise any finger-prints on the metal and make identifying the perpetrator of this trick unidentifiable. Even though, of course, he fully well knew who'd done it.

With your dream in mind, I'm off to see my next patient. I think today's session went quite well. I look forward to thinking over this prob-lem more.

Goodbye, Doctor.

See you soon.

23

Matthew Brady couldn't bring himself to tell his supervisor about the mousetrap experience, so he kept it a secret. He thought often about Nancy Buffet's ingenuity as he nursed his wounds. He'd obviously underrated her cunning. And, he continued to visit the secret room under the roof of Building J.

One day, after staring at the hole for maybe an hour and waiting to see if Nancy might make a mistake and visit the secret room while he was still there, he had a revelation. Maybe he'd been had in more ways than one. Was it possible that there was another secret place further down in the flue into which he'd repelled, slithered, and butt whipped himself down?

So he more carefully checked the area below the entrance to the secret room.

At first it seemed impossible she could have placed something further down. The flue narrowed to a smaller diameter, one much smaller than he could fit through.

At the same time he noticed that the metal had many thin scars on it, as if someone had, in fact, gone down further into the flue space. He thought back to Nancy's weight, size, and girth, and figured she might be able to make it.

Was there another entrance to a different room further off to his right and down—one he couldn't see, and located in the direction the flue took from his vantage point?

Was that where the *real* action was?

Had he been so taken with the first secret room he'd found that he'd completely missed the spot where she'd hidden the recorder?

Morning, Joe.

Morning, Doctor.

We need to talk.

You seem a bit agitated.

I am. The scuttlebutt going around is that a guard has discovered a roof entrance to Building J, the one we're currently in, and that someone has breached security and possibly entered the building illegally.

Wow. I had no idea such a thing was possible. How did they get past the guards at the gate?

No word on that yet, only a rumor so far.

Is anyone sure the rumor is correct?

Probably not. I thought I'd ask you about it.

Why me? I'm on the inside. I have no way to contact anyone on the outside. Besides, why would anyone want to get in here? And why would I want them to spring me? I've already told you, I love it here. The meds make me incredibly happy and I'm left alone exactly as I want to be. Do you think I'd rather be back on the farm, or standing trial for something I didn't do? Not on your life.

I suppose you're right.

How did you come to the conclusion that it might be me?

Because you're intelligent, Joe, much smarter than anyone else in here including me and the guards. We've already confirmed that. I can't imagine the guards are involved, so that leaves the inmates. Most of them are drugged much more thoroughly than you as you can tell by watching them stare at the walls and talk to themselves. You're the only one I think that poses any kind of risk.

Well, I haven't anything to contribute to your idea. I don't want out. No way. And I have no desire whatsoever to communicate with anyone on the outside. Are you sure my dream didn't influence your thoughts on this matter?

You mean, by you not doing anything, the monsters in your ship were defeated?

Something like that. Though now that I think of it, that makes no sense.

Right. And I doubt you could make up a story that ridiculous and pose it as a dream. Didn't mean that. Only that it slipped from your conscious mind to your subconscious, and appeared as a part of one of your own dreams. But, again, that doesn't make any sense.

It doesn't.

The more Matt thought about it, the more reasonable his idea became. Whatever had brought Nancy to this particular spot was located somewhere further down the flue than he'd gone. But now he was confused, for he couldn't proceed more than a foot or two further into the flue without getting caught and having to wrench his way backward to where he'd begun. This was a job for someone much smaller than he, someone like a teenager or a woman. But not Nancy. Then he remembered one of the other guards. Wiry and useful, tall and skinny. As if he didn't eat enough, or was one of the lucky few who burned off fat as quickly as it developed. Before he could ask this guard, though, he had to get permission from his supervisor.

Sorry I mistrusted you, Joe.

No apologies necessary. I'm actually flattered you think I'm the smartest guy in Building J.

Hell with Building J, Joe, you're most likely the smartest person I've ever met.

Probably not true, but I'll take it for a complement anyway. Thanks.

Do you have any idea what might be going on?

You mean you want to take advantage of my intelligence?

Yes.

I don't see how I could have an idea. Besides you, I don't know anyone in here. Remember, I'm a loner and keep to myself. I'd be guessing. You see these guys more often than I do, maybe you'd be better at this than I.

I'm limited by my code of confidentiality. Even if someone confessed, I couldn't tell anyone about it, especially the authorities.

I see. I guess I should have figured that out for myself. Why did you ask me about it?

Figured I'd ask you because it would very much help my attempts to figure you out.

So, no luck with my dream?

Well, according to your dream everyone is involved in this business in some way. At least from your point of view. That's why the monsters you felt were invading your rocket were monsters plural, rather than monster singular. Do you actually feel that way?

That everyone I know is involved?

Yes.

No. I couldn't imagine my mother involved, for example. Or Missy or Carla. My father's dead and everyone else we've discussed I know little or not at all. Besides, I'd be paranoid to think that.

Matt's supervisor gave him permission to recruit the skinny guard for the purpose of further investigating the flue below the secret room. While Matt was not optimistic the guard would fit, he took him up to the roof and they gave it a try. No go. Not only that, it wasn't even close. In fact, neither Matt nor the skinny guard could figure out a way that *any* human, even a small child, could fit through the space. Matt then let the guard return to duty.

After all our discussion on this, you don't have a good candidate any more than I do?

I don't, and that's the sad part. On one hand, there are not that many people to consider, and on the other none of them singly or as part of a group seems to have the motive or skills to carry it out. That is, whatever I imagine it is.

And you still don't want me to tell you?

No.

Then we're at a stalemate.

May I ask you a question?

You already have. Several times.

May I ask you several questions?

Yes. At the same time, you understand, I'm under no obligation to answer them.

I completely understand. You've made that very clear.

All right, what do you want to know?

Do you have dreams?

Me?

Yes.

Of course I do. Everyone, whether they want to admit it or not, has dreams. They're inevitable. An escape mechanism for the many problems we face each day of our lives.

Do you analyze your own dreams as you do mine?

Yes and no.

Why that?

Well, sometimes my dreams are purely reflexive. They represent something so obvious that there's no point in my wasting time analyzing them.

Such as?

Well, I don't want to get too specific here. After all, I'm not the object of analysis, you are. But typically they take the form of wish fulfillment, obvious fears, and imaginative representations of fairytale-like stories.

Can you give me an example of each of these?

Not from a personal point of view, no, though I can from a professional's perspective.

I'll take that.

Well, wish fulfillment in patients typically involves dreams of people we'd like to have sex with, or in some way connect with them that's typically out of bounds in real life. Obvious fears would include things such as me being constantly late for appointments with patients or meetings I'm required to attend. Fairytale-like stories often involve the ability to avoid gravity in some way. Like being able to go where you want in the air, like on a magic carpet.

You've had some dreams in each of these categories? Without being specific.

Sure. Again, everyone has.

These are the dreams you don't bother to analyze?

No, I don't. And I'm sure, without giving it much thought, I've excluded these types of dreams of yours from our conversations because I know they wouldn't get us anywhere.

I understand. The other dreams you have that you do analyze are more complex?

Yes.

Dreams like we've been discussing, for example.

Not exactly, of course, but dreams of more complexity, yes. In fact, again, everyone has some of those.

Which type do you have more often?

The simple type, of course.

Of course.

Why all the questions about dreams?

I'm getting to the point.

Good.

Of those dreams with more complexity, the ones you *do* analyze, are any of those analyses of significance?

Yes.

One or more of these dreams have led you to important conclusions about your life?

I suppose so. I mean it depends on what you call important conclusions.

Important conclusions of a type meaning that they turn out to be of use to you.

Yes.

And have they turned out to be true?

What do you mean?

Well, in our discussion about my dream, the one in the spaceship, I get the feeling you think it might reveal something important about me, and maybe resolve a situation ultimately threatening my life.

Your life?

Well, if we were to figure out who did what I'm accused of committing, then I might not stand trial, be convicted, and sentenced to die from lethal injection. Right?

Or hanging. Yes. At least in the way you put it.

Hmm.

By that I mean dreams represent one perspective of things. The perspective of the person dreaming. Therefore it may or may not have the effect you describe.

But it could.

Yes. Certainly.

After the skinny guard left, Matt sat inside the secret room next to the obviously deliberate opening created in the metal of the flue, and stared down into the narrowing continuing flue in both confusion and dejection. It had seemed so obvious. How could he have failed to solve this problem once again? Nancy Buffet was clearly a worthy opponent. She'd ably set him up time and again for false solutions, and each time he'd fallen into the trap. Matt was nothing if not patient, what some might call obsessive, so he was not prepared to give up. Yet.

Can you recount a dream one of your patients may have had, or create one yourself, that would clearly demonstrate the difference between a reflexive dream and an important and revealing dream?

Where are you going with this, Joe?

You'll see. I think this is important, or I wouldn't be taking your valuable time with it.

All right. This is a simple made-up dream. A man is standing all alone on the shores of a very large sea. The waters are tranquil. Suddenly a storm rises in the distance and the scene becomes ugly. The clouds turn black and lightning and thunder bristle in the air. The waves grow to mountain size. He runs, though cannot escape. Then he wakes up.

That would be a dream not worth analyzing?

Right. I hear accounts of those kinds of dreams all the time in my work. Simple and foreboding. Fear dreams that everyone has.

Couldn't it, though, relate to the dreamer's life in a very real way?

Sure it could. And I'd briefly discuss that with my patient. Usually, however, it means that the dreamer is caught in some real-life situation from which they feel they cannot escape.

That makes sense. Sounds like the dreamer in this case could analyze their own dream without your help.

I've never thought about it that way, but yes, you're right.

Now, could you give me another example, this time of a more complex dream?

Like the science fiction one you gave me?

Exactly. Though different.

Without taking too much more of our time on this, I guess that might be useful. Here's a synopsis of a dream that's often referenced in the literature. Thus, don't take it as one of my own.

I won't.

A woman is lost in a forest. She's wearing very little and it's cold. It's a moonless night. She's frightened of being molested and she begins to hear sounds around her. Some of the sounds are clearly from animals in the forest. One of them is human, though, and she can tell from its low pitch that it's male. It's growling. Now, so far, it's your standard rape dream that wouldn't mean a whole lot. Here comes the more complex part. She wakes up. In her dream that is. And finds her husband snoring next to her in bed. She's still scared, so she gets out of bed and tries to escape. He wakes up and growls like the man in her dream within the dream. She opens the door and falls out of a ten-story building. In broad daylight. Dressed in her nightclothes, the same ones she wore in the dark of the forest. As she falls, she gets further and further from the ground. The building was apparently far taller than she'd initially thought it was. Now she notices people looking out of windows laughing at her, pointing in her direction and laughing hysterically. She tries to scream to let them know she's going to die, but they don't hear her. So she continues to fall with the ground strangely getting more and more distant. And the dream ends.

What's it mean?

Well, the most obvious analysis would be that she feels trapped in a marriage with someone different than the one she married and wants out. He's a beast. Escape, however, is impossible, for her friends will think it's her fault, not his. They admire him, and would think it strange she'd want out.

And the complex version?

That she had a deep-seated problem with the institution of marriage. That her husband has nothing to do with it. The people in the building are laughing because they think she might be a lesbian. She's gotten herself into this situation because it's expected of her. And there's no way out. Not even suicide, reflected in her falling out of a large building yet going up instead of down.

How do you come up with such analyses?

Symbols. Always symbols. The man in the forest represents not her husband, but *all* men. The fact that she can't see him, only hear him, evidences that. Her husband plays a very small role in the dream. He snores and wakes to prove he's another one of the type she heard in the forest. The number of people laughing at her clearly suggests they're not only her close friends, but the world at large. After all, the whole building is laughing, not just a few select people. Therefore, they represent society. Do you see?

I do. Quite an interpretation. And would you tell the patient about this analysis?

Probably, though maybe not immediately. It would depend on the patient. I might tell her later, or explain it to her by metaphor so she could understand without immediately relating it to herself.

In other words, slowly.

Yes.

Very good. This explains a lot of things.

It does? About what?

About you.

Me?

Yes.

Such as?

I think I'll save that for a later meeting.

As Matt stared down the funnel of the flue and attempted to read the indentations that signaled usage of some kind, he suddenly got an idea that might solve his problem. If he could penetrate the hole in the secret room without sticking his hand in and getting his fingers caught in a damn mousetrap, why couldn't he do the same thing here? Send down a rope of some kind with a slipknot on its end, and see what he could pick up with it. Without a second to lose, he crawled backward, up and out of the flue onto the roof, and went looking for a long thin rope that he could manipulate in the same way he had his shoelace.

You're having fun with me.

No, Doctor, I'm not. It's only that I'm not a professional. I can't come up with a quick diagnosis. I'll have to give it some thought.

You've inverted our relationship.

What do you mean?

You've maneuvered me into a situation where I've become the patient and you the analyst. Do you see?

Yes, I suppose I do. It wasn't intentional.

I doubt that. It was deftly accomplished. I'm now wondering what you'll discover and tell me about myself, the same way patients feel about me when we part. It's a very real aspect of psychiatry and you've fooled me into taking the bait.

Not at all. If it appears that way, so be it. But my questions were very real. I want to understand. Not so much *you*, but the process. What you've told me has been very helpful.

To you. Not to me.

If I'm going to help you help me by giving better responses to your questions, though, knowing how the process works will greatly facilitate it. Isn't that so?

See, you're asking questions as a psychiatrist might. As I might.

The only way I can understand. Don't you see?

I've got to go, Joe.

You're not angry with me are you Doctor?

Not at *you*, I'm not. No.

Goodbye.

24

atthew Brady brought a long thin rope with him this time, designed to do exactly what he wanted. He'd made sure of that by choosing it carefully, taking great care to add stiff string to its end so the rope would pick up small objects by any available protrusion it found.

Good morning, Joe.

Morning, Doctor. Did you by any chance think over the conundrum we faced last time?

No. I've been very busy.

You're still angry with me.

No. I was never that. Just disappointed in myself.

Because you felt I'd manipulated you in some way?

You did.

Certainly not intentionally, I can assure you of that. I simply wanted to know if when you analyzed my dreams, and for that matter my situation in general, you were piece-mealing your analysis through your view of my case, or telling me what you actually thought.

Joe, from almost the very beginning I've considered you an extremely intelligent guy. The test proved that as well as your logical and somewhat unemotional behavior. Therefore, I would never toy with you in regards to my interpretations of your dreams or any other aspects of your case. I've been extremely candid with you from the outset.

That's good to hear, Doctor. I've pretty much come to the same conclusion myself. Does that calm you down a bit about my attempting to turn the tables on you?

It does. But that you so deftly did it still worries me professionally.

That you might be losing your touch?

Yes.

Well I can assure you of this. I *am* intelligent and, I suppose, clever. My mind is, as I've said before, deceitful at times. So now I'm worried that I might have inadvertently been playing you. I hope that's not true. And I hope now that you've heard it from me, you realize my lack of guilt in leading you into this situation.

Matt wiggled the rope back and forth after sending it though the flue opening and quickly realized he was getting nowhere fast. The size and extreme flexibility of the rope would never do. He couldn't actually feel the end of the string, the slipknot there, and thus what he'd created was fundamentally useless. Nevertheless, he continued searching for a time before calling it quits. Then he sat back in frustration, and gave his situation more thought.

He could certainly get a less flexible rope and hope that would work. Or, now that he thought of it, he could ask his supervisor if he could search from the bottom up. That is, could he drill holes in the ceiling from below instead of attempting to find whatever it might be from above? He doubted his supervisor would give such permission, probably since Matt had no idea of the whatever-it-was's position and would most likely have to tear up a good portion of the ceiling before he found anything. If, in fact, something was there.

But I bought it. I fell for it hook, line, and sinker.

No you didn't. You kept it simple and merely quoted from textbooks on the subject. You revealed nothing to me at all.

Let's get back to the situation at hand, shall we? I'm concerned that we're well off base here, and no matter how I feel about the problem we've been discussing, nothing will help me feel better about it.

Okay.

Where shall we begin?

How about you start by asking me questions?

I have no more questions to ask. Maybe we're through.

Maybe. But I have a feeling you've not gotten everything you want out of me yet.

You do?

Yes.

All right, I'll ask something broad. What other things that I've not asked do you think I need to ask before deciding the question of your ability to stand trial?

Good.

You think so?

I do.

Then what's the answer?

Yes.

I've forgotten the question.

You wanted to know if there are things left to discuss with me, and I've answered yes.

What?

Ask me about any scars I have.

Do you have any scars?

Yes.

Where?

Here.

On your hand?

Yes. Do you see it?

Hard not to. I'm surprised I didn't notice it before. What happened? Something to do with the tractor?

No. It's self-inflicted.

Now *that's* interesting. How did it happen?

See? You've not lost your touch. We're off and running.

Stop trying to encourage me. I'm fine. How did it happen?

My father had given me a severe whipping with his belt, and I was incredibly angry with him for it.

How old were you?

Most likely ten or eleven.

So what happened?

I went to the barn and sulked. Planned for ways to get even with him.

Such as?

Wreck the tractor. Something big, like that. Something he'd *really* feel.

Did you imagine getting back at him violently?

Not on your life. He was still twice as big as I was, and strong from having been a farmer all his life.

Did you break the tractor?

No. I couldn't. See I was smart even then and knew that if I managed to mess up any of his equipment, it would harm our family as much as it would hurt him. I'd suffer as well as he. Made no sense. So that was out.

And?

I found this screw on the floor of the barn. A big one. Maybe an inch in diameter at the top. Pointed at the other end. Very sharp. It looked like it had fallen from the roof or something, but it also looked shiny. New. Like it had never been used before.

Matt was running out of ideas at this point. So close, yet still so far. He knew something important was hidden down that chute, yet he had no way to prove that or get at it. No way to retrieve the evidence of what Nancy Buffet had been doing down here. He'd considered everything. Creating a curved piece of wood that could follow the angles of the metal flue, for example. That, of course, would never work. He had no idea what further angles the chute might take beyond where it disappeared from his sight. He thought of using the rope with a magnet on its end, in hopes that the object he was after would be attracted by magnetism. That, of course, was hopeless, too. It might not be attracted, or the metal of the chute might be magnetic itself, making pushing the magnet down the flue impossible. He considered tearing up the metal chute itself until he found what he was looking for. That would, however, be illegal, and therefore make anything he found inadmissible as evidence. And he'd most likely be sent a bill for the necessary repairs. He was completely stuck.

So what did you do?

I stood the screw pointed side up on an anvil in the barn and slammed my left hand, palm open, down on it from above. Right on that pointed end.

You did *what*? Why? What did you expect to gain from doing that?

Just wait. The first thing I did, of course, was scream bloody murder. Blood was squirting everywhere. Hurt like hell. I'd somehow rammed my hand completely down to the other end of the screw. Gone completely through me with most of the thing sticking out the back of my hand. Seeing that scared me more than the blood and the pain. It was horrendous.

What happened then?

My mother heard me from the kitchen in the house and came running. By that time I was crying and staring at the screw protruding from the back of my hand. It was a mess.

Did your father come out, too?

No. My mother saw me, grabbed me by the other hand, and pulled me into the house and over to the kitchen sink. I had no idea what she was going to do to fix this.

How did she?

She didn't. My father walked in to see what the ruckus was about, looked at my hand, grabbed my arm, and pulled the damn thing out. That hurt more than me slamming it down in the first place. Of course, more blood came rushing out from the open wound. Then he walked out. Just like that. Without a word.

Your mother?

She pulled me into the bathroom and doused it with rubbing alcohol. Just kept doing that as I screamed, more from the pain the alcohol was inflicting than the wound itself.

What then?

After a minute of letting the alcohol enter my hand, she took a clean cloth of some kind and wrapped it tightly around my hand to stop the bleeding. And nothing further was ever said about it.

Nothing?

No. My father had nothing to say as usual, and my mother probably blamed him for it but didn't want any trouble.

Did they take you to a doctor?

No. I wanted to tell my mother that my father had done it to me in addition to the whipping, but I didn't. She wouldn't have believed it anyway, since he'd been in the house when it happened.

What do you imagine she thought?

That it was an accident. I'm sure of it.

So, she never said a word, even as she was washing it, using the alcohol, and wrapping the bandage around it?

No. Nothing.

This is incredible.

It is, isn't it?

Do you know *why* you did it?

Not for sure. I think it must've had something to do with my damn alter ego. It was mad at me for not confronting my father and at least trying to stop him from giving me the whipping. I don't know. Why does anybody do anything?

Interesting question to be asking a psychiatrist.

Suppose so.

I'm sorry for not having noticed the scar before.

Don't be. I don't use this hand much, and often keep it out of view when I'm talking to people. Subconscious, I think.

Can I get a closer look?

Sure.

My God, it's as bad on both sides of your hand.

Not surprising since it went clear through.

Do you have mobility with that hand?

Yes, except it's never been right again. Must have cut some bones, muscles, nerves, tendons, and the like when I did it.

So you keep it hidden.

Not hidden. Just don't make a big show of it. Someone might ask me how it happened and I'd have to make up a story.

What kind of story?

Probably about how it was an accident with the tractor, just like you thought before I told you.

Matt's obsession refused to let him give up on his search. He drew pictures of the inside of the continuing flue based on architectural drawings he had of Building J. He imagined Nancy, who he now knew could no more have gone into that extension than he or the skinny guard could have, placing the whatever-it-was in its place, and then retrieving it.

Then it struck him. The obvious. The coiled wire. It had seemed fairly pliable but strong as well. Something that could be curved with enough force though not at the slightest touch. Could that be the thing she'd used? Attached whatever-it-was to the end of that wire and shoved it down in the flue as far as it would go, and then somehow bounced the whatever-it-was off and recoiled the wire? This would be consistent with the scratches he saw on the metal outside the secret room. It would also account for no one being able to crawl through the flue to place whatever-it-was there. And it would probably make it accessible after the fact in much the same way.

My God, how could you have forgotten to tell me maybe the most important thing we've discussed yet? This is amazing and truly helpful.

How so?

It suggests both your innocence and, possibly, the psychological problems that made you unfit for trial.

Tell me.

By impaling your hand on the screw when you were angry proves you'd rather hurt yourself than hurt others. You're a masochist. Someone incapable of hurting others. I could testify to that in court. Of course, we'd have to prove your story, but your mother could help verify that. And, of course, the scars. I'd need to get your permission to tell the story. Then, if it didn't convince the district attorney before the trial, I could easily prove your inability to stand trail in the first place. This story could be the crux of the entire case.

So I could remain here in the facility?

Yes. Or have the charges against you dropped.

And the meds?

You can get meds like your taking without being in a psychiatric ward. Plenty of people do. You'd be happy and out being a farmer again. Both of which I think you'd like to do.

Yes. But what if this doesn't work? Either way?

He jests at scars that never felt a wound?

Shakespeare again.

Yes.

Matt thought back to when he'd discovered the coiled wire. Had he taken it, or had Nancy? Then he remembered handing it over to his supervisor as part of the evidence he was gathering at the time, and his supervisor returning it to him. And therefore where it was.

So you think my stupidity is a way out of this mess?

Not your stupidity, only your emotions making decisions for you.

I thought you were not supposed to take sides in this case, just tell the court whether I'm sane enough to stand trial?

You're right, of course. There's no assurance that in this situation I would be called by the defense to make a statement. Although they'd be crazy not to if I told them what I know. As for informing the court you're not ready to stand trial and that you may never be, I could at least argue to keep you here. Both acceptable.

Though neither guaranteed to put me back on the farm with my meds without a trial.

No. Probably not. But those solutions would work for you almost as well.

You know I have to thank you for all you've done for me. It's truly incredible the amount of time and effort you've put into this. Faithful friends are hard to find.

Again, don't consider me your friend. My job, Joe, only my job.

Matt returned with the coil of wire to the flue outside the entrance to the secret room. He uncoiled it and stretched it out to see how far it would go. Of course, he had no idea how long Nancy's arms were or whether they were stretched to their limit when she'd done the deed. Nevertheless, he got a clue of how far down the flue the whatever-it-was was. Maybe eight feet, and he knew now that his first impulse—that the coiled wire had been a part of the horn system—had to be wrong. So what, he thought, and pushed it until it reached a dead end. The place that no doubt Nancy had left the thing.

He had more information now. Of course, knowing how far it was wouldn't help him that much. It might tell him if the end were still above the kitchen or above another room, but little else. He realized that he needed to study the drawings of the building more to see if this possible new room might be more interesting a place to record conversations than the kitchen with its cooks and bottle washers.

So, what do we do now?

You don't do anything, Joe. You continue like nothing has happened. Don't get your hopes up. Keep thinking about other things that might help prove what you've told me today. Let me do the thinking about what it means. I'll meet you again in a couple of days and maybe have an idea or two. All right?

Yes.

Goodbye for now, Joe.

Bye, Doctor, and thanks.

You bet.

25

Matt discovered two things when he looked over the drawings of Building J. The first proved quite encouraging. Indeed, the location of the end of the no longer coiled wire was directly over what the building designers had called the Interview Room. Here, as he understood it, psychiatrists met with inmates to determine if they were qualified to stand trial. Unfortunately, as he discovered this, he also discovered that the wall and ceiling of this room were soundproof. As he read the drawings, this soundproofing consisted of several acoustically impenetrable walls cemented together to make it impossible to eavesdrop on conversations within the room. One good thing. One bad thing. What, then, could Nancy have hidden outside these walls that would do anyone any good? And, why would she want to record conversations in there anyway?

Good morning, Joe.
Morning, Doctor Amador.
How are you doing today?
Good. You?
Fine. Any dreams?
None of any consequence.
Then I'll leave that decision up to you now that you understand the difference. At least from a psychiatric point of view.
I do have a question, though.

Not one of those questions that will lead us to switch our positions again, I hope.

No. Not that.

What, then?

Who did it?

Who did what?

Whatever I'm supposed to have done.

How would I know?

Because you know everything I can think of, even many things you may have surmised from what I've told you about my dreams and other things I haven't thought about in years. All that, and you know what it is that I'm supposed to have done.

True. But I still don't know who did it.

Are you convinced I didn't do it?

Not my job to be convinced of anything, Joe, except your ability to stand trial. That's it.

That's all you're going to say on the matter? Even with the scars on my hand?

That's all I *can* say. At least for the moment. If you go to trial and they call me to the stand I'll say more than that.

Does that mean you actually do have an opinion on my guilt or innocence but won't tell me?

Matt studied the drawings more carefully to see if there was anything he might be missing. He looked over the specifications for the insulation. That interested him for some reason, so he studied the plans for the building very carefully. That's when he had a true epiphany. The room, any room, must have light fixtures. And in rooms such as those in professional buildings such as Building J, particularly in the Interview Room, this lighting must be placed inside walls or ceilings, still making light but recessed. Standing lamps will not suffice. And lights that protrude won't do either, since they might provide an opportunity for anyone inside to dismantle them for use in escaping. Therefore, such inset lighting would exist within walls and maybe these lights would provide less secure soundproofing than the rest of the walls and ceiling. True inspiration on his part. This was it. Somehow, Nancy Buffet had figured out a way to tuck a tape recorder down into the built-in lights in the ceiling of the Interview Room and was collecting conversations of those meeting in that room.

I'm a professional, Joe. We've gone through this before. Whether or not I have a personal opinion about you and the situation you're facing is irrelevant. My only job is to determine whether or not you're fit to stand trial in a courtroom.

But *do* you have an opinion?

Not pertinent. I won't answer.

I understand. Could I ask you how you're leaning at this point regarding my ability to stand trial?

Anything's fair to ask.

Okay. How are you leaning at this point?

I'm not completely sure we're done yet, but assuming we are, then I would reaffirm what I've already told you.

And that is?

That the most recent thing you've told me, the reason for the scars on the front and back of your hand, suggests that you are not fit to stand trial. Of course, that being said, I'll still have to write up my findings and in so doing may come to a different conclusion. For I'm not just weighing that one factor, but all the factors we've discussed.

So, as I understand it, were you to have to report at this very moment, it would likely be that I'd remain here. Otherwise, you can't say.

Yes.

So here comes the dicey part. I assume that this issue of my ability to stand trial will come up again in the not so distant future, and that someone else may be deciding my fate. And that person may not be as thorough or as caring as you. Is that right?

Correct.

When might that new review of my sanity take place?

Whenever the judge deems it so.

Meaning?

If he or she doesn't think I'm a competent judge of your sanity, then maybe tomorrow. If he or she deems me competent as I imagine will be the case, then more likely in a year or so.

This keeps up, then, until I'm judged sane and stand trial or I remain here until I die.

Exactly.

So what have we accomplished over the weeks you've been coming to see me? Particularly if I have to go through this entire process again next week, next month, or more likely next year?

We've most likely, again no promises, given you a year or more distance from the crime.

Why do you put it that way?

Because that's precisely what it is. You see, Joe, the further we are from the crime, the more people forget, the more they get sick and die, the less interested those most affected become. It's not fair to the innocent on the outside who are most affected by these delays, but it's a fact. The longer the process takes, the more likely it will be forgotten and that you will remain incarcerated and, therefore, not a threat to society.

I never was.

Probably correct, though this is the way the law reads.

So I could remain here for the rest of my life?

You could.

And whoever actually committed the crime I'm charged with committing is free to commit more crimes.

Unfortunately, yes. That's true as well.

Matt reported his most recent findings to his supervisor who, in turn, told him that Nancy Buffet had not visited Building J at any time since he'd spoken with her based on observations by others in the Administration Building now charged with keeping a watch. Matt was not surprised by this, since he'd spent so many hours up on that roof. He couldn't imagine him not seeing her if she had. Matt then posed a question to his boss. He asked if sometime during his night shift when the Interview Room was not occupied, he could enter that room and inspect the light fixtures in the ceiling there. No drilling, no hammering, no anything else but to see if Nancy Buffet had placed something there by using the coil of wire he'd found.

Matt's supervisor argued that the lights in the walls and ceilings of Building J had no access points. Matt, however, knew differently. He'd studied the plans for the Interview Room and discovered that, because of the flue above the ceiling in the room, the only way lights could be replaced was from within the room itself. With that, his supervisor gave him permission in the form of a typed release to make sure the investigation could not be interpreted in any other way. And, of course, with the express order for Matt to bring anything he found there directly to his office before attempting to investigate it further himself.

Then I don't see how we've accomplished anything during these weeks except postpone the inevitable and keep me inside and someone on the outside free to commit more crimes.

And understand a great deal more about your situation that you can use to inform the next psychiatrist whoever and whenever that may be.

Is that worth anything?

I didn't agree to these sessions for the sake of anything but to do a professional job of examining you to see if you're fit to stand trial, Joe. Once again, I'm not here to decide whether you're innocent or guilty. Do you see that?

Yes, I see it. But I don't have to like it.

No, you don't. Unfortunately, though, it's all I'm here for.

So what do I do now?

Assuming we both feel our sessions are over, you go back to your room and do what you usually do until either I or another psychiatrist shows up and begins interviewing you again.

Does it have to start over?

No, though it usually does.

What do you mean?

My file on you is turned over to anyone new involved, and they can read it thoroughly. But I have to be honest, psychiatrists are like everyone else, they tend to make their own decisions and not rely on someone else's. So, as much as I'd like to tell you that the questions would begin where you and I left off, the only realistic way that would happen would be if I was the next psychiatrist to see you.

Understood.

So, is there anything else you want to tell or ask me before we finish these sessions?

Matt waited until he was confident the last interviews had taken place in the Interview Room that day and entered it with the key his supervisor had loaned him. He'd brought along a complete toolbox that went with his job as guard and those on loan from a member of the utility staff, moved a chair in line with what he guessed was the ceiling light below the duct, and proceeded to look it over for methods of replacing its internal bulb. It didn't take a genius to find the screws along both sides and ends to figure out how to accomplish the task and, within a couple of minutes, he'd removed the outer translucent shell protecting the long fluorescent bulb inside. What he also found there was a curved metal reflecting unit above the bulb and between him and the inner ceiling area that gave no hint on how it could be removed. Clearly, whatever Nancy Buffet had placed above had not fallen into the area below this barrier, so he'd have to remove it as well to get further inside.

I'd like to tell you how much I appreciate the work you've done, Doctor. You are a true professional and a good man. I'm not sure I could have withstood anyone lesser for this job. You're intelligent, honorable, and truly refreshing. If everyone in the world were more like you, I wouldn't be such a loner.

Thank you, Joe. I believe I could say the same about you. I'll miss our meetings.

Goodbye, Doctor Amador.

Goodbye, Joe.

Matt was surprised to discover that with a normal screwdriver he could pry the reflective metal shielding from its mooring without damaging it. He did so and it fell off. Not, of course, to the floor, since he'd not removed the fluorescent bulb yet. So he removed both carefully, set them aside, and used his flashlight to see further inside. The first thing he checked was the shield itself to see if anything had fallen onto it since it had been placed there. Nothing had. Then he used his flashlight to scan the area below him to make sure something hadn't dropped onto the carpet without him hearing it fall. Not there either. So he inspected the inner workings of the area in the ceiling below what he presumed was the ductwork of the flue. He found nothing obvious by way of holes drilled through the metal. Then he realized that Nancy Buffet could not have created a hole here since she would have had to enter the Interview Room to do so. Why do that, while creating the elaborate entryway above? Made no sense. Whatever it was that she'd used to compromise the Interview Room was still inside the heating and cooling flues. Was he stuck yet again?

Wait, Doctor.

What?

I just realized that I still have more information to give to you.

About my evaluation?

Yes.

You don't need to. I'm already willing to give you what I think you want. More time in here with your meds.

Actually you told me you still needed time to consider *all* the facts before you made your final decision. But that's not why I want to tell you this.

Remember, deciding your status is my sole reason for evaluating you.

Is all our time together not worth a few more minutes?

Okay, Joe. You've earned that, I guess.

Matt was sometimes slow, but he wasn't stupid. He'd attended college and, though it hadn't done him much good by way of a better job, it had taught him a few things. One of those things was that he should think through matters thoroughly before giving up. This was one of those things. If Nancy's incursion into the building had landed in the area above the lights, he should be able to prove it by knocking on the metal in much the same way contractors do walls to find studs behind them. The sound should change whenever something above but touching the ceiling, or metal shield in this case, was present. So, he took his time knocking quietly and listening carefully, moving slowly from one end of the exposed area to the other.

And he found it.

Nearly at the end of his sonic analysis, something radically changed the resonance of the sound. Something inside the duct. Something small, since he could hear it bounce from his knocks. Something clearly not part of the ductwork in that it only resonated in that one spot. Knocks on the areas around the spot proved completely free of similar sounds. Thus, it was not a connector between one duct and another. This was a freely moveable object inside the space either blown out of the cooler or heater, or, as he now knew it to be, something that one Nancy Buffet had placed there with a long wire.

What if I remembered something that was so incredible that it might alter everything we've discussed?

How could that be? I thought you've been telling me the *complete* truth.

I have been. But, as I told you quite some time ago now, I'm not to be held responsible for my deceiving alter ego.

All right, Joe. How long will this take?

I'm not sure.

Then you'll have to hold onto this information until I can see you again. Unfortunately, I'm already late for my next appointment. So, goodbye again. I'll see you soon.

Goodbye, Doctor Amador.

26

att had to sit on the new information he had until morning when his supervisor arrived. He then told him of his discovery and asked what could be done to retrieve whatever it was inside the duct. For the first time in their relationship, the supervisor had no idea what could be done. This question had, apparently, never been asked of him before. So Matt had to wait longer for a decision on how to proceed.

Good morning, Joe.

Morning, Doctor Amador.

I'm going to skip the usual formalities and get right down to this new piece of information you need to tell me.

I've remembered what it was I'm innocent of doing.

You mean you've remembered the crime that you're accused of committing?

I have.

Since when?

Not sure exactly. It's hard to say because it first came to me in a dream, and then I slowly pieced it together over time. So exactly when is hard to pin down.

When's not *that* important, Joe. So, now, tell me exactly what you remember.

Matt finally received a call from his supervisor with the good news that the construction company responsible for installing the ducts in Building J were still in business, and they would visit the facility and drill a hole in the appropriate place, retract whatever was in there, and weld the hole shut with appropriate replacement metal. All Joe had to do was wait a day or two until the workers capable of doing the job were free, and he and his supervisor would know for sure what the hell was going on.

I remember nothing about the actual event because I wasn't there. I'm innocent, as I've maintained since the beginning of this mess.

I understand. Go on.

So I only know what the newspapers reported.

And the arresting officers. And the judge.

I don't remember those things at all. Just what I read in the papers.

So, you're saying that you read about it in the papers before you were arrested?

Yes.

That's not possible.

Why?

Because you were arrested immediately.

I don't remember that.

So, what did you read in the newspapers?

That Nancy was murdered.

Nancy?

Yes. Didn't you know?

Let's forget that. How did she die?

She was shot in the back by an unknown party.

Nancy?

Yes, Nancy. And Bradley did it. I'm sure of that.

Bradley?

Bradley did it. He killed the blond girl as well. I'm sure of it. And he's out there now attempting to murder other people as well.

Stop it, Joe, you're not making sense.

I am making sense. It's so clear to me now.

Did you take your meds this morning?

Why?

Because you're a different Joe from the one I usually see in the morning.

Nancy's dead, Doctor. Bradley did it. Aren't you concerned about this? More deaths may have already occurred. Something needs to be done.

Joe, listen to me. I want you to return to your room. In about ten minutes, I want you to go from there to the pharmacy. Take what they give you there so they can see you consume it, and return to your room. I'm your current doctor in such matters, and I more than request that you do it. Do you understand me?

Yes, I do.

When the workers from the construction company arrived, it was late in the evening. A strange time for them to show, but perfect for Matt since he was on duty at the time. He showed them the room and the light fixture, and told them where to find the whatever-it-was inside. They followed their instructions, and before long Matt was treated to what he'd worked so long and hard to find—the hidden tape recorder, though he now knew it couldn't be that. It was too small. What he saw when the workers brought it out of its hiding place was a cylinder standing half-an-inch high and the same wide with a flat top and bottom. Couldn't have weighed more than a few ounces and it appeared to consist of solid metal. Knowing what he did about such things, Matt was aware that weight could be deceiving. He also knew about miniaturization. But, he would have to wait still longer before he got an answer from those more trained to recognize such things. But, at the least, he figured his search had been successful. And maybe, whoever was responsible for identifying it, might be able to pull fingerprints from it as well. Those, he knew, would tell the tale.

27

ater the next day, Matt got word that his supervisor wanted to see him. Even though he was asleep when the phone rang, he dressed quickly and arrived at the supervisor's office within minutes. Once there, he had to wait as two policemen spoke with his boss. When they left, Matt was told that the device the workers from the construction company had found was a microphone-transmitter that apparently could hear everything that went on in the Interview Room. The supervisor also told Matt that the range of this device was no more than an eighth of a mile, so anyone listening would have to have been on the premises of the facility to hear the conversations as they occurred. Nancy Buffet's desk in the Administration Building was obviously within that range. Interestingly, when the supervisor had gone to visit her that morning to search her desk, she'd apparently vacated her job without informing anyone. She'd also taken her belongings with her. He described the situation as *very* suspicious and congratulated Matt on a job well done. That a significant new position awaited him. While Matt was surprised and delighted at getting this promotion, he was also frustrated. Apparently, the time he'd taken in resolving the situation had only helped discover what had happened, not what had been collected or why.

Good morning, Joe.
Morning, Doctor Amador.
How are things progressing?

Fine.

Any dreams?

None. I've slept well every night since I last saw you.

Good. I think you needed the rest. Don't you?

Apparently so.

Do you remember anything about our last meeting?

It's kind of fuzzy. I do remember that you were angry at me.

Not angry, Joe, concerned. That's all.

I see.

You don't remember anything else?

Nothing in particular.

You had an epiphany of sorts. You claimed to remember what you'd been accused of doing that eventually placed you in here.

I did?

Yes. Don't you remember any of that?

No.

You told me that Nancy was dead, and that Bradley had murdered her.

I thought Bradley was dead.

Me, too. Although there was a time in our discussions when we considered that since you only had the word of your father on that, that he might still be alive. You also said you were sure he'd killed the blond girl found in the hole out in the forest that day you met Bradley for the first time.

Well that might be true. But the part about believing he's still alive is strange. I wonder where I got that idea?

Now, Joe, I'm going to suggest something. It's only a suggestion. I'd like you to think about it, all right?

Sure.

Is it possible that, fearing I might turn in a report that you were sane enough to stand trial, you actually contrived the entire thing to make me think you were truly insane?

I don't know. Doesn't sound like me.

So, you don't remember?

No.

There's nothing you can say to contradict or enforce my supposition?

No.

Does it make you angry, even the slightest bit, that I've now accused you of strategically making yourself seem insane. All as an act?

No. I don't remember.

Are you telling me the truth, Joe?

About remembering?

Yes.

Yes.

Try as he might, Matt couldn't get the whole plot that Nancy had completed out of his mind. While he'd been relieved of duty on the case, no one could keep him from thinking about it. He knew this had become a kind of obsession, but it had brought rewards to his life, most recently a promotion, and he'd learned to follow his intuition on such matters. Thus it was, that he spent the morning, his usual time for sleeping, thinking over and over what had occurred. Nancy Buffet, a new employee, had entered Building J through a vent in the roof and planted a microphone/transmitter in a flue above the Interview Room where inmates were typically interviewed by their psychiatrists. She'd recorded said interviews probably while at her desk in the Administration Building and made off with the records of them precisely at the time she was about to be caught. Her multiple trips to the secret room and beyond with her wire coil were probably necessitated by repositioning the microphone/transmitter for better reception, not picking up tapes or discs of the recordings themselves since she most likely did that at her desk.

His first question had to do with how she'd known she was about to be caught? Red handed no less. Obviously one of the conversations that had taken place in that room was of great interest to her. Considering all of them as equally important was illogical. Therefore, his next step, probably on his own since his supervisor had turned the case over to security and the county sheriff's department, was to get a case list of interviews that took place in the room during the time period he considered important to see if a relationship existed between Nancy and any of the persons being interviewed. Not easy, but doable. He knew someone in the billing office who would have this information, and who owed him a favor. Two favors actually. So he fell asleep thinking about this strategy, and how he could carry it out without his supervisor knowing.

Do you remember taking your meds before our meeting that morning?

No. But I take my meds regularly like clockwork. If I don't, I get a little crazy. Depressed and full of anxiety at the same time. Not a good combination, at least for me. Was I that way that morning?

Yes, Joe, you were.

My guess would be that I forgot to take my meds. Sorry about that. It won't happen again, I can assure you of that.

Good.

So, now where are we?

We are where we were before my last visit took place. Do you remember that meeting?

I do.

Tell me about the last part of our meeting. What you said.

If I remember correctly, I told you something about having discovered something important.

Do you remember what?

Not exactly.

What *do* you remember?

Just what you said. That I had something important to tell you about remembering something, and you had to leave because you were late for an appointment.

Yes, that's right. You don't remember anything else?

No, should I?

Well I was hoping you'd remember what you were going to tell me.

Can't think of it.

Nothing about Bradley or Nancy?

No.

We discussed that.

Where were we before that?

Well before your telling me you'd remembered something important, we were saying goodbye to one another. I was then going to visit my next patient and later that night write a report for the judge informing him of your ability to stand trial or not.

What were you going to tell him?

I didn't know that until I reviewed your entire case and made up my mind. My feeling when we spoke was that I would probably tell him you weren't ready.

Did you do that?

No.

Why not?

After you told me what you now don't remember, it didn't seem that I had all the information from you that I needed.

I see.

So I guess that's where we are now.

Saying goodbye?

Yes.

Will I ever see you again?

That's not up to me, Joe. Possibly. A lot of things can happen between when I turn in my report until the next regular visit would take place. Probably in a year or so.

Well, goodbye, Doctor Amador.

Goodbye, Joe. Are you sure now there's nothing else you want to tell me at this point?

I'm sure.

I wish us both the very best of luck.

Me, too.

28

att had no trouble obtaining a complete list of psychiatrists and their associated patients from the friend that owed him a favor. The question for Matt, though, was what exactly would he do with the list. How could he possibly figure out from roughly twenty combinations of names, which one Nancy Buffet would be interested in overhearing? But, he gave it a shot anyway, using the Internet as his research weapon of choice. No go. After only fifteen minutes, Matt realized his chances of success were next to none. He had to find a different approach.

After considering his problem for a couple of hours, Matt decided to risk his friend's loyalty by asking yet another favor. He knew he would be pushing the envelope, but he had to try. So he called and asked his friend if he would send Matt a copy of Nancy Buffet's application for a position at the facility. His friend did not agree initially. After all, providing a copy of those being interviewed in the Interview Room was one thing—these were as near to public information as one could get without actually *being* public information—but applications were confidential. So, rather than beg for her application, Matt then asked for the entire file, including the vetting that the business office had done before she was hired. He knew that piling on more requests might make his friend more likely to give up just his first one. It had worked before, and indeed it worked again.

Within the hour, Matt was reading the handwriting on Nancy Buffet's application and learning a good deal about her. Most importantly, of course, her telephone number and local residence. With that information, he took his personal jeep out of the facility's garage and drove to the local town where Nancy Buffet lived. He was, for one of those rare times, actually glad he mostly worked nights so he could follow hunches during the day.

He was shocked when he arrived at the address given on Nancy's form. A set of apartments, and not too well kept. Since the form had no apartment number on it, he found the super's residence and rang the doorbell. When the old man answered, Matt asked about Nancy Buffet. Being of sound body and looking rather intimidating to the skinny superintendent, he clearly intimidated the old man who quickly identified Nancy's place of residence. Matt also got directions, and followed them to an open door and a living room full of scattered junk. The place was a mess. He couldn't imagine anyone living there. Pictures off the wall, the floor scattered with broken dishes, tables turned upside down, and so on. Clearly the place had been tossed by amateurs. Someone looking for something. Maybe Nancy, though that seemed improbable given the mess. Could be that they'd found her and she'd put up a struggle. Or they hadn't found her and were paying her back for not being home. It didn't matter much what had happened. Nancy had either been abducted or, more likely, had already left when the thieves had come looking for her.

Before leaving the complex, Matt told the super about the mess and apologized for being the bearer of bad news. The skinny old man then rattled off a series of swear words that Matt had not heard since his days in the Naval Academy. He finally left, and returned to the Forensic Psychiatric Facility. He parked his car and walked across the brown snowless lawn toward Building J to get some sleep in the secret room, and think over what he'd just found. As he did, he heard two harsh pops in the distance as he felt two devastating blows to his midsection. He jerked twice from the force, began to lose consciousness, and slumped to the ground as his breath escaped from his lungs. For the last time.

Joe?
Good morning, Doctor.
You placed a call for me?
Yes.

This is highly irregular. I'm not your regular psychiatrist. You know that. I'm simply the doctor the court appointed to provide my findings on the state of your mental health. Nothing more than that.

I know, but I felt I owed it to you.

What?

To explain a few things about our previous conversations.

Explain what things?

About what's been occurring around here.

You mean like the shooting this morning?

Shooting?

You don't know about that?

No.

One of the guards was shot and killed on the way into Building J.

One of the guards?

Yes.

Have they found the perpetrator?

Yes, they have.

Thank goodness. Who was it?

Don't know. They're keeping it under wraps for the time being. Typical cop stuff. I do know the guard's name, though. He was Matthew Brady. Did you know him?

Matthew Brady? The Civil War photographer? How could that be?

I think it was a different Matthew Brady, Joe. Did you know him?

Don't have any idea. I suppose if he worked here, I would have seen him around. I don't know any of the guards by name. Haven't spoken to most of them.

Understood. Let's forget that. Tell me what you have to add to our interviews, so I can get back to my regular patients. Please. I'm short of time.

Have you turned in your report about me yet?

Why?

What I have to tell you might change your mind.

No, I haven't. I didn't feel well last night, so I went to bed early.

That's great.

You're happy I didn't feel well?

No. That you didn't turn in your report yet.

I see. Is this going to take more than a few minutes?

I believe so.

Well, let me cancel a couple of appointments before we begin. I think this takes precedence over them given what just now occurred outside your building.

All right.

Okay, what's this new information that's possibly going to change my mind about the report?

Well, to begin, I haven't been completely honest in everything I've told you.

Because of your alter ego?

No, because I haven't been telling the complete truth.

That's twice you've used the word 'complete.' Does that mean you've erred more on the side of not telling me true things as opposed to telling me direct lies?

Mostly.

So, you *have* told me lies?

Yes. One I've already told you about.

I remember that. Give me an example of another lie.

My memory of what event caused the police to arrest and charge me with the crime. I've known it all along.

So you lied not once, but many times about that?

Yes, though I'm counting it as one lie repeated, rather than several lies. Do you see the difference?

Not really. But what does it matter? I now have to take the things you told me that are true in a different light because of those lies. That lie, as you call it, will color everything you've told me. I'll have to rethink the entire ensemble of statements you've given me. Do you see that?

Yes. Maybe you should always doubt truth to be a liar.

True, but now, rather than picking lies and new things you want to tell me randomly, why not begin at the beginning. And as you do, it would help if you'd tell me the things you said that were true. At least in general. You don't have to go into specifics.

I understand.

Good. Now begin wherever you think's best.

Well, everything I told you about my parents, grandparents, the Bible, my injury, all that stuff was completely true. I may have inadvertently left a few things out, but as far as I remember my family history is exactly as I made it out to be.

That's good to hear. So your father did whip you, put you in the barn for a night, gave you pneumonia, those kinds of things?

Absolutely.

Go on.

What I told you about the blond girl, whether she was both the one I met in my father's house and the one that Bradley showed me, is also true.

She was mutilated, and we don't have any idea whether there were two that might look alike or not?

That's right.

What about Bradley's suicide?

Exactly as I said. My father told me about it. As far as I know, Bradley's dead.

When are you going to get to the parts where you consciously left out information or overtly lied?

I'm getting there. You asked specifically that I verify what I told you previously *was* true.

You're right. I did. Sorry.

No problem. I understand your anticipation of what's to come. Maybe I can whet your appetite by telling you that a lot of what I told you I didn't remember that I later revealed to you was a direct lie. I've remembered the entire story from the beginning.

Well, now you'll have to be more specific. Offhand, I don't remember exactly what you revealed or when.

Understood, and that's why I'm taking things slowly.

Okay.

Before I go on, though, you should know that the meds I've supposedly been taking I've *not* been taking.

How so? I prescribed them and, according to the pharmacists, they witnessed you taking them. That's part of their job. To watch patients take their meds before they leave the pharmacy area.

True. Do you remember our discussion on magic?

Yes. You're going to tell me that you magically didn't take the meds?

Exactly. Easiest thing to do in the world. Put the cup with the meds in it up to your mouth while tipping it a little early and palming the pills in the hand you're lifting the cup with. A high school trick. I could teach you how to do it in a minute.

Why do that? I thought you wanted to stay in here because of the meds.

Another lie. As you'll see, I wanted to stay in here for quite different reasons.

All right, so you didn't take the pills I prescribed. Probably flushed them down the toilet.

Exactly what I did. Sorry to waste government money, but the government's probably doing a better job at that than I am, therefore it doesn't bother me that much.

Go on. So you were completely sober the entire time we've been meeting?

I was. Am. And, since you've now gotten me to uncover lies before truths, I purposely did the test wrong as the tester suggested.

Why?

Because I wanted you to think I was not only smart, but that I wasn't completely in control of myself. I needed you to continue thinking I was a savant. At that point, I desperately had to remain in here for reasons I'll explain shortly.

Go on.

Fine. Let's go back now to where I left off in telling truths. My description of meeting Missy and of Nancy's jealousy was completely correct. We met at Niagara Falls and fell in love there. She visited me later on and I asked her to marry me, just as I told you.

Good.

What I described to you about Nancy's continuing to harass me was the truth as well. She had a fixation on me for some reason and wouldn't let go. No telling why, but she did.

Continue.

The next part is true as well. I'm infertile. Not impotent, mind you, infertile. Many people don't know the difference. Can't have kids. I didn't know that until after Missy and I got married. Obviously we got tested and I found out. Missy wanted a child. Given my background I wasn't particularly interested, but to make her happy I agreed.

What did you do then?

Discussed the possibility of adopting. But she wanted to birth the child herself. Given the choices, we opted for artificial insemination as I told you. To make that story short, everything I told you about my father and Missy is true. I don't know whether the insemination was by injection or from my father, though I don't think Missy would've lied to me about such a thing. But I'm not completely sure of it either.

Good. A lot of truth there.

Yes. I've lied mostly by being incomplete rather than outright lying.

Go on.

Well, Carla was born and we were both very happy. Things were going very well. My farm was in good shape, Missy seemed satisfied, and I was surprisingly overjoyed at having a young child in my home. Whether she was blood mine or mine by default didn't matter. Carla was a great kid. Now here comes one of the parts I left out.

Go on.

Sometime during the fourth year of our marriage, Nancy contacted me again.

Still harassing you?

Not exactly. She'd changed. Told me she'd seen a psychiatrist of all things, and he'd helped her as she put it, 'grow up.'

How did she contact you?

By email. My first reaction to this was, of course, to tell her I was glad, but that we were still through and that was that. I was happily married and had a child.

Did she continue to badger you?'

I wouldn't actually call it that. We continued to communicate through email, and things progressed. Mostly my relationship with Missy began to disintegrate.

Because of Nancy?

I don't think so, though I can't rationally imagine she wasn't a part of it. No, Missy and I were growing apart.

Why?

We were not a good match as it turns out. It had appeared that we were initially, but we were too much alike. Logical. It meant we got along well, didn't argue, but it slowly became obvious that our lives were too similar in that regard. Our marriage was virtually passionless. We'd make love, of course, but it was like going through the motions. We did it for reasons we could express verbally. It soon became clear to both of us, I believe, that things were not supposed to work that way. The old adage that opposites attract apparently has some validity.

So you slowly grew apart.

Yes. At least in a way. Carla kept us together. We both knew she was the lynchpin, and that without her we'd be pretty unhappy together.

And Nancy comes in where?

Nancy was very different than Missy. She was emotional, argumentative, and critical of what I did. You'd think that would turn me off, and, of course it had before I met Missy. But it also turned me on. I guess I didn't want someone around me continuously agreeing with everything I did or said. I wanted to be with a better stranger.

Makes perfect sense. So what did you do?

Well, one thing led to another and, before long, I was seeing Nancy on the side.

You had an affair.

Yes. That sums it up nicely. I had an affair.

Didn't Missy get suspicious?

How? I'm a farmer, remember? Gone all day. Missy stayed in the house. Even though we had a smaller farm than my father, we had windbreaks of trees on my property. No way would she come out of the house to check on me. She loved to cook, take care of Carla, and read. We had plenty of books. So I would plow the fields, or whatever, go into a windbreak, and have lunch and other things with Nancy. It couldn't have been more perfect.

How did you feel about this arrangement?

Rotten. At least when I gave thought to it. Nancy was not only a real beauty, but she was a wonder with sex. I certainly felt guilty about cheating on Missy, though not to the extent that I would tell her.

How did Nancy feel about this?

She wanted me to leave Missy and Carla, and her and me get married. Natural for her to think that way.

I noticed that you left the word divorce out of that equation.

Did, though not intentionally. I know what divorces can do to people, and I surely didn't want to lose my farm.

So, what did you do?

I kept stalling. Any way I could to keep the status quo. And I worked it quite nicely for a time.

Until?

Until the day I came home and discovered the thing I'm accused of committing.

Tell me about that.

I'm still in a state of shock over it. Even after a year now. Worst thing I've ever seen in my life and hope never to top it. I opened the door to a house full of flies and a stench I'll never forget. The walls were covered with blood and shreds of what appeared to be pieces of skin.

You don't have to get graphic here if you don't want to.

I don't. And won't. Suffice it to say, Missy and Carla were carved into pieces. I couldn't believe it. Thank God the maggots had not had time to appear. That would've probably put me over the edge. As it was, I came close to a complete breakdown. Right then and there. I screamed bloody murder and ran around the house somehow still expecting my wife and child to be alive and hiding in a corner somewhere. But, instead, I found their heads. Posed, as no doubt you know. Just like the blond girl in the hole. Each with hardly a mark on their faces and with red ribbons in their hair.

What did you think about that?

I thought Bradley was still alive, and for some reason had revenged me for something he thought I'd done to him when I hadn't done anything to him at all.

You called the cops?

Didn't have to. Someone else had. No more than five minutes had passed before the swarming flies were replaced with swarming policemen. Arresting me for the murder of my wife and child. I couldn't believe it was happening.

What did you say to the policemen?

I told them about Bradley, what he'd done to the girl years before, and how he must be still alive. They took notes, except there I was, knee deep in the blood of my family. What could I do? What could I say? The evidence was all around me.

What else?

I guess I picked up a knife from the floor. Probably the murder weapon, and was wildly waving it around as I spoke. Hell, I would have thought I was guilty myself given that scene. A wild man who was about to attempt more murders. The cops in this case. So they tackled me, handcuffed and footcuffed me if you can believe it, read me my rights, took me down to the station, and booked me for double homicide. Of course, you know about this from the report.

I do, but it's different hearing it from you. So, when you told me you didn't know why Missy and Carla had not come to visit you all those times, you were lying?

Yes. It was part of a larger plan. I regret it. Knowing what I do now, though, I'd do it over again in the blink of an eye. I had no choice.

Why?

That will become evident as I explain the rest of the story.

Go on.

Well, I went to jail with a five million dollar bail set. No way I was going to borrow that, so there's where I stayed.

How did you feel at that time?

Feel? I felt like I'd stepped on a landmine. My whole life had gone up in smoke.

I meant emotionally as well as logically.

Angry, first of all. I wanted desperately to find Bradley and kill the sucker.

Even though you thought he was dead?

Yes. But I figured he couldn't be. Not with the heads posed like that. Like the girl in the hole. It was insane.

And?

And what?

What else did you feel?

I guess I felt guilty. Not of the charge, but of having the affair with Nancy. After all, I'd been doing that during the time of the murder. If I'd been in the field or home at the time, I might have prevented the murders. But I'd been off seeing my girlfriend. It was a low blow. Let me tell you, I cried a lot of tears. I slammed my fist against the wall of my cell many times. In both anger and guilt. Blood will have blood, I thought.

That's when they put you under suicide watch?

Yes. I guess I wasn't very rational at the time. I'd broken my hand, my good one without the scars, and was screaming and crying and must have seemed insane. Even when I came into court for a hearing, I couldn't keep quiet. I kept screaming, crying, and beating on things.

That's why you were seen as potentially unfit for trial?

Somewhere in there, yes.

But you weren't brought here at that time. Just to the local psychiatric ward.

True. Except I couldn't restrain myself there either. I was a mess as you can imagine. And, of course, my being so, at least in the minds of the prosecutors assigned to my case by the district attorney's office, didn't do my pleas of innocence any good. They made the charges against me stronger. An unbalanced man went berserk and killed his wife and child.

Did you have any visitors to either the jail or the hospital when you were there?

No. None. My wife and child were dead. My mother probably believed I'd done it. Nancy was smart enough to stay away, knowing that seeing her there might make them investigate her as well as me. And, as my mistress, make me a more likely candidate for the killings. After all, I'd be worried about divorce and would be more likely to knock off my wife and child in order to marry Nancy. It might also implicate her as an accessory to the crime, which neither of us wanted.

You didn't know this for sure?

No. She didn't contact me at any time.

Later?

Well get to that.

All right.

For now, let me say that she was out of the picture entirely. I was on my own. One of the penalties for being a loner, I guess.

So, eventually you were remanded to this place, and that's where we eventually connected. Right?

That's the short version, yes.

There's a longer version?

Yes. One you'll want to hear, I'm sure.

I do. Immediately, if you please.

My only way out of this mess was to turn off my tears and anger and get back to the real me. A logical person who figures things out carefully. Without emotion. So while I spent time in jail, in the infirmary, and here, I thought clearly about the situation. Was Bradley *really* still alive? Who else might have done this thing? I realized, actually very quickly once I got to it, that there was one other person who was perfectly suited to commit these crimes. Nancy Buffet.

I thought you loved her. That you were getting along fine together. That you thought she'd matured.

I did. I also knew she was someone so different than me, so more emotionally driven than logically so, that she might have done it. After all, look at her motive. She wanted me as her husband. Had wanted that since before I met Missy at Niagara Falls. But she also knew I wasn't eager to divorce Missy and give up my child. Like any person in her place, she was no doubt terribly conflicted about what to do. And it could have been, could easily have been, that she decided her only way to get what she wanted was to murder Missy and Carla and set it up as if Bradley had done it. She knew the story of Bradley by then, and that in some small way I believed him to still be alive. He'd make the perfect candidate for the crime. So she could have committed the double murder before we met that day.

Sounds foolproof.

In some ways it was. Though she wouldn't and couldn't know how badly I'd react to the killings. That I wouldn't act as a sane man. That I'd tell the cops about Bradley still being alive and that would make them believe my words the ranting of a murderer. Besides, I still wasn't sure if Bradley was alive. Maybe the cops looked into it, maybe they didn't. I'm guessing they did and discovered country cops don't keep such good records and found very little about the blond girl's murder.

So Nancy did it?

I certainly thought so. More so as you and I went through all the people I knew and everything that had gone on in my miserable life. I remembered particularly my first relationship with Nancy, and the way she reacted to my meeting and falling in love with Missy.

Why didn't you tell the cops this?

I certainly needed it to be her. I needed some way to prove her guilt and, of course, to relieve my own in the matter. But I still loved her. There is no evil angel but love.

Incredible. This is truly amazing.

Well, I hope before I finish telling the story that you'll think it's credible, not incredible.

Sorry, I didn't mean to use that word. It slipped my mind how you take explicit meanings from words. Anyway, keep going.

Well, one day, maybe a month back, while I was waiting for you to show for our every other day interviews, I heard a metal on metal rattle up above me in the ceiling. Actually, not in the ceiling itself, in the fluorescent lights up there. Unusual to say the least. Clearly not something you'd expect to happen in a building this well constructed and maintained. Particularly not in the lighting of the most carefully sound-proofed and guarded room in this building. Confidential conversations occur constantly here. But there it was. A relatively loud sound of metal on metal. It took me by surprise. At the same time I saw no reason to tell you or report it to the guards. After all, what did I have to lose if anyone heard what I or you had to say? Actually, I had everything to gain, since I constantly reiterated my innocence to you and that I'd forgotten the crime I was supposed to have committed. Could only do me good. So, if someone was listening, and that's all I could figure was happening, they'd get the true lowdown rather than what the police thought.

You obviously didn't tell me. I certainly would have remembered that.

I didn't. But as I screwed the thing around in my mind, it occurred to me that if the whatever-it-was was some kind of recording device, that Nancy might be doing it. She was deranged enough, as I'd come to think of her at that point, to do something like that. She'd record me telling you I'd done it, turn it anonymously over to the cops, and she'd put the final nail in my coffin. It made perfect sense.

Why didn't you tell me about this?

I'm not sure. I guess I decided to go with the flow. Punish her with the truth. That I didn't do it. All her work in getting the thing in the lights in the first place would be for naught. I don't know.

I understand.

Good. So, while I sat there day after day on my bed in my room staring at the walls, I got an idea that maybe I'd been wrong about Nancy's motives. Maybe she wasn't trying to convict me of the crime, but wanted to exonerate me instead.

How could she do that? After all, you were simply telling me what you'd told the police all along.

True. Though as emotionally reckless as Nancy has always been, she was equally clever. And, as I've told you more than once, obsessive. It could be that she was attempting to get me to tell her who the real murderer was.

How could you? You didn't know, did you?

Not at first I didn't. Then it occurred to me that maybe Nancy did.

How could that be?

Well, she was on the outside. Maybe she knew something I didn't. Or had gone through the same list of potential suspects and come to a conclusion that I hadn't.

And?

That's when I decided to stall you by telling you things that were generally true about possible suspects. I didn't know for sure which one it might be, but I hoped that one of my magical excursions would give her an idea of some fact I'd forgotten to tell her. I wanted, basically, to fill her in with as much information as I could possibly give her in order to help her with whatever she was up to.

All this on the basis that you'd come to the conclusion that it was her that had dropped the whatever-it-was in the ceiling lights, and that you now believed she was on your side? Both of these conclusions based not on communicating with her in any way, but on hunches you had.

Yes. Based on my having known her for a long time.

Understood. At the same time, this could have been caused by something natural, a sound you heard that didn't mean anything at all. Maybe the building was groaning as buildings often do as they settle.

Yes. Or that it was what I thought it was, but meant to record someone else in the room in some other interview at some other time for some other reason. I know it's hard to believe, but I was desperate and bored, so why not? It was a game. I like games. Remember backwards chess?

Yes, I do.

It's true that you can't lose a game if you don't play the game. It's also true that you can't win a game if you don't play the game. So it kept me occupied. A good thing as far as I was concerned. After all, without such things in a place like this, with all the people I could talk to being pretty much out of their skulls, I'd probably go bonkers myself.

What happened next?

I decided to believe that she'd figured out who it was that killed Missy and Carla and, as I said before, she wanted me to give her proof of it. But, since I didn't know who did it and not believing it could be Bradley, I had no idea what I should do.

So what *did* you do?

I figured out who did it.

And gave her the kind of information she needed to turn him in?

No. She would have wanted me, rather us, to taunt him.

What?

You know. Give her some ammunition to drive him crazy and do something else. Try to get him to kill me, if possible.

How did you come to this conclusion?

Easy. It was what I would've done in the same situation. My game, which is what it was at that point, was to pretend I was right about what she was doing, figure out who'd done it, and help her taunt the guy into believing I was giving him up to the cops.

I don't understand.

She's making a recording, see, and on that recording are my accusations of who did it. She could easily edit the recording—these days you can do that with free software over the Internet—send it to the perpetrator thus driving him crazy, and hope it was enough to bring him out of hiding and prove his own guilt.

My God. Do you realize how impossible this sounds?

Does, doesn't it? That's how games are played. You make up some rules and follow them carefully until you win or lose. That's the fun. Not so much if you lose, but certainly fun if you win. And I had plenty of time to waste in here. Lots of time to think.

So who did it?

Surprisingly, that was the easiest part. In our interviews we wandered around it over and over again without realizing we actually had it.

How?

By process of elimination. We were constantly attempting to test people, individually at first, and by putting them together in combinations later. I took the same direction as the chess game. Played it backwards.

When you took all the people out of the equation who could not possibly have done it, what are you left with?

Who, for God's sakes? You're driving me crazy.

Well, we know that Missy and Carla didn't kill themselves. So that's two gone. We also know my father's dead. A slight thought that he might have rigged his own death, but knowing my father as I did I knew he couldn't have imagined such a thing, no less carried it out.

Correct so far.

I know my mother couldn't be the culprit. She was the only sane person in my life growing up. And why would she do it? How could she manage it? Made no sense. So she's out of the equation.

Go on.

Nancy's still a possibility, but according to the game I was playing she was out of the picture as well. To play the game, the rules required that she be innocent. The same being true for Missy's brother who, you'll remember, was not in the picture in the first place.

Right.

That leaves one possible blond girl who could have mutilated her twin sister with a shovel. Not likely. Not even vaguely likely that the blond girl had a twin sister in the first place. Remember, we made that up from almost no evidence whatsoever. The little blond girl's father, who I couldn't believe would think I could have killed his girl, would be much more likely to think Bradley did it.

That leaves Bradley who you think is dead.

I still do.

Then who's left? You're not going to tell me George did it are you?

George?

Your cousin. We spoke of him a time or two.

No. I forgot about him. George didn't do it.

Then who's left?

That's what had me stumped at first. Then it came to me like a freight train and, believe it or not, in a dream. You were right about dreams, Doctor, they can be revealing.

If, of course, whoever you're now going to name, given that you and me are about the only ones left and I know I didn't do it, proves to be correct. Otherwise your dream is still fantasy.

Correct.

Tell me about the dream.

All right. I'll leave out the graphic parts if you don't mind.

Not unless they actually pertain to the crime.

They don't.

Go ahead.

Here's my dream. I'm walking in a forest at night with Bradley and come upon a shovel matted with hair and covered in blood.

So far, exactly as you told me the scene looked when he convinced you he had something to show you. Except for it now being nighttime.

Yes. And that's followed by him showing me the girl's mutilated dead body in the hole. Again, just the way it happened. That's where it changes though. Radically changes. This time Bradley's father is sitting on the edge of the hole with his face in his hands crying.

My God, you're not telling me . . .

Hold it. Let me finish. Bradley tells me this is how he really found the little girl. I look at his father and realize that he's completely covered in blood.

He killed the girl?

Apparently so. I'm not sure yet. So I ask him—and remember this is my dream, not reality—if he's all right. He looks up at me as if seeing me for the first time. And he realizes something. So he tells me quietly that he found his son holding the shovel, took it away from him, and was trying to bury the dead girl so Bradley wouldn't have to spend the rest of his life in jail.

You believed him?

It's a dream, Doctor. But no, I didn't believe him. How *could* I? Bradley had no blood on him. In fact, both in the dream and in reality now, Bradley looks like he'd come from a shower. Clean as a whistle. His father tells me not to tell anyone about this. It's not fair for a kid to have to go through what Bradley's going to have to go through by spending the rest of his life in prison or in an asylum.

And?

I tell him I can't do that. A crime has been committed here and it can't be swept under a rug. I wouldn't have used those words in real life at that age, but this is a dream. He tries to grab me, except he's slippery from the blood and I get away and go tell my father about it. He comes out just as the police arrive, and Bradley's father is now cleaned up and

Bradley has blood and bits of skin on *him*. Looking like he killed the girl.

Son of a bitch.

A dream, Doctor. Just a dream.

Though a powerful one. What happened next?

Nothing. That's it.

That's it?

Well, my belief is that Bradley's father eventually killed Bradley and made it look like suicide. Since Bradley was the only suspect, the girl was eventually buried and the cops forgot about it.

Where does this put Bradley in relation to Missy and Carla?

Well, this part is my conscious mind, not a fact or in a dream.

I got it.

Bradley's father never forgets that I turned his son in.

But you didn't. You simply told your father about seeing what you saw.

You know that and I know that, though Bradley's father can think whatever he wants. All he sees are the cops appearing right as my father does, they see Bradley covered in blood, arrest him, and off we go. Eventually, Bradley's father puts up bail, brings Bradley home, kills him, and makes it appear as a suicide. Even though he committed each of the crimes, from his perspective and as warped as he is, I've destroyed his family. Pain is lessened by another's anguish.

Jesus. But why wait until now to do this horrible thing to your family and not to you?

Good question. Not easy to answer, since reason is not an insane man's best quality. As I see it, though, Bradley's father stewed in his juices for many years. Suffering over what he'd probably convinced himself of, his son's murder of the girl and his son's committing suicide, when actually he'd committed both crimes. It began to wear on him. Maybe his wife had left him by then. Maybe not. But he was miserable. Deep down inside, he knew he'd committed both murders. In his conscious mind, though, he thought that I, even as a boy, was responsible for everything. And his obsession grew until it boiled over. He decided to get revenge.

That still doesn't explain why he murdered your wife and child.

No, it doesn't. But I have two scenarios for that and I think I now know which one fits and which doesn't. One of those scenarios is that he came to my farmhouse one afternoon expecting me to be there. When I wasn't, he did the ugly deed because the time had come, and he couldn't wait. The other scenario is that he deliberately came when I wasn't there to make me understand what he'd gone through during those many years of his self-punishment. He killed them with the express desire that I find them and go insane like he had. Either scenario works.

You presume the latter one is correct, right?

Yes. For me, at least, it fits better.

What has this got to do with Nancy and her plans?

Yes, I forgot about that. I think she came to the same conclusion as I did on her own. But she, like me, realized that going to the cops would only exacerbate my situation. Just like my going to them would. So she created an elaborate plan to force Bradley's father into the open.

How?

By sending him anonymous recordings of me declaring his son to be the murderer.

Why would that send him into a rage? Wouldn't that verify his contention that you caused it anyway?

No. If my theory is right, Bradley's father had by this time idolized his son in some fanatical way. Or maybe convinced himself that he and his son were the same person. In any event, I interpreted Nancy's desire that I say the right thing for her recording, me railing against Bradley as being the culprit.

Thus the reason for that day when I came in and you were ranting that Bradley had killed Nancy.

Yes.

It was my idea that if Bradley's father was guilty, as I suspected, this would drive him over the edge. He'd go bonkers. After all, what had Nancy to do with anything? I was painting his son as a serial killer. And he'd try to get at me in any way he could.

How?

I didn't know. I've been thinking since I've been talking to you today about the guard shot outside this building. I'd hate to think I was responsible for that, even indirectly, but I'm guessing the suspect responsible for that murder would be Bradley's father. He bought, or already had, some kind of long-range rifle, and come up here not knowing that I can never leave the inside of this building. He then shot the first person who, at long distance, resembled me. That could have been anybody. By this time, he's mad as a hatter.

Unreal.

Unreal, yes, though only until it's proven real. Why not put it to the test? Call the front desk. See what they've discovered about this. Then we'll talk some more. If I'm wrong, it'll be short and sweet. If I'm right, we'll go from there.

You'll stay in this room until I return?

I will. As long as they don't drag me out of here.

They won't. I'll make sure of that.

You were right, Joe. At least I think so.

What do you mean?

They've tentatively identified the man who shot the guard as Bradley's father.

And?

And nothing. They tell me he denies any involvement in the death of your wife and daughter. Claims you did it.

He would, of course.

They won't say anything more about him in regards to your case. If you were hoping for immediate exoneration, I'm afraid you're out of luck. At the same time, however, the cops have reopened the death of the girl-in-the-hole's case and Bradley's apparent suicide. So, there's a chance you'll be released.

Good to hear. At least as a possibility. Though I still wonder.

About what?

Nancy.

How so?

Is she trying to get me released in order to kill me herself? Did she murder Missy and Carla?

I thought you were sure she was on your side.

I was.

But not now?

I don't know. Nancy's unpredictable.

If you're released, she puts one between your eyes?

More likely do it slowly and in a way that doesn't implicate her. Arsenic, or something.

To desperation turns my trust and hope?

Yes.

So now you're fearful of being released?

Possibly.

Maybe I'll not tell them then.

Tell them what?

About our discussion. You called me here not as your doctor after all, and not as someone required to submit an opinion on your ability to stand trial. I came, against my better judgment I might add, as your friend. That's it. We met in this room because it was the only place we could meet in this building. Therefore, I'm not bound to silence.

Won't our discussion affect your final ruling on my ability to stand trial?

Not anymore.

I thought you hadn't filed it yet.

I haven't, but I have made up my mind.

What's your decision?

That you are sane, Joe. Ready to stand trial, even though it now seems that it won't be necessary. I thought that would make you happy.

It does. Were you to have chosen differently, I might have to remain inside for another year given that being unable to stand trial due to insanity does not bode well for my returning to society anytime soon.

Yes.

Now I'm having second thoughts.

It appears that way. So what do we do now?

We?

I need you to confirm my decision.

You do?

Yes. Your response will put my answer directly on one side or the other.

I'm sane, Doctor. I'll have to deal with Nancy one way or another eventually. Why not now?

Good. Then that's solved. At least as far as I'm concerned. Then I'll leave you. For the last time. At least under these circumstances I hope.

All right.

Thank you again for being so thorough in your remembrance of the details of the events of your life.

All? You don't know half of it, Doctor.

What do you mean by *that*?

As with anyone's life, there are many more events in it than can be covered in the amount of time we've spent, even though our conversations have been quite extensive.

You mean there's more? Of significance to this case?

I'm sure you'd find that so. You didn't actually ask *all* the right questions.

I missed some?

While it's true, I am a man more sinned against than sinning, much of me remains in darkness, even to me.

Shakespeare again?

Who is it that can tell me who I am?

Right. But Joe?

Yes?

Are you telling me now that you may have played a more sinister role in this?

Only that there's much more to think about.

Such as?

Well, me for example.

Yes?

I'm the only one who has first hand knowledge of all the experiences. I found Mutt. Bradley showed me the girl's body, but I was there. I found Missy and Carla's bodies.

Sure. But you didn't attempt to rape Missy.

No, though I could have convinced my father to do it. To keep my genes in the family.

Again, are you now telling me you did these things?

No. I'm *sure* I didn't do these things.

Now you're just sure, when before you *knew* you didn't commit them?

Our doubts are traitors, Doctor.

Joe?

Yes?

Never mind.

Goodbye, Doctor.

Goodbye.

Readers Guide

1. What rationale did the author use to make most of the book a dialog not using double quotes or references to who's speaking?

2. Do Amador (the psychiatrist) and Barnum (the patient) actually exchange roles during the course of the book and, if so, why?

3. The guard's name, Matthew Brady, is not explained until later on in the book when it's connection to the civil war photographer is revealed. Does this mean anything in the context of the narrative?

4. What role(s) do drugs play in the novel?

5. In most books there's a clear protagonist with whom readers can self-identify. Is there a protagonist in this novel and if so, why, and if not, why not?

6. Would this book make a better play or a better film or best left as is?

7. Truth and lies play diverse roles in this book. Can anyone be trusted? If so, who?

8. Shakespeare quotes abound in this novel. Why? Is any one of his plays more important than the rest to this book? Why?

9. Does Joe really want out of the Forensic Psychiatric Facility? If not, why not?

10. Are the various characters in this novel simply characters, or do they represent certain aspects of the human condition?

11. Why western Washington state for the location of this story? Could the choice of place be changed and have any effect on the novel's plot or outcome?

12. Two parallel plots (the interviews and the use of the secret room in the attic) are notable here. Are there more? How many?

13. One of the themes of this book is its violence and sexual conflicts. Nothing new in that, except here we find the two related some of the time and unrelated at others. Why?

14. Family relations and interrelations often play opposing roles here. Do these resolve in some way or are they left as loose ends? In fact, is anything truly resolved by book's end?

15. Aside from the scant references to the weather, the basic layout of the facility, and the two proximate buildings involved, the book consists only of dialog and brief accounts of movement taking place outside Building J. Where does the action actually take place then? And do these two places give it different meanings?